FROZEN
ASSETS

Also by James Leasor:

FICTION

Passport to Oblivion
Spylight
The Yang Meridian
Passport for a Pilgrim
Follow the Drum
Mandarin Gold

NONFICTION

The One That Got Away (with Kendal Burt)
The Millionth Chance
The Clock with Four Hands
Wall of Silence (with Peter Eton)
The Plague and the Fire
The Uninvited Envoy
Singapore: The Battle That Changed the World
Green Beach
Boarding Party
Code Name Nimrod
Who Killed Sir Harry Oakes?

FROZEN

ASSETS

James Leasor

St. Martin's Press
New York

Library of Congress Cataloging-in-Publication Data

Leasor, James.
   Frozen assets / James Leasor.
      p. cm.
   ISBN 0-312-03347-8
   I. Title.
  PR6062.E24F76 1989
  823'.914-dc20   89-32755
                        CIP

First published in Great Britain by Grafton Books, A Division of the Collins Publishing Group.

First U.S. Edition

10 9 8 7 6 5 4 3 2 1

Frozen . . . 'congealed by extreme cold; subjected, or exposed to extreme cold.'

Assets . . . 'Sufficient estate or effects . . . The origin of the English use is to be found in the Anglo-French law phrase *aver assetz*, to have sufficient, viz. to meet certain claims.'

Oxford English Dictionary,
Clarendon Press, Oxford

PART ONE

THE 1670s

All that day – and on every other day for as far back as any
of them cared to count – snow had been falling steadily. It
was not snow as the three travellers remembered from
winters in England – how very far away that land seemed
now – gentle and soft, like tiny feathers floating from a
friendly sky, but in solid flakes thick as thumbnails, hard
and sharp and hostile as chips of broken glass.

Around them as they walked, the lower slopes of mountains stretched up to unseen and immeasurable heights, lost
in perpetual clouds that even at noon did not part to show
the sun. The air felt so cold that the tiny hairs in their
nostrils froze, and they breathed through scarves wrapped
around their mouths. Their lips had cracked and split, and
even fat rubbed on them from goats and ponies they had
killed and eaten on the journey could not ease the constant
throbbing pain.

Above their jerkins and thick trousers they had wrapped
sheepskins bought in the bazaar of the last village, long since
left behind them. Now the tufts of this stinking greasy wool
had grown icicles, the shape of large frozen tears. These
icicles clanked like chain links as they moved slowly on,
heads down, shoulders hunched, bodies bent into the perpetual and probing wind.

Before the sun had retreated sullenly above the clouds it
had blazed with such ferocious intensity that when they

blinked their eyes, raw red images of fire still burned dazzlingly on their eyelids. In the last bazaar they had therefore bought strips of polished copper with tiny horizontal slits cut into them; these the locals wore like masks when they went out into the snow. Now the three men peered through the narrow openings at infinite wastes of snow, a white desert seemingly without beginning or end.

Speech was a luxury they could now only afford in emergencies. To form words caused their lips to bleed again, and then the blood froze like crimson ice. They trudged for miles in silence, thumbs around the leather straps of the packs to ease the weight on their aching backs. The cold had numbed their feet to such an extent that one man, at the end of a day's march, discovered that a stone, sharp and hard as a nail, had pierced the sole of his right boot – and he had never felt a moment's discomfort.

The three men had roped themselves together for safety and for physical reassurance. In this silent white world, empty of all recognizable landmarks, wreathed from time to time with drifting fog, so that it became impossible to check where ground ended and clouds began, always chill as death, anyone who fell even a dozen paces behind his companions could be lost instantly and possibly forever. Earlier on, this had happened to one of their group. One moment he had been with them, and the next he was gone. They heard his shouts for help, piteously magnified by some echo of the hills, and although they retraced their steps, calling out to him, they had not found him. Their feet made no sound on the snow, and his cries echoed and re-echoed from banks of snow and hills of ice they could not even see, repeating themselves into oblivion. Gradually, his voice tailed away and died, until the only sound was the hollow whistling of the wind.

Snow lay thick as a thousand shrouds, so that where they had walked seemed as featureless as the way ahead. Swirling mists that moved with a life of their own in unseen eddies of the air obscured their route.

They took it in turns to lead, stopping every hour to rest, crouching close together for warmth and comfort, each secretly surprised by the grim faces of his companions. Everyone felt certain in his own mind that he could not look as wretched, had not suddenly aged as much as they had done, with beards matted by ice droplets, lips cracked and bleeding, lower eyelids drooping loosely and red-rimmed. Their hands were encrusted and caked with dirt, fingernails long, broken and chipped. Even in that freezing altitude, where it seemed that no man from the west had ever marched before, their flesh crawled with lice and stank with the odour of the grave. They had travelled for so long that time had ceased to have meaning; days had stretched into weeks and then to months. Were they really any closer to their destination, or would death overtake them before they could reach the East and all its fabled riches?

More than a year earlier, they had set out from London, and nearly two years had passed since they had first decided, with what now seemed all too little preparation or fore-thought, to make this astonishing journey. It was difficult now to marshal sufficient willpower and resolution to control weary limbs and force them to keep moving east, always east. But although they had no energy to speak, images and memories crowded their minds. They saw the past with the exaggerated clarity and sharpness of men wearied to the edge of endurance, breathing thin air, living high on the spine of unknown and terrifying peaks.

Ralph Ballantyne, the prime mover of the expedition, was leading them, aiming for a pass that herdsmen of the last village had assured them existed. That village was now many days march behind them, and how could they see the pass when visibility by day was as poor as visibility by night? Had these herdsmen who spoke of it ever actually crossed this pass, or had they only heard of it from others – as they had heard stories themselves, of huge wild shambling creatures who lived up in the snows, walking upright like men, with the strength and size of giants, capable of carrying off a traveller before he even realized his danger?

Perhaps the good Lord who had guided them so far would now reveal the track they must take in a desert of snow unmarked by the feet of man, beast or bird? Ballantyne prayed that this would come about, as he recalled stages of their journey, back to its earliest beginnings in the Lion and Unicorn coffee house off Leadenhall Street in the City of London.

Every day in that summer, now so far away, there had been much discussion in City coffee houses about the astonishing success of the newly formed Honourable East India Company. The prodigal riches showered on merchant adventurers who had financed it to trade in spices with the East Indies and the Spice Islands, and other islands that lay beyond the last charted seas, aroused great envy in those who had not been shrewd enough to do the same. They assured themselves that fortunes of at least equal size must surely await others with courage and capital enough to finance ships, and promised huge bounty to captains and crews, to be paid when their vessels returned heavily laden with the spices that commanded such extraordinary sums from the rich.

The spices were prohibitively expensive because they were so rare and therefore greatly sought after. Without them, the tables of the wealthy in England and France throughout six or seven months of every year would lack any meat save salted beef or mutton. There was no way in which cattle could be kept alive in quantity throughout the bleak winter months, so they were slain in mid-September and the carcasses salted down.

The salt destroyed the meat's natural flavours. No amount of boiling or soaking could restore them satisfactorily and all meat tasted so salty that many people could not stomach more than a week or two of eating it. Spices, however, provided a welcome change of taste. They also preserved the flesh, and in addition added to it their own rare and individual aromatic flavours. It was always a pleasure to eat spiced meat and, having tasted this, unthinkable to return to tough and indigestible salt flesh.

But not everyone who invested in the East India Company's imitators became rich quickly. Some did not become rich at all. For a year they would have no news whatever about ships or their cargoes, because the East was many months' sailing away. Consequently, some backers lost patience or interest, or both, and sold their shares at a discount. They would regret such short-sightedness when, long after the ships had sailed from Gravesend on the Thames, they returned, holds crammed with spices which fetched more than their weight in gold.

The scent of these cargoes would drift on the wind to the City of London. It was the smell of wealth for those who had retained their shares, the smell of bitter regret for others who had not.

But although a regular system of ships going east and others returning west was set up, unexpected hazards soon began to threaten and often destroy the huge potential profits. In the oceans around India, pirates in fast sloops lay in wait for these defenceless vessels as they wallowed along, heavy with treasure. The profits of the trade could be great, but the risks of loss and death were at least as large.

The East India Company bought bases in Indian ports and reached agreement with local Indian rulers to build warehouses to store the spices so that they could be moved at the safest time of year, usually before the monsoon, when sailing conditions were most treacherous and so even the pirates would be less active.

French and Portuguese traders followed the British example. They set up their own companies to trade in spices, and soon found they need not actually visit the East Indies to make a profit. They could simply raid the British warehouses in India when they were full of spices, and make off with the contents.

To stop these attacks, British merchants engaged locals as

11

guards. The Portuguese and the French did the same, and because, to European eyes, all Indians tended to look alike – as the Chinese most certainly did – each country's traders dressed their guards in copies of the uniforms of their country's armies. This was becoming ruinously expensive, and the meeting at the Lion and Unicorn coffee house had been called to investigate a new and exciting proposal – an overland route to the East. This would be relatively safe across Europe as far as Constantinople. From there, through Afghanistan and India and the unknown lands on the road to China, it was known that local merchants with camels made regular journeys in each direction, and generally arrived safely. They followed what was called the Silk Road, pioneered centuries earlier by Marco Polo and his father and uncle on their journey to China to bring back silk and other treasures from old Cathay.

Surely it could be possible for young British merchants of energy and enterprise to do the same? Could they not come to agreements with local rulers to supply guides, and possibly guards, and so ensure the safety of their persons and their trade? They would not then be at the mercy of waves and the winds of heaven, and there would be no pirates to attack them.

This seemed such a good idea to the men in the crowded upstairs room of the coffee house, with their glasses of brandy and long pipes of tobacco, that many expressed surprise that others had not thought of this before them. Ballantyne knew that other Europeans had indeed attempted the journey and then abandoned it because difficulties and dangers overwhelmed them. They had not been so well equipped as these London merchants would be. And as Paul Mapperley had said, 'There has to be someone who is first.' They all nodded vigorously; of course he was right. Mapperley was a tall, well-favoured man, the younger son of a younger son, thus without land or wealth himself, and hence intensely eager to acquire both. He was a natural leader, everyone agreed.

He and five others had borrowed money at huge rates of interest from parents, relations or Hebrew money lenders to finance their trip. They equipped themselves with the stoutest boots and suits of the thickest cloth, as well as rough everyday apparel. They engaged servants, all burly men, and promised them a share of the spoils. Swordsmiths fashioned specially strong blades and splendid scabbards. They carried flintlock pistols and small clocks and knives and trinkets – strings of beads, polished metal mirrors – to distribute as gifts to men of importance they might meet on the way, as an earnest of their wealth and good intentions.

And so they set off, with letters patent from the Sovereign, obtained through the good offices of Ballantyne's uncle, who was a friend of the Lord Mayor of London. These documents granted them the sole right to trade with the Indies and England by the overland route. Such a letter had seemed of immense value in the City of London. Now, in its thick leather folder, embossed with the Royal Arms in gold, it was only one more piece of impedimenta to carry through the snow.

In Constantinople they had hoped to secure passage aboard a ship trading with the west coast of India, but they arrived only days before the rains began, and during the monsoon few ships sailed east, and aboard those that made the voyage all berths were already bespoken.

The city was expensive, and this delay of several months ate deeply into their funds. After all, they were gentlemen and had to live as such, else local merchant princes would dismiss them as travellers of little account. In Constantinople, one of their party succumbed to fever, thought to come from the foul stench of open sewers under the rain. Ballantyne let blood and fed him with the richest soups he could obtain, but all to no avail. He died within weeks, ravaged with disease, his skin yellow and as tightly stretched on his bones as an old drumskin.

The servants became uneasy at the terrible manner of his passing. They did not like the city or the climate, and the death of this gentleman distressed them. If he could not survive, what hope would a valet have, should he fall ill with the same fever? Several were offered places with Turkish families, largely on account of their ability to train and ride horses. They accepted, and the merchants were not altogether sorry to see them go. They told themselves it would be more sensible to engage locals in India who spoke native languages and knew the customs.

With the end of the monsoon, they persuaded a ship's captain to take them on to India, but he lacked space for all the party. The young merchant-adventurers (as the City of London had described them) therefore paid off all remaining servants, and set out on their own. In Bombay they presented their letters of authority to the new British Governor. The city had only lately come under the control of the East India Company as part of the dowry given by the Portuguese for the marriage a decade earlier, in 1661, of Catherine of Braganza to Charles II. The Governor welcomed the travellers, but counselled them most strongly against continuing their journey without adequate preparation.

'You will be going where no European has travelled successfully since the days of Marco Polo,' he explained. 'You will cross mountains so high that clouds continually – and I am told, mercifully – conceal the height of their peaks, which are quite measureless to men. You will pass through lands controlled by fierce tribesmen who may strip you of all your belongings and then subject you to a terrible death. Others have already attempted what you seek to do. Most have died. The few who survived have struggled back, wholly demented by the horrors of their experiences. I know, my friends, I have seen them. This is an impossible journey, through totally hostile lands, where the customs and habits of the natives are worse than those of any brute beasts. I beg of you to turn back now – while you still can do so.'

Ballantyne remained undaunted.

'I expect we shall have strange adventures, and the risks

are clearly much graver than we imagined in London,' he admitted. 'But it is not too long since many seafarers believed that off the west coast of Portugal the sea descended over a vast cliff to an unfathomable depth. That was said to be the edge of the world, the end of the earth – *Finis Terre*. But now we know that this is not so.

'You mentioned Marco Polo. In his account of his journey he told how he had met men who would ascend into the air, attached to giant kites to test the strength and direction of the winds. Stay-at-homes did not believe Marco Polo, but he was right. Perhaps, one day, voyagers will fly in such aerial kites over these hills about which you now warn us, for men may harness the winds of the air as they have harnessed the winds at sea. In the meantime, although we value your counsel and the kindness of Christian spirit that prompts it, we must go on. We have come so far. We cannot go back.'

One of their number took a different view. He became enchanted by the charm of the Governor's youngest daughter. He stayed behind to marry her, and remained in Bombay as a merchant. This left four out of the original six who had set out from England with such enthusiasm and high hopes.

An Indian who had made one fortune out of the spice trade and now saw the prospect of another, at no personal risk to himself, advanced money to them on the understanding that he would take a handsome share of their trade going through Bombay. With this sum, Mapperley engaged coolies and an Afghan overseer who spoke some English. They bought pack ponies, small, sturdy animals, capable, so the overseer assured them, of living off the land. In the direst extremity, they could also be killed for their meat. Then, with food and skins to wrap around themselves against the expected chill of high altitudes – about which many had warned them in such terms that they felt they must be grossly exaggerated – they set off.

They were marching without maps, for no one before

15

them had charted the journey; they travelled with the sun by day and the stars at night as their only guides. First, they headed north, hoping by this means to be able to avoid the worst of the mountains. If they could keep to the foothills, then surely their journey must be easier.

There was a track to follow. They passed strings of camels laden with bales of cloth, coming along it from the East, and they were overtaken by other local traders more used to the route and the conditions. Each night they camped, pitching tents made of skins sewn together, organizing a sentry system with the coolies.

As they changed direction and began to climb towards the East, the soft dust on the track became increasingly irritating to their throats and eyes. Two ponies went lame and had to be abandoned, their load distributed among the others. Several coolies fell ill with fever and were left behind in a village.

In the distance, they could see foothills, grey and brown, like pumice-stone, where the wind had blown away the snow. Behind them, mountains soared on and up, peaks perpetually out of sight in drifting clouds. But they remained miles away, almost like a mirage or a painted backcloth in a theatre. The ground became harsh to their boots. Stones and rocks as cruel as razors stripped away the leather, and oppressive clouds hung low over the horizon, veiling the hills.

Outside one village – simply a huddle of huts made of stitched skins with mud roofs and walls, where children with running noses cowered fearfully under their mothers' skirts as they came by – a great bird suddenly and unexpectedly took wing from a clump of trees. This terrified the pony Mapperley was riding so much that it threw him, and then dragged him along by his ankle as it galloped away.

By the time the others overtook the pony, Mapperley was dead. His skull had been hammered by boulders on the iron-hard ground that had cracked the bone like the shell of an egg. Thomas Drayton, the eldest son of a Suffolk squire

16

who had mortgaged his estate to pay a gambling debt that his son was now risking his life to repay from profits expected from the spice trade, and Jonas Travers, the second son of a Cornish landowner, helped Ballantyne to scratch a low grave for him. They fashioned a crude cross from the peeled branches of a tree. Drayton had a Testament with him, and read a few verses over the shallow grave.

They stayed on in the village for a few days to rest the animals and themselves. The people were poor and had no use for money, indeed had apparently never seen a coin. They had to barter for provisions, using the trinkets they had brought out from London. The head man appeared friendly, and Ballantyne, through the overseer, explained how in the West, day and night were divided into hours, and how clocks measured out men's lives.

The head man agreed to supply them with salted meat and dried, shrunken apricots to chew, with small skin bags of nuts and rice, and chopped-up lengths of straw which could start a fire. But he insisted that the price for these was the last of the clocks they had brought with them. He was tall, with a light skin and red hair, and he sat watching the clock, seeing the tiny wheels turn one against the other, cog meshing with cog, fascinated by the complexity of the movements.

'I have given you the best thing I possess,' Ballantyne told him through the overseer. He was not happy with the amount of rice and food they had received in return, but realized he was in no position to argue. Yet they had many miles still to travel and little of value left to barter for more food. He had to do all he could do to gain more here.

'We still have knives,' Ballantyne said. 'Take five knives instead of the clock.'

'We do not wish your knives,' replied the man. 'You have shown them to us. The blades rust. Look.'

He motioned to Ballantyne to slide his own knife from its leather sheath. The blade was indeed edged with rust.

17

'You see,' said the man, 'you do not know the secret of the river of roses.'

'That is true,' agreed Ballantyne. 'What is its secret?'

Perhaps this knowledge might later, somehow and somewhere, be exchanged for food or help on their way?

'It is far from here, at the base of the mountain with the face of a man. It faces another mountain, with the horns of a goat. Between them the rose-red river flows.'

'Where does it come from? Where does it go to?' asked Ballantyne. He always felt impatient with this roundabout way of speaking, almost universal in the East.

'It comes from a secret source no one has seen, and flows through plains towards the five great rivers of India. No fish live in its waters, but they flow over something else of infinitely greater value. The rose-red riverbed.'

He paused again, as though reluctant to surrender the secret. Ballantyne pushed the unwanted dagger back into its sheath, buttoned it on his belt, picked up the clock as though still undecided whether he should give it or keep it.

'What is that?' he asked pointedly.

'Half of knowledge is the question,' the head man replied enigmatically. 'The other half is the answer.' He reached out for the clock.

'The secret is hidden in the red sand, my friend. It is found nowhere else – and look at its power.'

With a quick movement he released his tulwar from its metal sheath. The long, etched blade glittered like burnished silver in the afternoon air.

'I can leave this anywhere,' he explained. 'In water, in snow, in rain. It will never rust. It is always clean. Life eternal comes only from the river of roses, and the rose-red sands over which it runs, and from which it takes its name.'

'What is its secret?' asked Ballantyne, not really concerned, thinking that this was just talk, as there had been talk of giant men covered in hair, who lived in the highest reaches of the hills, and possessed almost supernatural strength and agility.

18

'I know not what the power may be, but you can see what it does,' replied the head man. 'We burn this sand, and from the ashes comes a liquid metal with a strong and pungent smell. Your swords will rust and rot, and have to be sharpened again and again, growing smaller every time, but our blades have a long life. That is the secret of the river. I will give it to you in return for this machine that can measure out my days and nights.'

'It is already yours,' Ballantyne assured him; if he did not give it, this man could so easily simply seize the clock and kill them all. 'How will I find this river?'

'I will tell you exactly where the mountains are, between which it flows. To my knowledge, there are no other hills like that in all the world. Find those hills, and you find the river. Find the river and, my friend, you have a gift of priceless value.

'Look, I will write down the names of the hills for you, and directions to help you find them. Then you may seek out the river, and share its precious secret.'

He called for writing materials and a square of goatskin and began to write in his own local script. Ballantyne could not understand it, and neither could the overseer, but no doubt they would meet men of education on the journey, who could translate. This was certainly not the moment to admit ignorance, so he accepted the skin with every expression of gratitude, and folded it carefully and put it in his pouch. He would have preferred more rice or meat, but he felt it would be impolite to admit this when apparently the head man had given him what he genuinely believed was his most valuable possession.

They then set off, all more conscious of the dangers ahead, and the fact that much of their original optimism and certainty of fortune had vanished. Survival now seemed almost as important as success. Days merged together, and Ballantyne, writing a brief note in his diary each day, making ever shorter entries, because his inkhorn was almost empty, was surprised to see that they had been forty days on the march from Bombay, and had no means of knowing how much longer their journey would take.

On the afternoon of the forty-first day, they came over the crest of a hill, through a gorge cut into the rock – and faced a hundred silent horsemen.

Their horses were small, like Shetland ponies. The riders sat on blankets thrown over the animals' haunches, their feet dangling only inches from the ground. They were dressed in furs, some with the fur turned in towards their bodies, some wearing skins with the fur outside. They waited in a row, watching them.

Ballantyne halted his small column and raised his right hand in salutation. None of the men responded. They sat in silhouette against the sun, which was moving slowly down behind the rim of the further hills.

'Hail! We come in peace,' Ballantyne shouted, as though they could understand. The overseer translated, his voice echoing from the peaks. Still no one spoke or replied. Then, at a signal from a man in the centre, the horsemen turned abruptly, wheeled away, and vanished down the hillside.

Had they been there, or was this a vision brought on by the burning, blazing sun, reflected from snow on tired and aching eyes?

As Ballantyne shook his head to blot both the image and the frightening thought from his mind, he felt panic rise within him like a tide. They had all imagined other sights before this: a palm tree, of a kind they had only seen in paintings of the East; a man as tall as a house; strange beasts with claws and tails and scaly bodies. But when they cried out a warning to the others, they said they could see nothing. Ballantyne had seen the beasts clearly. Travers had seen the man, and Drayton, the palm tree, and they had looked at each other, reassuring each other beseechingly that these things *had* been there. But what was reality and what was fantasy? Reality meant the rocks and the mountains and the snow and the bitter piercing cold. Fantasy must·control the pictures in their minds and eyes – or could they be part of the same vision, the same nightmare?

Ballantyne turned to Drayton.

'Do you think they are hostile?' he asked.

Drayton shrugged, but did not reply. Ballantyne felt a strange relief that he had also seen them. They must be real, not a vision; he was not imagining things. He put his head down and started to walk on. Then he heard a cry of anger and surprise from Drayton, and turned. Drayton was pointing back down the hillside. The bearers were retreating, some on ponies, some on foot, all moving hurriedly, not looking back, and the overseer was leading them. Within seconds they would be out of earshot. Ballantyne shouted: 'Come back! *Come back!*'

They did not even look towards him. In seconds, they had disappeared and then the sun died behind the hills. They had timed their departure deliberately. No one could pursue them in the dark.

'We'll camp here,' said Ballantyne flatly. There was nowhere else to camp, and a camp now meant lying wrapped in fur skins they had bought in the last village. His fingers and toes were numb beyond all feeling. His joints felt locked with the freezing cold. He should make a fire, cook some of the salt meat they still had, but he felt too weary, too lethargic. They all lay down, wrapped the skins around them, rolled over to tighten them and prepared for sleep.

Some time in the night Ballantyne woke. Snow was falling. He had tried to wrap his head in the skin but the wind had blown it open and his face was covered with ice. He felt it crack as he moved his jaws, wiped away the ice. He could see Drayton near him, looking uneasily like a corpse under the snow. He leaned across to him, shook him. There was no response.

'Drayton! Drayton! *Wake up!*' he shouted desperately. He pulled the fur from his colleague's face and realized he would never wake up again. Ballantyne stood up, calling to Travers.

21

'Get up! We'll freeze to death! *Get up!*'

Under the moon, through the falling screen of snow, he saw Travers move, writhing like a serpent in the skins, scattering his covering of frozen snow. At last he stood up.

'Drayton's dead,' Ballantyne told him.

Travers did not speak; there was nothing to say. Death had stalked them silently, keeping pace with them, step after step, but they could not turn back; they were too far along their way. They stood, stamping their feet, beating their arms about their bodies. Ballantyne sensed that if they stopped they could freeze to death. Gradually, the moon waned and the sun came up from the hills. The snow ceased. What about the horsemen they had seen?

'We must bury him,' said Ballantyne.

'The ground's too hard,' replied Travers. He prodded his sword through the snow. The blade snapped against a hidden rock.

'Then we will wrap him in skins and leave him, God rest his soul.'

Afterwards, they moved a little way off. Ballantyne took out a tinder and flint, and using some scraps of straw he still kept in his pouch, lit a tiny fire. They melted some snow in a pan, added honey, bought like so much else in the last bazaar, and sipped the weak warm liquid, blowing on their hands and fingers to try to restore some feeling and circulation.

The two survivors set off now over the hill, keeping the pale sun behind them. They went down into a shallow valley, walking slowly because the air was rare and they were tired, and also because secretly they both feared that the snow might conceal a hole, a crevasse, a ravine into which they could fall or break a leg and then be left to die. No help could come their way here; they were on their own. But once through these mountains, surely they must discover a more hospitable land? The snow could not last forever, even in this freezing desert of despair.

As if to disprove these comfortable assurances, snow

22

began to fall more thickly now, blotting out the sickly sun. The wind was gaining in strength and blew great sheets of snow in front of them, then round about them, so that they faced a soft hill of snow into which they ploughed, and half-way through this, the wind blew the snow away again, and they were standing on rough grey rocks.

Ballantyne heard a cry of warning or alarm. He paused and looked behind him. The horsemen were following them. As they rode expertly through the driving snow, Ballantyne saw a glitter of diffused sunshine on raised blades. Swords swung like scythes in the sky. They wheeled and came towards them.

The two men drew their swords and stood, waiting. The horsemen surrounded them and then they paused. Ballantyne noted with curiosity that the hoofs of the horses were wrapped in leather, presumably to protect them from the cold. He had never seen that before; he would tell them at home about this when he returned to England. He would tell them so many things when he went back – if ever he went back.

The leader of the horsemen shouted at them, but they could not understand what he said. Ballantyne raised his hands above his head, waving his sword to show that he did not intend to attack them.

They rode in close to him. Suddenly, a blade winked like a heliograph and Travers dropped. His severed head rolled, eyes and mouth still open, down the white slope of the hill. The body, streaming blood like a crimson fountain, col-lapsed like a sack on the stained snow. Ballantyne charged the nearest rider, brought down his sword on the man's thigh. The horseman screamed in agony and his horse took off, galloping wildly across the snow. The other men drew back for a moment – and in that moment, the mountain roared.

A huge wave of snow rolled down from the clouds, like a tidal wave. The horsemen spurred their mounts frantically to escape the avalanche. Ballantyne also started to run, but up the hill, through the streaming, steaming flood of snow and ice and earth. He stumbled on, falling, rising, falling again until he could run no longer. The mountain now was still. Far beneath him, out of sight, snow and small rocks rumbled on towards the foothills. His heart pounded and thundered like a captive hammer in his chest.

He paused for a moment, weak with altitude and exertion and the lack of food. Then he toiled on slowly, head down against the driving wind, all sense of direction temporarily gone. If he could only reach this peak, go down the other side of the mountain, he might be free of this accursed place. Step after step he trudged. The cold had frozen all thoughts from his mind except the basic will to survive at whatever cost.

He was already half asleep, dazed by misery and chill, when for the first time on his journey, his left foot did not touch hard ground through the thick soft covering of snow.

Instinctively he drew back but in doing so he lost his balance and, weary with his exertions, could not regain it.

He slipped forward slowly, and the snow opened and swallowed him. He felt himself slide, not quickly but gently, almost gracefully, between two sheer and vertical walls of shining ice, smooth as glass. Frantically, he dug his sword into one of them to try and arrest his progress. But he could not even slow his fall. The blade simply scored the ice and then broke.

Ballantyne looked up. He could see a narrowing, shrinking slit of sky. Snow was still falling, even down to the depths to which he was sliding. He cried out, but there was no one to hear him, no one at all. He tried to pray but he felt too cold, too stunned, too exhausted, to think of words, let alone to voice them. Gradually, a chill deeper than anything he had previously experienced, ever imagined, began to grip him with ever-tightening fingers. Soon, he dozed, and then he slept.

Snow kept on falling. Within seconds, it had covered the crevasse into which Ballantyne had fallen. Within minutes, it was as though no one had ever been there. Once more the mountain was virgin, unclimbed, unclimbable. The only sound was the sigh and sough of the ceaseless, freezing wind, and the endless feathery flutter of falling flakes.

PART TWO

THE 1980s

The wise man always keeps his balls in the air.

Dr Jason Love lay on his back in the centre of his swimming pool in the garden of his Wiltshire home, pondering the essential and unarguable truth of this seemingly inelegant recommendation as he enjoyed the warmth of an unexpectedly sunny March afternoon.

The advice had been given to him years before when, as a medical student at St Bartholomew's Hospital in London, he had examined an out-patient, a retired circus juggler. This man had explained that this philosophy had formed his whole basis of a happy life. As a three or four ball juggler, so long as he could keep all the balls whirling round in the air above his head, hand to hand, his mind was totally concentrated. Nothing could ever be allowed to break that concentration or the balls would fall, and he would be out of a job. Severiano Ballesteros, the golfer, put it another way: 'If I lose concentration, I lose the hole.'

Concentration was the key to so many achievements, and in the years since Dr Love had been in practice in the West Country, he had often passed on this maxim to patients who frittered away their energies and content in needless worry, crossing difficult bridges before they had even been built.

Now Love concentrated his mind on his own immediate plans. Early next morning, he was leaving for his house in the Algarve, driving through France and Spain in his supercharged Cord roadster. As he floated, he checked that he had done everything required of a bachelor country physician about to go on holiday. A locum was arriving later that afternoon; his housekeeper, Mrs Hunter, had already prepared his room. As a Judo brown belt, Dr Love took a weekly class in the village hall for members of the local branch of the Royal British Legion; he had persuaded a retired paratroop sergeant to carry on these sessions in his absence. He had carefully serviced his car in preparation for the long drive to the sun. What might only be a routine trip for a modern vehicle was something more important for one more than fifty years old. He had also arranged for his collection of car badges and mascots, accumulated over many years from old-car graveyards, autojumbles and sales in many countries, to be placed for safekeeping in the bank while he was away.

He derived particular pleasure from these badges and their simple heraldry, evocative of more leisurely and gracious days, when symbols for speed and silence were not stylized rockets or spaceships, but the outspread wings of a bird. The German Adler – the name meant eagle – understandably bore a badge of an eagle's wings. The Hispano-Suiza, which translated meant, more prosaically, simply Spanish-Swiss, displayed a stork as mascot. This commemorated an association during the First World War, when the company provided engines for French Spad fighter planes, and so adopted the stork insignia from one of their squadrons. Morgan displayed a winged wheel; wings bore aloft the initial 'B' for Bentley. But the badge which Love held in the highest, if somewhat quizzical regard, was the Cord crest of three hearts and three arrows. This was said to be based on the coat of arms of the Scottish M'Cord or Mackorda family. Love thought it doubtful whether Mr Errett Lobban Cord, the American entrepreneur salesman who had founded the company to produce the car that bore his name, had ever enjoyed any right to bear these arms. But so far as Love was concerned anyone who, at the height of world recession in the 1930s, could conceive a car not just as a means of transportation but as the fulfilment of a dream of speed and elegance, had the right to choose any crest he coveted.

For reasons almost impossible to explain to people who drove modern cars, Love liked the Cord, despite its fits of unpredictable temperament – or maybe because of them. Of course, such behaviour in a dull car – as pique in a plain or dowdy woman – would be unforgivable, but curiously became an endearing individualistic peccadillo in a beautiful creature – and no one could criticize the Cord's good looks.

Many might have reservations about a car with a gear change operated by vacuum servos and electric solenoids, through circuits so complex that the driver could actually engage two gears at the same time, but the New York Museum of Modern Art called the Cord one of the eight finest automobiles ever designed. Love could never contemplate its long, coffin-nosed bonnet with two stainless steel exhaust pipes protruding on either side, its steeply raked split windscreen, more suitable for a speedboat than a car, without experiencing a thrill of pleasure. It was of an age – the 1930s – and yet somehow ageless; not so much a car as a personal statement.

The car bristled with innovations that had taken nearly half a century to be generally accepted: supercharging, front wheel drive, independent front suspension, retractable headlights, total sound proofing, integral construction. Indeed, it had been too advanced for the mass of drivers and, as with many pioneers, its makers had paid the price of being unacceptably far ahead for public acceptance and taste. And when the Cord ceased production in 1937, the body dies were sold to two other car manufacturers and then shipped to Russia – and never heard of again.

That morning, Love had received from an antiquarian bookseller a copy of *Religio Medici*, which the seventeenth century Norwich physician, Sir Thomas Browne, had spent many years writing. A previous owner of the book had

28

marked a passage in pencil, which Love now recalled, because it summed up his own opinion of the mass of careful, cautious people who were always mulishly reluctant to accept anything new, strange or daring.

'If there be any among those common objects of hatred I do contemn and laugh at,' Browne had written with feeling, 'it is that great enemy of Reason, Virtue and Religion, the Multitude: that numerous piece of monstrosity which, taken asunder, seem men and the reasonable creatures of God; but, confused together, make but one great beast, and a monstrosity more prodigious than Hydra.'

Well, thought Love now, as he floated gently towards the shallow end, such views would not win votes at any election, or in a seminar for package tour operators, but then Browne was not standing for election, and neither was he. Love was his own man, or as people used to describe such fortunate persons, free, white and over twenty-one. Nowadays such a description could not be used on the grounds that it could be racist. What rubbish, he thought, and dived to rid his mind of the idea. As he surfaced, he heard the outside telephone bell ringing loudly. Usually he carried a portable cordless telephone outside with him, but this afternoon he had not been expecting a call.

He climbed out of the pool, pulled on a towelled dressing gown in the blue and silver stripes of his old Oxford college, and walked towards the study door. Probably his locum was ringing; there could be some unexpected problem. Perhaps his wife was ill, his car would not start? This must be the punishment for congratulating himself that, in the metaphorical phrase of his father, long since dead, his hat was on his head and his troubles were covered. Love picked up the receiver with one hand, held a pencil poised above a notepad with the other.

'Hello,' he said without notable enthusiasm. 'Dr Love speaking.'

A man's voice said: 'You won't remember me, Doctor.'

The speaker paused dramatically, obviously hoping to be

instantly contradicted. Love rolled his eyes heavenwards. Who could this be? Probably some former contemporary driving west, seeking a drink, a free meal, maybe even a bed for the night, on the strength of a brief association forgotten over many years until it suited him to remember. This happened frequently when such acquaintances, driving west from London, would ring on their way and announce that they would call in. They seemed to assume that people living in the country maintained a full staff against such social eventualities, delighted to prepare a meal, a bed, perhaps even a dinner party without more than the briefest notice.

'You *don't* remember me?' the voice went on, in the aggrieved tone of one who imagines no one would ever forget him.

'No,' Love admitted. He began to dab the towel on his damp hair; it was cold out of the sun. Who could this clown be?

'Then I'll put you out of your misery,' the caller continued more briskly. 'Richard Mass Parkington.'

'*Really?*'

Now Love remembered. Years before, he had met Parkington briefly in Teheran, long before the Iran-Iraq war. A certain Colonel Douglas MacGillivray, who worked in a department of the Foreign Office that seemed to lack a precise name, only a mixture of letters and numbers, had heard that Love was going to Teheran as a delegate to a medical anti-malaria conference. He had asked him if he could possibly spare a few moments to try and find why a colleague in that city had not been in touch with him as he promised. Love had agreed, without envisaging any complications – never imagining the true nature of this colleague's calling – or the fact that he had been murdered. Richard Mass Parkington had come to his aid, and he had been grateful for his help. But that was a long time ago. That was then; this was now.

'Where are you?' Love asked him in a more friendly tone.

'I would like to see you,' Parkington replied, not answering the question.

'Well, whenever you're down here,' said Love, expecting him to be in London or Paris or Rome or wherever he lived now; the line was not very clear.

'I'm leaving for the Algarve tomorrow,' he added. 'Driving through France and Spain. Perhaps you could ring me when I'm back? I'll be away for about three weeks.'

'You are driving your Cord?'

'Of course.'

'It's about a Cord I would like to see you.'

'Really? Well, please drop in on my return.'

'I'm here now,' replied Parkington. 'I'm speaking to you on my car phone. I'm actually in your front drive. I rang the doorbell but there was no answer.'

'That bell doesn't work,' Love explained. One of the minor hazards of living in the country was that you always intended to repair such items, but so often more important or more interesting matters interfered. And, after all, everyone who knew you simply opened the door and came into the house. Others could wait their turn.

'The door's on the latch,' he explained. 'Come right in.'

He had half expected Parkington to have changed; most people he met after a space of years had, sometimes dramatically. Their hair had thinned, their waists had thickened, but Parkington looked exactly as he did at their first meeting. He had not changed at all. He was lean and fit and clear-eyed. Love hoped the visitor could say the same about him. They shook hands.

'What brings you here?' he asked, with not too much enthusiasm. What brought old acquaintances here, if not a request for hospitality, could too often be a medical opinion for nothing. 'Apart from wanting to talk about a Cord, of course, which I find odd from you. Never knew you were so keen.'

'I'm not. I have this curious pain, Doctor, this odd spot,

31

this funny feeling. My own quack doesn't seem to understand me. I wonder if you could tell me what the score is, man to man, for old time's sake, eh?'

'No way. You look fit to me.'

'Ah, but fit for what? Seriously, I want to tell you about a very rare car. The Lost Cord, if you like.'

He glanced around the hall appreciatively. 'I didn't know you country doctors did so well.'

'It's being single that helps,' Love explained. 'Now, what can I do for you? As I said, I'm off tomorrow and my locum is due any minute, and I'm growing colder every second.'

'You can't do anything for me, Doctor, I am glad to say. But maybe I can do something for you.'

'What have you got to offer?'

'Give me a drink, and I'll tell you.'

They went out on to the patio. The sun had warmed the mellow stone, and a strong late afternoon scent of honeysuckle and roses sweetened the air. Love opened the outside refrigerator, took out his usual bottle of rum, added lime juice and ice, mixed two long drinks.

'You didn't ask me what I'd have,' said Parkington, aggrieved.

'You'll have that or Adam's wine,' Love replied. 'All alcohol's bad for you, but this less than most. Helps the blood sugar. Or so I tell myself.'

'I believe you. And I'll drink to that.'

He drank, held out the empty glass to be refilled.

'You still have the same Cord?' he asked as Love poured out a further four fingers of rum, added juice and ice.

'Of course.'

'To such constancy in all relationships,' said Parkington, raising his glass. He looked quizzically at Love.

'I'm not working flat out for the old firm any more,' he explained carefully. 'I was pensioned off. More or less.'

'You're young to draw a pension, surely?'

'True. But I figured it was better to go voluntarily and perpendicularly on my own two feet, than horizontally in an ambulance or a hearse with a bullet up my arse or in my brain.'

'Agreed. Although some patients of mine would not know the difference.'

'The Chinese in olden days believed – very wisely, in my view – that the stomach and not the head was the repository of all knowledge. But the backside?'

'Such considerations apart, what can you do for me?'

'I'm working for the Midland Widows Insurance Company.'

'Then let me make one thing clear as gin. I don't want to take out a policy. Not even from you, for old time's sake, for your sake, or even for mine. My view of insurance is like my view of marriage. You have to die to beat them both. That's why I've never been keen.'

'On either?' asked Parkington.

Love nodded.

'On both.'

'Well, you have a point. I have been married three times, so I speak with some experience. I pay alimony to my first wife. My second pays alimony to me. My third ran off with a Bahamian millionaire, so we called it quits.

'Now, I don't sell policies – or even buy them. My task is checking out on odd claims. Someone will insure a restaurant or hotel, say, that's losing money. It has been valued highly and everything is kosher, above board. Then – wham – there's a fire when no one's in the hotel or the restaurant, but curiously five drums of cooking oil have been left in the kitchen. Open. All goes up in smoke – even the books that could show the place was making a loss. I look into fortuitously unfortunate happenings like that. And other aspects of the business.'

'Like what?'

Love poured two more drinks.

'Like asking people who really know their subject what something might be worth. A rather special Cord, for instance.'

33

'Depends on the model, where it is, the condition. And how is it special?'

'That's what I want you to tell me. It seems to be one like yours,' Parkington explained. 'But it's in Pakistan. The owner wants to sell it at auction, Sotheby's or Christie's, and needs it insured before it comes back to this country, in case it gets damaged on the journey.'

'That shouldn't be too difficult to assess,' said Love.

'Maybe not. But it's not quite as simple as that. In my experience nothing ever is.'

'In mine, too,' agreed Love with feeling. How often had he faced patients who lied deliberately and consistently to him about their symptoms, either through fear or shame, and yet still expected an accurate diagnosis – and an instant cure?

'According to the details we have, it's a Cord 812, supercharged two-seater. Known in the catalogue as a Sportsman coupé. And it's in perfect condition.'

'Every secondhand car over 20 years old always is,' Love pointed out drily. 'And this is over 50 years old. They have usually been owned by a district nurse. Never had a spanner on them. Original toolkit still unwrapped. Or again, only used for religious purposes. Taking someone to a mosque, a temple, a synagogue, a church. Or for funerals.'

'Well, maybe that's all this one has been used for, too. It doesn't seem in too bad a shape. Here are two photos.'

Parkington took the polaroids out of an envelope. Love examined them. The car's chromium and silvery paintwork seemed in good condition; so did the upholstery leather.

'What would you say it's worth?' asked Parkington, watching him closely. 'On the basis of these pictures.'

'Very difficult to give a price. I assume the engine is original and so on? If so, it all depends on who wants the car. If, say, you found the original owner, who is now an oil baron or a property tycoon or some such, he might give you up to half a million pounds. Or again, he might not. Probably not. The richer they are, the meaner they become.

34

And if it went to auction on a dull day, it might only fetch a fraction of that sum.'

'What would *you* value it at, then?'

'I could not give a price without seeing it,' said Love, handing back the photographs. 'But at a rough guess, it has probably a fairly interesting history. Maybe owned by a maharaja or someone like that in the days of the Raj? I'd say between a hundred thousand pounds and a quarter of a million.'

'No more?'

'It's quite a lot for a car that wouldn't have fetched three hundred a few years ago. But again, as I say, if someone *really* wants it and there's an under bidder or two or four, it could go for several times that. Are you offering it to me at my valuation?'

'No way,' replied Parkington sharply. 'I'm offering you – on behalf of the company – a trip to Pakistan to look at it yourself and then give me a detailed and written valuation, based on your knowledge of this rather esoteric make.'

'But I am off to Portugal tomorrow. This Pakistan thing will have to wait until I'm back. I can't just abandon my trip. I've booked my passage.'

'Unbook it, then. Be our guest. With a fee thrown in.'

'How much of a fee are the Midland Widows throwing?'

'What about £50 a day walkabout money, plus all expenses, and £500 in your back pocket?'

'What about it? And by cancelling my holiday I could save the Midland Widows half a million? They ask for a labour of Hercules – and will not pay for a labour of Love!'

'All right,' said Parkington resignedly. 'I know you are half Scottish. Double that fee. And we refund whatever you have paid out on the Channel ferry. What do you say to that?'

'I say, yes.'

'Good. You should feel at home out there.'

'I will. I was in Pakistan years ago. I have always wanted to go back.'

'I didn't mean that,' said Parkington. 'I meant you will be among your own kind. The car is owned by a doctor, one S. Khan, according to our agent in Rawalpindi. Curious, don't you think? Two doctors. One here, one there. And each with a Cord.'

'I'm not paid to think,' Love retorted. 'But why don't you ask a dealer to value the car? They must be closer to market value than I am.'

'No doubt. And eager to get into that market and start trading. It's really a matter of trust. Horse copers and dealers in exotic old cars share one thing in common. They'll screw you if they get a chance. And I'm not giving them the chance to screw the Midland Widows, any or all of them. My job depends on it. At least, you're honest.'

'At least,' repeated Love ironically. 'Although I have been called other things, and often. Let me look at those pictures again.'

Parkington handed over the two photographs. Love picked up a magnifying glass.

'Dr Khan wants it insured for ten million pounds,' said Parkington, closely watching Love's reaction. 'That's why we need your expert opinion.'

'I can tell you now, without moving an inch from here, that figure is absurd,' said Love firmly.

'Possibly, on the basis of two photographs,' agreed Parkington. 'But remember that Christie's have sold a Bugatti Royale for five and a half million, and in the States a Mercedes 540K will fetch almost as much. So will a Duesenberg, the Cord's stablemate back in the thirties. I've done some homework on prices, you know.'

'So it seems, but much as I like the Cord as a car, it isn't up in the ten million pound league. At least, not yet.'

'Maybe not. But the fact is that some cars *do* fetch millions if there is something special about them. And according to Dr Khan, this Cord falls into that category.'

'Any reasons why?'

'None. But you will find out for us. Perhaps this Cord is

so special that it would appeal to the very richest collectors, men or women to whom money is of no consideration whatever. When they want something, they buy it, and to hell with the cost.

'We're not talking about bank clerks owing mortgages on semi-detached breeding boxes in Bexley Heath and Tulse Hill. Here, we're talking about serious collectors. This might be the only Cord of its kind in the world, totally unique. The owner says it is.'

'Every owner of every old car feels the same – especially when they want to sell it. But how *can* it be so valuable?'

'That, my dear Doctor, is why we are flying you out to Pakistan. I am going on ahead and will meet you in Rawalpindi. Bowker's Hotel. We only ask the question, remember. The Midland Widows look to you for the answer. Now, if you are offering me another rum, I will accept. Pakistan is a dry country and my throat is already parched at the prospect.'

The explosion was so powerful that ten miles away it rocked the Russian Yak helicopter like a child's toy. The huge machine fell clumsily for nearly fifty feet, while the pilot desperately feathered the blades and raced his engine, and the three men strapped in the big passenger compartment looked at each other in alarm.

They were flying above the snows of Afghanistan, well off their usual preset course. They felt it was safer that way – although, of course, they would not admit this to each other, scarcely to themselves – but there seemed less chance of being fired at. Also, they could see any enemy more easily against the snow, using their special binoculars which would pick out the colour of a sheepskin cape or fur hood, the darkness of a machine gun or one of the dreaded Stinger or Blowpipe missile launchers.

It was easier for the Afghans, the Mujahideen, the rebels out in the hills, fighting their ferocious rearguard against the retiring Russian forces, to hole up in rocks and crevices, or beneath scrubby bushes that grew like scabs on the harsh raw rock of the hillsides, than to venture out on a white landscape that offered neither cover nor protection. This war was said to be over; only those involved knew that it had simply moved into another phase.

The men in the helicopter were nearing the end of their tour and although, naturally, they did not admit their feelings, even to each other, they were reluctant to take unnecessary risks. Within days they should be out of this terrible country, out of danger, and with any luck, not returning. So long as they kept radio silence, no one at base would know exactly where they were. After this reconnaissance sortie they would return and make the brusque signal, NTR, nothing to report.

Vorbachov, the KGB colonel, was the first to react. He pulled a wry face, shrugged his shoulders, glanced at his companions questioningly.

'Theirs or ours?' he asked briefly.

Rominsky, the scientist, did not reply. It was not worth attempting to answer such a question: he could only give a guess, and that was no opinion at all. He needed facts, certainties before he voiced any view on any serious subject. The third man, an infantry major, said nervously:

'Could be a rockfall. They have avalanches this time of the year. Someone shouts or fires a rifle, and sound waves react, and a whole mass of snow on the upper slopes starts to slide. It gathers weight, and there's a sound like a gun going off.'

'That wasn't a gun,' said Vorbachov shortly. 'That was something else. And who are those men down below? Have we any patrols out this far?'

'Shall we go back over the foothills, Comrade Colonel, and take a closer look?' the pilot asked him without enthusiasm. He had made too many sorties over other foothills, had landed to pick up too many wounded, usually horribly mutilated, to wish to take any further risks. But Vorbachov was in charge, just as someone back at base was in charge of him. This could be a man who appeared to be an orderly, a driver, someone no one would suspect of working on two levels, but who Vorbachov knew and feared. Even the scientist, or this nervous infantry major could be his superior, but the pilot doubted this. The major looked too uneasy. Like the pilot, he had been out here for too long.

'Keep on course,' Vorbachov ordered. 'Go directly towards the heart of that explosion.'

'There may be another,' said the pilot. 'Then if we are too close, we could lose more height – more than we did just now. And that's it.'

'Well, go up higher. But we must see what caused it. I don't believe it was an avalanche. Not with such force.'

The pilot nodded, and began to gain height. He was pleased to do so; the last time he had landed, he had picked up six wounded men. The sight of their wounds had haunted his dreams ever since. Their thick trousers had been hacked away with knives, their testicles cut out and stuffed into their mouths – and then their lips sewn tightly together with a tentmaker's needle.

Worst of all, they were still alive, writhing in their giant agony on the abrasive rocks, their unspeakable wounds black with flies. Afghan women had done this, so the only one who still could speak eventually told them. It was their tradition to treat captured enemies in such a way. Every invader who had attempted to occupy the country had faced this risk.

Even the British, years ago, had been forced to withdraw to the relative safety of the Khyber Pass and into their Indian empire south of the craggy hills, leaving this harsh, horrible land to the people who could be as cruel as its climate.

The blades of the rotor beat the freezing air like a giant egg whisk. The shadow of the helicopter and its flickering hammering blades moved steadily across the white expanse. Soon they flew into thick white cloud. But as they entered it, they realized that this was not really cloud, but snowflakes which had blown up from the ground through the force of the explosion, and had not yet settled.

It was like being in the centre of a child's snowstorm toy, thought the infantry major. He had two children in the workers' flat shared with his wife, her mother and his aunt, on the outskirts of Leningrad. His younger child had been given one of these toys for a birthday present. He remembered shaking it and seeing the flakes slowly settle on miniature cone-shaped fir trees, and little figures wearing blue parkas and red shoes, until all was covered in white, just like this accursed landscape.

And in thinking of this, he thought again of his family. The smell of stale cabbage water and blocked drains was suddenly sharp in his nostrils, and he heard a child crying in the tiny flat across the stone damp corridor, with the shared lavatory and the single tap for cold water, and the familiar, hoarse barking of a miserable dog, kept chained on the balcony.

It had been exciting to leave that dreary place, to fly south with a crack unit, to be told you would be warmly welcomed by the inhabitants of a country you would help to liberate from American Fascist imperialists. Reality had proved totally different from the dream. Fact was separated from propaganda fiction by pain, by death, by the all-pervading fear of capture that made him start up at night in his camp bed, sweating and gasping for breath. And the recurring nightmare that he had been cornered by the Mujahideen, and their honed sword blades felt cold against his naked body.

'Now go down,' Vorbachov told the pilot.

'You mean land, sir?'

'If necessary. Not many people are likely to be up here. Except ours.'

'I hope you are right, Comrade Colonel,' the pilot thought, as he brought down the helicopter through the flurrying snow. Suddenly, they were in bright sunshine, so sharp it hurt their eyes and they blinked against the unexpected

40

blaze. The pilot steered the helicopter to the right. A hundred feet beneath them they could now see a yellow vehicle; two long trails from its tracks stretched behind it into infinity. Several men were standing around this, looking up at them, shielding their eyes against the glare of the sun. One ran to the vehicle, opened the cab door and brought out a red flag which he began to wave vigorously.

'Who the hell are they?' asked Vorbachov, almost to himself.

'It looks like one of our vehicles. Snowcat.'

'What the devil are they doing up here? Do you think the Afghans have captured it? Is this a trap? Can you speak to them on the radio?'

'I'll do my best, sir.'

The pilot began to speak into his head microphone. The loudspeaker crackled; static roared and whistled and squealed against the drumming of the engine until he found the wavelength. The men on the ground were speaking:

'Ground to helicopter Zee five seven four oh kay. Can you land? Can you land?'

'Helicopter to ground, who are you?'

'We are party of engineers, number six-oh-one-five field service group, with orders to create an avalanche.'

'That was the explosion we heard?'

'Yes.'

'What is the purpose of landing? We may sink into the snow.'

'There is a hard patch in front of the Snowcat. It would be safe to land there.'

'But why, man, why?'

'We have discovered something we think Headquarters should know about. At once.'

Vorbachov took the microphone from the pilot.

'What have you discovered?' he asked.

There was a pause.

'We think you should see for yourselves.'

'Colonel Vorbachov speaking. We have no time for delay.

41

We are on patrol, and are already off course. We came here to investigate the explosion.'

'In that case, Comrade Colonel, we will take our discovery back on the Snowcat. But that will take a day, maybe two, maybe longer. We have trouble with the engine. You can be back with it in an hour.'

The pilot turned to the others, looked at them enquiringly.

'You think they're genuine?' the major asked nervously.

'Of course they're genuine,' said Vorbachov irritably, to convince himself as much as the others. He turned to the pilot.

'Can you get her off again if we go down?'

'Provided we don't sink into the snow too deeply.'

'Well, land where the man suggested. Look, he's running to show you the place.'

They all peered out of the side of the helicopter. The man with the red flag was stumbling through thick snow, up to his knees, until he began to run more easily. He was obviously on hard ground, packed snow or ice. He waved triumphantly up to them.

The pilot came down gently where he indicated. The great blades stirred the fluttering snow and blew it around them in a crisp halo. Freezing crystals glittered like glass: blue, green, purple, white under the blazing heatless sun. The machine's belly crunched a few inches into the hard surface, then the pilot cut the engine. The rotors slackened and drooped and stopped. The pilot undid his safety harness, came through the cabin, opened the door. The four men jumped down on to the snow. After the synthetic heat of the cabin blower, and the comforting roar of the engine, chill and silence hit them like a blow. The insides of their nostrils hardened with cold. Suddenly it became painful to breathe. Their teeth ached, their lips stiffened and cracked as they walked slowly, stiffly towards the man with the flag. He recognized Vorbachov's KGB tabs on his uniform and saluted smartly. He ignored the others.

'Well?' Vorbachov asked him shortly, acknowledging his salute. 'What is this discovery that is so important?'

'I will show you, sir.'

They followed him to the Snowcat. On the far side, in shadow, so that they had not seen it from the air, a tent had been set up hastily, using one side of the Snowcat as a wall. He lifted the flap, motioned them inside. They bent their heads, stooping in the confined triangular space. The canvas roof was already frozen, stiff as a board. Their breath hung like fog in front of them. On the ground, a green tarpaulin, stamped in each corner with a red star and a hammer and sickle, had been stretched and on this lay a block of ice, rough-edged and raw as though it had been crudely hacked from an even larger block. A layer of snow covered it, and the pilot thought for a moment that it looked like a huge piece of cake with white icing. The man with the flag brushed loose snow from the top with the edge of his flagpole. They peered closely at the ice. Inside lay the body of a man.

'Who the devil is that?' asked the scientist. 'One of ours or theirs?'

'Neither, sir,' the man with the flag explained. 'The ice is going cloudy now, but before that happened, it was clear as glass. He is wearing outlandish clothes, maybe from the last century or probably even older. They are made of leather and animal skins, and his boots are unusual. He has a pistol, what they called a flintlock, I believe, and a curious sword and a pouch and a copper shield for his eyes. They used to wear those hundreds of years ago in these hills before sun spectacles and eye shields were invented.'

'But where has he come from?' asked Vorbachov.

'We set a charge in the top of a crevasse, Comrade Colonel. We hoped this would blow away one side of the mountain, and the reverberations would start an avalanche. Our orders relate directly to scientific and mineral research. The explosion only blew a part of the mountain away. The rock underneath was far too thick for the charge we laid. It was totally concealed by snow, Comrade Colonel. We had not realized its depth. And this . . . this person must have been entombed inside the crevasse, and the explosion just spewed him out – literally at our feet.'

'Who do you think it is – was?' asked the major. He had seen the embalmed bodies of early Communist leaders, the great pioneers, Lenin, Stalin, and the rest, lying in state in Moscow, but their faces had appeared soft and unreal, like waxed fruit. Theirs might once have been the bodies of real people, or again they might not. There was no sure means of finding out. Of course, visitors were told they were who it was said they were, and crowds of hundreds, sometimes thousands, filed past them every day of every year. But then people were easily persuaded; everyone tended to believe what they wanted to believe.

The same thing happened, of course, in the West, so he had read. The bodies of saints and other holy people lay embalmed in churches and cathedrals, but again there seemed an element of trickery, possibly even substitution, about these convenient corpses. This man was altogether more believable. His condition owed nothing to the embalmer's art, only to the chill weight of immeasurable tons of ice and snow.

This man's blood, congealed through the centuries, must still be in his veins, food from his last meal still in his stomach, perhaps letters or maps remaining in his pouch. Death had come upon him suddenly and unawares; not by poison, the knife, the bullet, or after years of illness. One moment he must have been young, alive and healthy, the next, totally unexpectedly, he had begun a sleep of centuries within a mountain of ice.

'What do you want to do with this?' the Colonel asked, rubbing his hands together and stamping his feet against the cold.

'Headquarters should view this body as soon as possible, before the protective ice melts around it. All manner of facts could then be discovered, Comrade Colonel. It could also provide a great propaganda boost for us. In the middle of fighting a war against American Fascist gangsters and their lackeys here, we can still step aside to carry out serious and peaceful scientific enquiries.'

'How many men have you got with you?' interrupted Vorbachov sharply. He did not wish to hear a long speech about matters which he might not understand. He was ill-educated, and always felt uneasy in the presence of qualified professional people: lawyers, scientists, surgeons, engineers, and went to great pains to conceal his ignorance and lack of confidence when with them. He owed his position not to examinations and degrees but to ruthlessness and aggression, allies which had not failed him yet, and were the equal of paper qualifications.

'Six, Comrade Colonel,' the man with the flag replied respectfully.

'Well, then, get them here and carry this body between you to the helicopter. Now, we must be on our way. What is your unit identification so that I can report who made this discovery?'

The man gave him the details. Vorbachov noted them on a pocket tape recorder, with the map reference of the explosion, and walked back to the helicopter, not speaking. Silence always spoke loudest and to best effect with people like these; it also prevented a lot of questions he might not wish to answer. The body was loaded aboard and slid back into the narrow tail of the machine, then the huge block of ice was tied down securely with wide webbing straps.

The two parties saluted each other smartly, the helicopter pilot started his engine. The machine rose steadily into the air, bowed once in farewell, turned and moved gracefully across the face of the snow into the white oblivion. Long after it had disappeared, the peculiar whackering of its blades echoed across the hills. Only then did the man with the flag realize he had been so concerned to get the body they had discovered away safely and without damage, and so awed by the presence of a KGB colonel, he had forgotten to take the number of the unit to which he had entrusted it. He had given away a corpse, possibly hundreds of years old, and seemingly in perfect condition, to perfect strangers. He had no idea where the corpse had originally come from. Now he had no knowledge of its immediate destination.

All through the long flight from Heathrow to Islamabad, the capital of Pakistan, Love pondered what Parkington had told him and failed to find answers to the two questions that puzzled him. How could a Cord conceivably be worth so much? And why had its owner, Dr Khan, set such a high and apparently arbitrary figure on the car?

When the plane came down at Dohar to refuel, still seven o'clock English time, but nearly midnight there, neon lights flashed red and green and yellow with unidentifiable Arabic script. Under their intermittent glare, the runway shone in the darkness like a great expanse of liquid tar. What were they advertising? Or who were they warning?

At Muscat, passengers were allowed off the aircraft for half an hour. The airport was built like a long mosque, pale yellow under floodlights, with delicate filigree decorations and curved windows; the control tower resembled a minaret. Men with huge squeejees of rags and feathers continually wiped the black marble floor of the passenger lounge as Love walked up and down, seeking answers to his questions and finding none.

Quite inexplicably, he felt an increasing sense of unease about the trip, and his part in it. He guessed that Parkington must have felt the same, or he would simply have advised the Midland Widows that they should decline the business at such an inflated value. But he had not. So, why not? There must be a reason, but Parkington was keeping it to himself.

Love tried to rationalize his feelings, as he had taught patients to do if they expressed doubts or dreads about an operation; to concentrate and follow the advice of the juggler. The situation was really very simple. As an expert on Cord cars, he had accepted a fee to advise an insurance company on the value of one particular model. This he would do, then he would enjoy his holiday in Pakistan, instead of in Portugal, and that would be the end of the matter. But even as he assured himself he was being unnecessarily concerned, he could not rid himself of the thought that, far from being the end of the matter, his part in events might only be the beginning.

He did not feel like reading the paperbacks he had bought at Heathrow, and the daily newspapers the steward distributed seemed full of stories of disasters, kidnaps, terrorist bombings, aircraft hijacks. In search of lighter reading, Love skimmed through the magazine the airline provided, turning finally to the maps. The sight of routes in red, of distances, of figures for latitude and longitude always excited his interest; he had been born under a wandering star. Idly, he checked the map bearings of the Algarve, roughly 37 20N 8 35W and compared this with Peshawar, 34 3N 71 30E or thereabouts. The weather should be better than in Portugal: he was all in favour of that after a winter in England.

He had a theory that countries on roughly similar lines of latitude had much the same characteristics, both in their people and their products. Could this, in part at least, account for the fact that sherry came from Spain and Cyprus, and excellent table wines from parts of Chile, South Africa, Australia? Soon, he slept, and only awoke at half past four next morning as the airliner began its long, slow descent towards Islamabad.

Whenever Love travelled by plane, he packed everything he needed in a soft leather bag he could sling easily over his shoulder. This way, he was through the Customs at Islamabad airport before the luggage of other passengers had even been offloaded from the plane. Outside the building, behind a wire mesh screen, several people were waiting to meet relatives, friends, business associates. Some held up pieces of cardboard with names written crudely on them – Macnab, Ali, Glover, Rajib.

47

Against one wall stood a row of little booths, all closed now, with names of hotels above their locked doors. Nearby, a man sat behind a desk reading a vernacular newspaper. Love approached him.

'Yes?' the man asked him in English, without looking up.

'I want a taxi,' said Love.

'Then I want one hundred and fifty rupees. Five pounds, your English money.'

He pushed over a form, went on reading. Love filled it out with his name, home address, passport number, destination, price agreed. This was his first taste of Pakistani bureaucracy; he hoped it would be his last. The man pocketed the five pound note, shouted over the top of his paper, not taking his eyes from the printed page.

Another man, wrapped in a grey blanket, detached himself from the shelter of a pillar, where he had crouched, and led the way to a car parked amid rows of other almost identical vehicles. Behind the car park stood a lofty minaret garishly lit in blue and green. Love heard an electronic click, and then a recorded call to morning prayer: 'God is great . . . There is no god but Allah . . . Muhammad is the prophet of God. Come ye to prayer . . .'

They set off down wide streets into a dark and seemingly empty countryside. Over the previous two decades, this new capital, Islamabad, the home of Islam, in its literal translation, had been built at enormous cost around an original village in the middle of fields. Straight roads now radiated like the spokes of huge wheels from roundabout to roundabout; vast floodlit buildings shimmered in the distance like palaces in a celestial city. The road was double tracked, lit by huge overhead lights. On a hillside giant white stones spelled out three words: Unity, Faith, Discipline. But whose? Love wondered.

The driver overtook trucks festooned with coloured lights like travelling Christmas trees, and cyclists, wrapped in blankets against the early morning chill. Beside one, a dog on a string trotted along trustingly. Beyond silver leafed

48

trees, planted by the million to lay the dust, wildness still remained. In unclaimed patches of weed and swamp, Love could see the glittering resentful eyes of animals shine like green heads in the taxi's headlamps. What had been jungle once could be jungle again and, out there, the wild beasts waited. The unease he had felt on the plane returned; he felt surrounded by fear.

They turned off the Grand Trunk Road into the grounds of Bowker's Hotel. Dew glistened on metal tables and chairs stacked on a lawn beneath trees with whitewashed trunks. The cab stopped. Love climbed out, went into the reception office past a window full of souvenirs: a chess set in jade, elephants carved from camel bones. A clerk looked at him enquiringly.

'I have a room booked by Mr Parkington,' Love explained.

'Your name, please, sir?'

'Dr Jason Love.'

The man took up a card with a list of names, marked each one off with a pencil.

'Mr Glover?' he asked hopefully.

'No, Love. Doctor.'

'Not any booking for you, sir. Only for Mr Glover.'

'Probably that's me. There's been a mistake,' Love suggested.

'It cannot be, sir. Mr Glover is not taking up his booking. Regrettably, he is dead.'

'How d'you mean, *dead*?'

Then he remembered the man at the airport holding up a cardboard square with the name Glover.

'Just now dead, sir. In motoring accident on the Murree Road, coming from the airport. Very bad thing. We have just had telephone call.'

'Who from?'

'They are not saying, sir. Only reporting the facts.'

'I've heard of dead man's shoes. Now I'll have a dead man's room.'

'That would be difficult. It is not ready yet. We were told he was not using it.'

'Well, get it ready, for goodness' sake. Are you *certain* you've no booking for me?'

'I am now looking, sir. Positively no booking. That is the truth of the matter.'

'Well, you have one now. That is also the truth of the matter.'

Love filled in a card with details of name, address, passport number, expected length of stay, purpose of visit. Tourism sounded best and safest – an odd word to use about a journey like this, surely. *Safest?* After all, what danger could there be? Again he remembered his feeling of unease on the journey – and wondered whether someone else had mistaken Glover for Love.

If so, who had died in the accident – and had his death been totally accidental?

Room 101 of Bowker's Hotel contained two single beds and a table on which stood a basket of apples and oranges. Parkington had eaten two of the oranges the previous evening, and the air smelled vaguely acidic from their sharply scented peel. Now he lay on the bed nearest the door, a safety reaction, born from years as a secret agent. The motto for a successful spy, he thought, would find favour with insurance companies: never run a needless risk; the life you lose could be your own.

If he had chosen the far bed, he might trip over the near one should he be attacked. But who would attack him here? He was a tourist in a friendly land. Yet ten million pounds of someone's money – or someone's expectation – could be at stake. Such a sum could buy a lot of trouble.

On the other bed, Parkington had laid a large rubber-covered torch he had brought with him. This had a halogen bulb and a special reflector. A thin wire led from the torch, and he had looped it around his left wrist. By pressing a button on the end of this wire, the torch would illuminate the whole room in a blinding blaze, bright as a magnesium flash. The torch was also heavy enough to be useful as a blackjack – and who would suspect a harmless torch could also be a weapon?

He lay on his back, as always when on his own in a hot country, in that dreamy half-way state between sleep and wakefulness. His bedroom, like all rooms in this old-fashioned hotel, was in an annexe on the ground floor and furnished in a pleasantly outmoded way. He might have been back in the days of the Raj and, when in Rawalpindi, he always stayed at Bowker's, in preference to the modern Pearl-Continental or the Holiday Inn, because of this agreeable feeling of nostalgia. Time might not have stood quite still here but neither had it moved very quickly. After all, this was what one might expect; the Urdu word for yesterday was *kul*, the same as the word for tomorrow. He found this resistance to unnecessary change reassuring.

Not too much in Parkington's life had been so reassuring, and since being expelled from school at the age of sixteen, his career had been marked by too many changes. Nowadays, the prank that had warranted expulsion then would probably bring no more than a mild reprimand, but then it had quite irrevocably changed the course of his career. He – and others – had balanced half a bucket of water on a dormitory door, meaning to surprise another boy. Instead, an unpopular housemaster came in unexpectedly and was soaked. Worse, he claimed that the metal bucket falling on his head had seriously affected his hearing. The others involved vehemently and predictably denied all knowledge of the prank. Parkington did not, and since this was but one of several escapades in which he had taken a leading part, the headmaster requested his immediate removal.

Parkington was an orphan. His sole relation then was an old uncle, living on the south coast, a grumpy bachelor who suffered from heart trouble and sucked pills which he placed under his tongue several times a day.

'Nitro-glycerine tablets,' he would declare glumly. 'I'm a walking bloody bomb.'

Now he had something else to make him even more morose.

'That's the third school you've tried,' he told Parkington sourly. 'I can't spend any more money on you.'

'It's not your money you are spending, uncle. Father left it in trust for me.'

'I know that, boy, but I have to look after it for you – until you are of age. I suggest you cram for whatever examinations you should have taken at school and then apply for a short service commission in the Army. It's a pity we have so few colonies left. You might have done well out in some remote land.'

Parkington had scraped through the Regular Commissions Board and after a series of routine postings found he had a liking for what was carefully described as 'undercover work'. He was big and full of self-confidence. He could take care of himself in a tight corner, and quite liked doing so. More important, he could also fit well into that tight corner, as a labourer, an oil rig mechanic, as all manner of people.

Gradually, he moved sideways into the shadowy world where career structure was uncertain, because life expectancy itself lacked any certainty. Here, he worked for Colonel MacGillivray, in departments known by initials or numbers, or by curiously unapt descriptions such as Principal Co-Ordinating Costs Department, or the Central Advisory Committee.

These offices moved regularly – sometimes irregularly – around the capital: they could occupy a suite in Mayfair one month, a rooming house in Kilburn the next, then on to a bungalow in Balham. Overseas, their members might briefly be attached to an obscure embassy or consulate as a third or fourth commercial secretary, a second information officer. Parkington had worked directly under MacGillivray, who he much admired for the colonel's qualities of imperturbability and cynicism, which he described as realism. But there had been clashes of personality with others, because Parkington's natural inclination was to live for the moment, dangerously if need be, but always without much consideration for tomorrow. How could he think otherwise when today was still not finished?

Also, he often believed that he knew *instinctively* what should be done. Sometimes, he was right, sometimes not. Where he had been unwise was that he could not persuade his superiors – or even his colleagues – that he knew answers which had consistently eluded them. So this career had ended, with expressions of mutual regret – MacGillivray assuring him that he could still consider himself as being attached to the department in a loose, freelance capacity. With this in mind, he arranged for a regular fee to be paid every month into a bank account maintained for Parkington in a Jersey bank and under another name. They would call upon him if they needed someone on whom they could rely. The Treasury approved such arrangements; they saved money.

The Midland Widows had then approached him, as they regularly approached others retiring from police forces and the armed services, and appointed him as a Supernumerary Adviser.

Parkington did not always know who he was to advise, only that he was supernumerary in the sense that, in an insurance company specializing in pension plans, he must be one of the few on their staff not in pensionable employment. However, he had made his own bed and he could lie on it and he did – as often as possible with a pretty woman.

It was a pity he was alone now, he had thought as he undressed, and that Pakistan was dry. But he had seen the quaintly-titled Permit Room almost opposite his room, where a foreigner to whom alcohol was essential could buy a bottle of beer or vodka. He carried his own supply with him, for his head was the hardest part of him, so a former old mathematics master once informed him. Sometimes this hardness of head could be useful. Maybe this trip would be one of those times?

As he awaited sleep, he wondered drowsily about the huge value set on this Cord. Why anyone would be willing to spend millions of pounds on an old vehicle that only a few years earlier would have been sent to the scrapyard, was beyond his comprehension. But they did, they did. And right now, some unknown buyer would help to provide him with a living.

He wondered about Love; when he would arrive, whether he had changed much since they had last worked together and, if so, whether for better or worse. In Parkington's opinion, change was almost always retrograde. He instinctively equated it with decline, a theory based on words from the only hymn he remembered from his schooldays: 'Change and decay in all around I see.'

Beyond the French windows of his room lay a swimming pool, now empty, with a grass border around it. These windows were slightly open, not a wise move in India or Pakistan, when cats were prowling about at night, but he liked fresh air. A slight sound had disturbed his light doze. Now he was instantly awake, watching through the wide glass doors as dawn coloured the sky pink and gold, and prepared the world for another day.

The antennae of alarm in his mind assured him that this faint noise, as of a little animal moving carefully, had not been made by any small creature that walked on four legs, but by a larger one who walked on two. Parkington tensed, and his right hand went silently under the pillow. His fingers touched and then gripped the comfortingly serrated edge of his nine-millimetre Browning High Power pistol. He carefully drew the weapon down by his side as he heard a slightly louder squeak as the door knob was turned carefully. A faint rush of cooler air flooded into the room as the door opened fully. Parkington waited until he knew whoever was coming into the room was actually inside.

Then his left hand pressed the torch button. As his right

54

hand aimed his pistol, the room exploded into an incandescent blaze of light blinding the eyes of the intruder.

'Take one step further,' Parkington invited him conversationally, not raising his voice in case he awoke whoever might be sleeping in the room next door.

'Just one more tiny step, and I'll blow your balls right across the swimming pool.'

PART THREE

When the two Russian trucks came slowly down the road, Ahmed stood respectfully to one side and wrapped his khaki blanket round him, as much for concealment as against the bitter wind. Years ago – and not too many years ago, he kept reminding himself – when he had been Professor of Oriental Languages at the University of Kabul, others had shown him respect. Now that was all behind him, best left unremembered, unrecalled.

He watched, head bowed beneath his round fustian Afghan cap, as the breeze from the trucks flattened his thin pantaloons against his calves. He felt old and cold; he had stood like this, eyes averted from these hated invaders in too many places, for too long. Would there never come a time when, like other men of his age, he could sit in the most favoured place, and reap the reward of a lifetime of study?

He had always believed that, on retirement, this would be his right. But now it seemed that the only right which people like him possessed was the right to endure endless humiliations or to exercise their ultimate prerogative, the right to die. He was one of the dispossessed. In the early months of the Russian occupation, his home had been blasted apart by a bomb which fell short of its target. His wife had died instantly, his younger son after several days of agony, both legs blown away, and without any drugs to help him.

They had attempted to carry him on a litter across the mountains to the safety and shelter of Pakistan, where more than two and a half million other Afghans had already fled for safety, but his son could not survive the terrible jolting of the journey. He was buried on a rocky hillside in a grave unmarked on any map, but still vivid in his father's mind. Now, Ahmed was alone in the world – for his elder son was reported killed, fighting with the Mujahideen – without home or any possessions except the clothes on his body, the shoes on his feet. But weary as he was, he still felt he could do something – anything – to try and change this miserable situation and redeem his honour. If he had to die, he would die as a man, not as a slave.

He raised his head slightly as the trucks stopped so that he could see more clearly who or what was being taken out of them. The smallest item of news could have its value for those who doubted that the hated invaders would ever genuinely leave the country. Six men clambered out over the tailgate of the first vehicle and then crossed to the second. There was some shouting of contradictory orders, and then, between them, they carried a stretcher into the nearest building. This must be unusually heavy to require so many bearers, Ahmed thought, and whatever lay concealed beneath a tarpaulin thrown across it was at least two feet high and wide and possibly six feet long.

Ahmed watched the men come out of the building and drive off. He shuffled away behind some huts. A goat shambled off up an alleyway in front of him; a half naked little boy with a runny nose spun a home-made top; women sat gossiping as they picked nits out of their children's hair. No one noticed Ahmed. He fitted so well into the drab background, he was almost an invisible man.

He waited for several minutes and then, carrying a brush of twigs and a hammered copper bowl, flattened like a tray in the centre, he approached the building where the vehicle had stopped, knocked timidly at the door.

Someone inside called out a question in Russian. Ahmed

answered in the same language, asking them to let him in. It could be dangerous to enter any building without first announcing this intention. The Russians feared sudden movements; locals had been shot for much less. Now that they were leaving they were more on edge than when they were there in numbers. A man inside curtly told him to come in, and Ahmed opened the door.

Two Russians were standing by a zinc-covered table; they wore white coats and thick green rubber gloves. Ahmed recognized them; he had often seen them walking about the base. They looked at him enquiringly, then waved him away irritably; they must have thought he was a colleague or they would not have allowed him inside. Ahmed pretended not to understand, and crouched down, sweeping up dust into his bowl. Humble as a domestic animal, he moved around the room. They looked at him impatiently, uneasy in the company of a stranger.

'Get out,' one told him roughly. 'There's no need to sweep up now. Come on – *hurry!*'

Ahmed bowed and backed out of the door. He had seen what lay on the table: a slab of ice, rough cut, chipped and flawed, and inside this the entombed, frozen body of a man.

Could this be a Russian of high rank who had slipped down a crevasse, and whose corpse had only now been discovered? The war had been going on for nearly nine years, so this was possible. But Ahmed's brief glimpse of the body made him doubt this possibility. The dead man's face had not been Slavonic, with high cheek bones, and his skin looked sallow, with the bone structure of a European. His clothes, even though distorted by a foot of ice, seemed absurdly old-fashioned, like apparel taken from a museum.

Ahmed sought the opinion of a young man, a former student of his who was allowed to bring tea in a samovar to Russians in this hut. From him, he had already learned that the two scientists constantly carried out experiments on leaves, roots, and samples of earth and rock. They were searching for traces of minerals that could be mined and exploited. There was an economic as well as a political dimension to Russia's invasion of Afghanistan. And now that they were leaving – or at least giving this impression to the rest of the world – time added urgency to their search for any new unexploited sources of raw materials.

'I know all about that body, Professor,' the student replied at once. He was always polite to the old man, still mindful of their former relationship as teacher and pupil. 'A team of scientists were out trying to start an avalanche, to test for minerals in an area they had not tried before. The rock was far tougher than they had anticipated, and the explosion blew out a man's body that apparently had been wedged in a crevasse – for hundreds of years, so they think. They are all quite excited about the discovery.'

'Whose body is it?'

'A European's, so I have heard. It has been preserved amazingly. They will thaw it out here and then dry freeze it scientifically, and fly it to Moscow to be examined in detail. When the ice melts, it will flood everything, so they're transferring it tonight to the mortuary.'

The mortuary was a stone building, standing apart from the rest, and without windows. Its sliding metal doors were always kept bolted and padlocked. The only other opening was a vent in the roof through which came the constant hum of an air-conditioning machine that kept the temperature perpetually below zero. Here, on sliding trays like filing cabinets of the dead, were stored bodies of Russian soldiers awaiting group shipment back to Russia. Most of those killed in action were never recovered – it was too dangerous even to attempt to bring them in – and this suited the higher command because it had helped to conceal the true extent of Russian casualties in an increasingly unpopular war.

'There is a special room to one side, where they do post-mortems,' the young man explained. 'They will thaw it out there.'

'When is it due to go?'

'A cargo plane is going out the day after tomorrow. I

expect they will put the body on that. But why your interest?'

'Because *they* are interested,' Ahmed replied simply. 'If this were just another body, they would have left it where you say it has been for hundreds of years. There must be something about it that's important.'

'Probably only its age, Professor. They're scientists, you know, not politicians.'

'They are all politicians,' retorted Ahmed bitterly.

That night they both watched from the shadows as Russian orderlies wheeled the body on a trolley to the mortuary. The scientists were inside the building for more than half an hour. A sentry stood guard outside until they came out. He padlocked the gates, handed them the key, and the scientists walked back to their mess. The only sound in the cold night came from the air-conditioning plant. The young man told Ahmed that the temperature in the post-mortem room had been set unusually high; the ice casing around the corpse was melting steadily.

Next morning Ahmed sought him out again.

'Any news?' he asked him anxiously.

'I took tea in half an hour ago. The body was on the slab in the post-mortem room. Almost all the ice had melted. The body is of a man, probably in his early thirties. I saw bruises on his head where he must have fallen all that time ago. They have emptied his pockets, and his pouch.'

'What did they find?'

'A knife with a horn handle. An inkhorn, a crude quill pen. A sort of diary.'

'Who was he? Do they know?'

'Not yet. The diary was in English, but with quaint writing, and the melting ice had made the ink run. They brought in an interpreter to decipher it. He could not understand it at all, but they believe the man was one of several on a march to the East. His body was strong and well nourished, and his clothes of good cloth. There was also a piece of parchment or dried skin in his pouch, folded and flattened. And now, of course, rotten with water.'

'What was on that?'

'A few lines in some unknown script.'

'Unknown to them, perhaps,' replied Ahmed. 'But possibly not to me. I might be able to translate it.'

'They will find someone else for that, Professor. They have several interpreters here, you know. And in Moscow they have many more.'

'Not necessarily for something written hundreds of years ago – and in a script they may not recognize.'

Ahmed went across to the mortuary, knocked timidly at the door. A Russian orderly opened it. He had a Kalashnikov slung across his shoulder.

'What d'you want?' he asked, regarding the old man in his shabby clothes with disfavour.

'To see the senior scientist.'

'You? Why?'

'I think I can help them.'

'In what way?'

'Let him judge that,' Ahmed replied, and pushed past the man into the room.

The two scientists he had seen yesterday looked up from a computer screen, annoyed at the interruption.

'You again? What do you want?' The taller of the two asked him. 'There is no need to sweep the room now. Do it some other time.'

'Forgive me, gentlemen,' said Ahmed, bowing respectfully to them. 'I do not come to sweep the room, but to offer my services in another and hopefully more valuable way. I heard you had found a piece of parchment with some writing on it that you could not decipher.'

The scientists glanced uneasily at each other. Was nothing secret in this bleak and hostile land? Did every wall have ears?

'I may be able to help you,' Ahmed continued. 'I used to be Professor of Oriental Languages at Kabul University.'

61

'Why aren't you now?' asked the taller scientist sharply.

'I was then not a communist, so I had to leave. Now, of course, I fully realize the grievous errors of my past bourgeois thinking. I am hoping to be re-appointed, but, in the meantime, I thought that if I could help you over the translation, perhaps you might, from the goodness of your hearts, help me in return. Not that I could aim for total reinstatement of my old position. But at least I might work with academics again, instead of simply as a cleaner, a sweeper of dust.'

The other scientist turned to an Afghan orderly.

'Do you know this man?'

'It is true what he says,' the orderly replied. 'He was a professor in the old days.'

'How did you hear any translation was necessary?'

'The wind has ears, sir,' replied Ahmed.

'Pretty good ears, it seems,' said the other scientist drily. He exchanged a glance with his colleague. After all, no harm could possibly come from letting this old fool look at the script. It probably contained nothing of interest, let alone of value, if the contents of the dead man's diary were anything to go by. But it would be good for their personal prestige if they could present their superiors in Moscow with a translation. It might even help their own speedy repatriation, and any hope of leaving this wretched country must be pursued energetically – the more so if it could be achieved with honour and acclaim.

'Right,' he said. 'Let us see what you can do.'

The three of them went through the mortuary to a side room. Ahmed had never been inside the mortuary, had only glimpsed white hoar frost on the metal containers from the doorway. Their breath fanned out into the freezing air as they hurried past cabinets of corpses. The walls and ceiling of the post-mortem room were heavily insulated; and the air felt unpleasantly moist and warm. In front of them, on a polished metal table, with water dripping steadily into zinc gutters, lay the body of a man. He had longish hair, a sallow

62

face, a tarnished metal crucifix on a threadbare string around his neck.

'Who is he?' asked Ahmed softly. The dead man had a noble face; he had been a man of breeding, not a peasant.

'A traveller from long ago,' replied the taller scientist. 'We are having his diary translated. Not a very difficult job. But what is written on this piece of paper seems puzzling – at least to the interpreter who had a look at it. In Moscow, of course, it will not present any problems.'

'Of course not,' Ahmed agreed quickly.

The scientist pointed towards a side table. On this, flattened between two sheets of glass, lay a rough-edged square of animal skin.

'Don't touch it,' said the other scientist quickly. 'It may disintegrate if it is moved. We found it in his pouch.'

Ahmed nodded, peering at it closely.

'I need a stronger light,' he said.

The scientist adjusted a spring-loaded reading lamp above the glass. Ahmed examined the faded, watery writing.

'It's upside down,' he said, and moved around the table.

The writer had used some primitive pen, and the skin on which he had written was most probably placed on a rough uneven surface. The strokes were blotched and faded; Ahmed calculated that the wording had probably remained undamaged until the ice had thawed. Then the ink had run and blurred the letters.

'A magnifying glass,' he said in his more familiar professorial tone of voice. One was produced. He focused it. He could make out the writing now; it was an early Sanskrit script, unchanged from the fifth century for more than a thousand years, and now never used.

'Well?' the taller scientist asked impatiently.

'It is about a river,' replied Ahmed slowly, memorizing what he had read, deliberately not translating it all.

'What sort of river?'

'Impossible to say. The script is too faded. The name is unreadable. It is probably giving directions about crossing a river with a swift current. In Moscow, of course, with infra-red and other modern devices, it should not present any problems.'

'Is that all you can tell us?' the other scientist asked, disappointed. 'Can't you be more specific?'

'It says, so far as I can make out, that the river is shallow at only one point.'

'But what point? Where? What river?'

'I am sorry, sir,' said Ahmed in contrite tones, putting down the glass. 'That is all I can read.'

'It is not very much.' Disappointment roughened the scientist's voice like a rasp.

'With respect, sir, I do not think you will find anyone here who can interpret it more clearly. I am sorry, gentlemen, but I can only tell you what I have read.'

'Then get out!'

Ahmed bowed respectfully to them both and walked back through the mortuary. As he closed the outer door behind him, the scientists looked at each other, the same thought suddenly in both their minds.

'Do you think that *was* all he could translate?' asked the taller one.

'You think he is fooling us, eh? I have the same feeling. Well, we can soon find out.'

He called to the Russian orderly, who unslung his Kalashnikov. The three men hurried to the door – which opened as they reached it. Colonel Vorbachov stood looking at them all in surprise.

'Going somewhere in a hurry, comrades?' he asked.

'Not really in a hurry, Comrade Colonel. Just to check on some papers.'

'Three of you? Nothing to do with this corpse, I trust?'

'Nothing, Comrade Colonel.'

It was safer to deny it than to attempt to explain; no one trusted a KGB officer.

'I am glad to hear it, for I have just had a Most Immediate

signal about that. The body is to leave tonight, not tomorrow, as originally scheduled. And no one is to see any documents that I understand you have found. The whole discovery must not be mentioned anywhere until it can be announced at the highest level. Then due credit can be given.' He paused and added: 'To those who deserve it.'

The two scientists nodded, watched the colonel walk away. Fear now gripped their stomachs like pain after a poisoned meal. They must find that old professor before he could speak of what he had read on the parchment – *whatever* he had read. Security here was as leaky as a sieve. If some minion like him had heard that a message had been discovered, who else by now would know what it really contained? The taller scientist turned to the armed Russian orderly.

'Bring back that old man,' he ordered curtly. 'Alive if you can, dead if you can't.'

But Ahmed had also seen Vorbachov arrive and prudently vanished among the huts. He wrapped some chapattis in a cloth and tied the bundle around his waist with an elastic luggage strap he took from the roof rack of a parked car. Then he was on his way up into the hills, repeating to himself time and again what he had read on the parchment lest, with an old man's fading memory, it might vanish from his mind.

Love came through the French windows into Parkington's room, pushed aside the curtain and stood blinking in the blaze of Parkington's halogen torch. He regarded his colleague with disfavour.

'You should get off your bed instead of making absurd threats about castrating me from a distance,' he told him caustically. 'Then you might get somewhere.'

'Like where?' Parkington asked him, pushing his pistol back beneath the pillow, switching off his torch and turning on his bedside light.

'Like finding out why I have no booking here, although there was a booking in the name of Glover. Someone apparently rang the hotel clerk to say that this man Glover wouldn't need the room as he had been killed in an accident on the way from the airport. I saw a local holding a card with that name on it at the airport.'

'There are always men holding cards and themselves and probably each other at the airport,' retorted Parkington sourly, swinging himself off the bed and reaching for his trousers and shirt. 'What makes you think this Glover person was anything to do with us?'

'Nothing,' said Love. 'I would just like to know whether he was or he wasn't. For my own peace of mind.'

He did not add that in general practice a doctor soon develops the ability of an egg-sexer and a detective to spot something wrong that could have unexpected and unrevealed significance. In a court of law he could not give any reasons for this, but it was an extra sense: he felt that this unknown dead man had some relevance to him. How or why or what this might be, he could not imagine, but the belief lit a red warning light in his mind.

Parkington picked up the telephone, asked for a number. A man's voice answered.

'Hossein here.'

'Parkington. Bowker's. Room 101. As soon as you can.'

He replaced the receiver.

'Have a drink,' he suggested to Love.

'The place is dry, unless you fill in forms.'

'I carry supplies of refreshment with me,' Parkington replied. 'In a Muslim country, I am like a camel. Which is why questions like yours give me the hump.'

He crossed to the bathroom, came back carrying a large flask with a brightly coloured label: Superstrength After-shave. He poured two whiskies into toothglasses, handed one to Love.

'Who is Hossein?' Love asked him.

'The Midland Widows rep here. He'll find out if anyone can.'

'Do you trust him?' asked Love.

66

'I don't trust anyone as far as I can pee,' replied Parkington firmly. 'And I pee short these days.'

'You should have that looked at,' said Love.

'I will,' retorted Parkington. 'But not by you.'

Hossein was a small round man with very thick black hair. Parkington introduced them. He shook Love's hand energetically.

'It is my pleasure,' he said, as though he meant it.

'And it is my pleasure and your bonus at stake,' Parkington told him bluntly. 'Find out all you can about someone called Glover who is supposed to have died today in a road accident this morning.'

'Not a Pakistani name,' said Hossein.

'Agreed,' said Parkington. 'But the doctor here says a Pakistani was carrying a card with that name on it at the airport. So someone out there must have seen him, and probably knows him. Find out everything as quickly as you can. And as cheaply, of course.'

'Of course. I am just now doing this thing,' said Hossein.

He bowed and left the room.

Love sipped his whisky.

'What about this Dr Khan?' he asked. 'Shouldn't we have a word with him, tell him we're here?'

Parkington nodded.

'We'll drive out to his house.'

'Is the Cord there?'

'I hope so.'

He finished dressing, and they went out into the unexpectedly bright sunshine. Through the room's thick curtains the day had appeared dull, almost overcast. Now in the bright blaze of morning, the hotel's whitewashed walls appeared dazzling. An old-fashioned Morris Minor taxi, with a yellow roof and black body, cruised past. The driver slowed, looked at them hopefully, and stopped at Parkington's signal.

'Islamabad,' Parkington told him. They sat back on the cracked leather rear seat as the little car ground along past open-fronted shops. Outside one, huge rolls of carpet stood on their ends. Other carpets had been spread out nearby in a blaze of colour. Humbler traders squatted on the roadside, selling shoes, plates of nuts; boys fried dumplings in flat pans a yard wide.

An open-fronted shack was festooned with car wheel discs glittering like shields in the sun above sacks of rice and pyramids of oranges. Rows of tonga ponies waited, white towels thrown over them against the sun. They stood wearily, heads down, hoofs splayed out. And all the while the background rang with a ceaseless cacophony of car horns, whistles, bicycle bells and gongs on tongas. Seemingly, nothing had changed since Love had been there many years earlier – but then suddenly everything had, for they left the cluttered sidewalks behind and came out on to a wide motorway. Planted on either side were forests of silver-leafed trees. In the distance, mountains shimmered like a mirage.

'This is Islamabad,' Parkington explained. 'The new capital. When India became independent, they kept the capital city, Delhi, and Karachi was Pakistan's capital. Then they built this new city. It's split into sections. There's a diplomatic enclave, a government section, hotels, and private roads. Dr Khan's house is on one of them.'

'Have you met him?'

'Never. Don't even know his first name. His letters are always simply signed S. Khan. But he must be successful, to live out here. House prices are astonishingly high. Up to nine million rupees – three hundred thousand pounds at the present exchange rate – only buys a very modest pad. And there's so much money around that land out here now costs five thousand rupees a square metre – more than in New York.'

'I did not know Pakistan was so rich.'

'It isn't. But a lot of people who live here are. Drug runners. Arms dealers who supply the Mujahideen in Afghanistan. And possibly some who have helped the

Russians fight the Mujahideen. And no doubt the really wise are helping both – so whoever wins, they'll be on the right side.'

Parkington leaned forward and gave instructions to the driver.

'Left here, second right, now left again.'

They were now driving between large and impressive houses with high metal fences. Outside the gates stood swarthy uniformed guards armed with steel-tipped staves and revolvers. Most wore large brightly polished brass badges, stamped 'Security'. But whose, Love wondered. Theirs or their employers'?

The taxi slowed to a halt. Parkington and Love got out, told the driver to wait. On the gatepost was a polished brass plate: Dr S. Khan, MB, BS; Dr J. Khan, MD. The guard pressed a button and the gate opened electrically. They walked up the short paved drive. A manservant was already waiting in the doorway.

'Dr S. Khan,' said Parkington.

'Is not here, sir.'

'Dr J. Khan, then.'

'Is not here also, sir.'

'Where are they, then? We have come out from England to see them.'

'Dr Khan gone to Peshawar.'

'Both doctors?'

'Peshawar, sir.'

'When are they returning?'

'Tomorrow. Next day. Who can say? Inshallah.'

'The will of Allah,' said Love.

'Everything is the will of Allah, sir,' replied the servant sincerely. 'Blessed be His name, always.'

'Amen to that. Did either doctor leave a message for a Mr Parkington or a Dr Love?'

'I am just now looking, sir.'

The orderly left them at the door for a moment, rooted

through a pile of unopened letters on a brass tray. Somewhere in the house a clock struck the hour. There was a pleasant smell of wax polish and flowers. The hall felt agreeably cool. The orderly returned.

'Dr Parkington?' he asked hopefully.

'Half right,' agreed Parkington. He opened the envelope, read the note.

'This is Dr Khan's address in Peshawar. But it doesn't say why he has gone there.'

'Who can say, sir? I am not knowing. Many sick people in Peshawar.'

'Can we telephone him there?'

'Not giving me any number.'

'Could you let me see the phone book?' asked Love.

The orderly handed the telephone book to him. He dialled Directory Enquiries, read the quaint notice inside the cover while he waited for a reply: 'Observation sets are available in every exchange to detect the telephone number from which obnoxious calls are emanating. In case telephone subscribers receive frequent calls from one obscene source and feel themselves disturbed and irritated they can immediately contact the Divisional Engineer.'

That was comforting, Love thought. What was less helpful was that Directory Enquiries had no number in Peshawar for either Dr S. or Dr J. Khan and apparently no telephone at the address the servant had given them. There were any amount of other Khans – the name seemed as popular as Smith in Britain – but not the ones they wanted.

They went back to the taxi.

'We'll hire a car and get up there,' said Parkington. 'It's only a three hour run. And we have the address – though why neither are here beats me. Or why the doctors aren't on the phone in Peshawar. But then I didn't even know there were two Dr Khans.'

'Before we go, let's give Hossein time to find out what he can about this man Glover.'

Back at Bowker's, Parkington went to his room. He

70

wanted to finish the whisky and then have a sleep, what he called Egyptian PT. Love also felt reaction from the long flight creeping up on him. He remembered Sir Thomas Browne's admission and agreed with him: 'Though Somnus in Homer be sent to rouse up Agamemnon, I find no such effects in these drowsy approaches of sleep'. He would run a bath, have an hour's sleep and then pack what he needed for the trip to Peshawar. He picked up the key from the reception counter, opened his door.

Sitting in the easy chair next to the bed was a young woman, suntanned, smiling. She wore a silk shirt and trousers, and was more than pretty; she was beautiful. She stood up as Love came into the room, looked at him enquiringly.

'You've sure taken your time,' she said almost accusingly in an American West Coast accent.

'That can sometimes be a virtue,' Love replied. 'But just who are you? I don't think we've met.'

'I forgot. We haven't been introduced, and you English like to be formal, even these days. I am Dr Khan. Dr Stevie Khan.'

Wind swirling down the mountainside from hidden, freezing peaks lifted the rasping dust and blew it against Ahmed's face like so much sandpaper. He choked and coughed and turned his back, head down, for what comfort he could find. He was old for these conditions, and his heart hammered wearily at the strain of climbing at such a height. He guessed that others would already be seeking him out, following his trail, perhaps with the great tracking dogs the Russians used.

He had no time to spare, but he was not quite sure of his bearings. He knew where he should be aiming for, but distance at night and in the hills, especially when one was alone and fearful of forgetting a vital message, could be deceptive. He might have covered five miles, or it might only be three.

He paused for a moment, breathing slowly and deeply to

71

regain not only his breath but his equilibrium. Standing thus, head down, eyes shut, against the driving wind, he did not notice the two sentries move up behind him. The first he knew of their presence was when their hands gripped his forearms like metal vices. His heart fluttered within him like the wings of a frantic, imprisoned bird.

'Who are you?' asked one roughly. He spoke the local dialect.

'I was Professor Ahmed.'

'What are you doing out here, old man?' The question was not spoken unkindly, only with surprise, as the man released his grip.

'The same as you,' he retorted, recognizing the man's voice. 'Fighting.'

These young fellows thought they had it all their own way, that they were the only fighters. They did not realize there were others whose contribution could be at least as great, and in his case, with his new knowledge, of infinitely more value.

'You come with us,' the young man told him, wanting to believe but still not sure, not certain. You could be certain of nothing now: the most honest-sounding people could be spies, traitors put in by the other side to trap you, to turn your own voice against yourself.

They set off at a fast pace around the hill, possibly for half a mile, and then into a cave. Within the recesses of the cave, Ahmed saw a hurricane lamp, and the embers of a dying fire. They had been cooking some meat on it. He smelled roasted flesh and oil and fried rice and spices and for the first time that day was aware how hungry he was. Another man, slightly older than the two sentries, came out to see him. He wore ragged clothes, with two bandoliers of ammunition, a belt with a Webley tied to it by its lanyard. He was unshaven and in the dim light his eyes glowed red as the hot ashes.

'Who have you got here?' he asked the sentries gruffly, and then his voice softened. 'Why, my old professor. I did not expect to see you out here, far from home and late at night.'

The voice was faintly tinged with irony.

'I hope you are doing better in whatever task occupies your energies now, than when you were attempting to learn dead languages,' retorted Ahmed.

The man smiled.

'Now I am more concerned in mastering an enemy equally as difficult. But you did not come so far to tell me this?'

'No. I came to tell you that the Russians have found the body of a man buried in the ice and perfectly preserved, apparently for several hundred years.'

'A pity.'

'What do you mean?'

'It can't be one of theirs,' the man explained, grinning. He lit an American cigarette, offered one to the professor who shook it away.

'That remark is worthy of your powers of scholastic deduction, but no more,' he said shortly. 'What I have come to tell you is this. They are going to fly out this body to Moscow and use it for some propaganda effect – to try and prove to the world outside that even in the middle of war, they still have time for peaceful research.'

'Well, what can we do about that?'

'You can see the body never leaves the mortuary.'

'Where is the mortuary?'

'In Ramzak village. They have a big base there, and an airstrip. They fly in cargo, fly out wounded.'

'I know. There is a plane going out tomorrow night, so I hear.'

'Do not wait till then,' Ahmed implored him. 'Deal with it now.'

'You mean, steal the body?'

'No. Blow it up.'

'It is against our religion to mutilate the dead.'

'He has been asleep for many years. Were he alive to give his word, I believe he would understand the situation,' said

73

Ahmed, trying to convince himself as much as his listener. 'He was not of our faith. He wore a crucifix about his neck. He was a European, probably English. He had a diary in that language. He was a man of substance. I could see his character in his face.'

'It is risky, going in so close,' the other man replied, frowning. 'We had a bad mauling near there the other day. We lost fifteen men. They are impossible to replace quickly, if at all. Are you certain this is a worthy target?'

'I know.'

'Why are you so convinced, Professor? What do you know that I do not? One body can only have a limited propaganda effect, surely? The world does not greatly care what happens in this remote place – or to one dead body, however old it may be. Millions are starving, rotting in prison camps, dying in a dozen pointless wars. The world in the West is more concerned with their deep frozen meals, package holidays, television sets, bingo. Those things occupy their minds. Not realities, not freedom or slavery, as they affect us.'

'You may not have great powers of deduction,' said Ahmed with grudging admiration, 'but I am interested that you have guessed there is something more. There is something written down, that will be travelling with the body. A message he was carrying when he died.'

He told him what he had read in the mortuary.

'What do you think that means?' The other man looked at him blankly.

'It means something that could help us more than any other discovery since . . . since . . .'

His tired mind groped for words. 'Almost since the discovery of the wheel,' he added lamely.

'That is a strong claim to make. How do you intend to get that message out? You have not written it down?'

'Of course not. That would be fatal if they found me. I will keep it in my mind – until I get over the border.'

'You may never make the journey.'

'I am an old man,' said Ahmed, drawing himself up, 'but

74

I have fought in wars before you were born. I bore arms against the British once. In those days, battles were fought with honour. There were rules. It was almost a game played with live bullets. Not now. If I die tomorrow, if I die now, I have at least lived my life. If I am to die before I cross the border – and I do not agree that I will – let me do this last thing for my country. Is it not written, "This present life is only a toy"? This is the game I wish to play.'

'But what if you do not get through? Then you will have done nothing for your country.'

'Then it will not matter either way. Our foes will not have the secret – if you do as I ask you.'

'But our friends could use what you tell me,' said the man. 'Better write it down. Give it to a young man to take over.'

'I could not do that. Once what I have told you is written down, anyone who can read may know the secret. As it is, I am the only one. It is written on the tablet of my mind. No one else can read it, but me. And if, as you declare, I do not manage to cross the frontier, it will die with me.

'Do you know of this river where the water runs red as blood between two hills, one like the face of a man and the other with peaks like the horns on a young goat?'

'I have heard of these hills, yes. But I have not seen them. They are several days' march from here.'

'Show me on a map where they are.'

The guerrilla commander produced a map, folded neatly in a protective cellophane case. He pointed out a blue line that marked the position of the river. Ahmed worked out the map reference, and wrote it down on a small scrap of newspaper.

'If I am captured or wounded, I can swallow it easily enough,' he said.

His former student nodded, regarding him with grudging admiration. It could be a wise precaution, for the professor was old and the journey ahead more dangerous than he realized. The old boy was tough, all right. He would let him

75

go on – and do as he asked. He would destroy that body, and may Allah the all-merciful have mercy on them all for what they were about to do.

Love shook hands with Stevie Khan. He had not expected Dr Khan to be a woman, let alone an American, but then he had not known who or what to expect.

'You are Mr Parkington of the Midland Widows Insurance Company from London?' she asked, turning the question into a statement.

'I have been called many things, but not that,' Love replied. 'I'm a doctor, too. Jason Love.'

'So I am in the wrong room?'

'Most certainly for Parkington. But right for me.'

'I am sorry. The desk clerk told me that this was Mr Parkington's room. There must be some mistake. I came to see him on a business matter. So, if you will excuse me . . .'

'Of course. But before you go, could that business matter be about a Cord car?'

'Yeah. But how can you possibly know?'

'Because Mr Parkington has asked me out here to examine it. These cars are a hobby of mine. Almost an obsession, really.'

'I see. I had no idea. I thought he was on his own. You *are* a doctor of medicine, I take it?'

'You take it correctly,' Love agreed. 'And we have just been out to your house.'

'I know. My servant telephoned me. I have a mobile phone.'

'I cannot offer you a drink, for religious reasons unfortunately totally beyond my control. But would you like a coffee or lime juice, *nimbupani*, as we used to call it?'

'You have been here before then?'

'Years ago,' he admitted. 'I was in the Army. Almost every family in England has had some association with what we still tend to call India, meaning the whole subcontinent.'

Love picked up the phone, rang room service.

'Just a coffee,' she said, before he could speak. He ordered two.

76

'Let us sit in the sun,' he suggested. 'We see so little of it in England.'

'I would rather not, if you don't mind.'

'Of course not. If that is what you like.'

'It's not what I like, but what I think is safest.'

'*Safest?*' he replied. 'Do you mean your complexion is delicate, or something like that?'

'No,' she said, 'but *I* could be delicate.'

'You look very healthy to me – as a medical man.'

'Even the healthiest can die from a bullet.'

'What, here, in this hotel?'

'You have been away a long time,' she replied enigmatically.

'Perhaps too long?'

'Well, then, let me tell you just how things have changed. There are nearly three million refugees from Afghanistan just up the road from here, in enormous camps. One alone is fourteen kilometres square. These people have all sought sanctuary here and Pakistan, which as you know is not a rich country, has tried to help them. They share the same faith, the same outlook. They are neighbours, so they try to be good neighbours. As they say in Pakistan, a moment of love is worth more than seventy years of worship without it.

'I married a Pakistani some time ago – I met my husband as a student in the States – and so I work here with an American medical team. There are others from your country, Germany, Sweden. We have specialists, surgeons, physicians out here for a few months, then they go back home. Some of us are here all the time. And it is a very sobering task. The wounded who come in are often in a terrible state. They could be patched up more quickly – if we had enough equipment and specialists. But we are lacking in both.'

Love nodded sympathetically. For him, refugees meant childhood memories of newsreels showing groups disembarking at Tilbury or Southampton, carrying their belongings in brown paper parcels or in untidy bundles and cheap cardboard suitcases. They came then from Austria, from Germany; little children wearing outlandish clothes, sad old men who did not speak the language, who knew their qualifications would be useless in a strange and alien land. All had faced an uncertain, unhappy future. The sheer number of Afghans now destitute was difficult to assimilate, even to understand. Where, then, there had been hundreds, now there were millions.

'Are there many problems with them, apart from medical and surgical ones?'

'There is some friction, sure, with the locals, but not much. Some shopkeepers, for instance, resent the fact that these people produce goods and try to sell them. They don't like competition. But these refugees have to use what skills they have. They are proud people. They are not beggars. However, not all in the camps are refugees. Some are Communist agents. They look the same, they dress the same, they *are* the same – *outwardly*. But inwardly, they are here for a set Communist purpose, to ruin whatever we do, to harm those who help them. Some are saboteurs or killers. Americans are an obvious target. So for the moment, at least, you see why I think it would be healthier for me to have coffee with you inside.'

The coffee arrived. Love poured out two cups, black, without sugar.

'Now,' he said. 'Please tell me about the Cord.'

'What did Richard Parkington tell you about it?' she asked him.

'Not much. Only that there was a car here like one I own myself. It was to be insured for a very large sum of money – ten million pounds. He showed me two photographs.'

'And what did you think?'

'It seemed in good condition, but totally overvalued.'

She looked at Love for a moment, as though deliberating whether to dispute this opinion, then she said: 'That is a very special car.'

'For that money, it must be. Anyhow, when can I see it? Is it at your house?'

'It was going to be, but it hasn't arrived. It is up near Peshawar.'

'I was told by your servant that you and Dr Khan had gone there?'

'I told him to say that to any callers.'

'We couldn't find a phone number for you in Peshawar in the book.'

'No. I do not have a phone.'

'And the other doctor, Dr Khan? Your husband, I assume?'

She paused and looked away, stirred the coffee almost absentmindedly.

'Yes. He believed in more active help to the Afghans than just patching them up after they had been shot, or bombed. He was in there fighting with the Mujahideen, and helping the injured as they were wounded.'

'Was?' asked Love carefully.

She nodded.

'He was killed. I received a bloodstained jacket, which I recognized, with two letters from me in a pocket. He died bravely, so I was told.'

'He must have been a brave man,' said Love, conscious of the cliché; wanting to say something more comforting, if only he could think of it. She sat there, disconsolate and beautiful, with almond eyes, a trace of lipstick on her lips, firm pointed breasts outlined against her silk blouse. In some situations silence seemed more eloquent than any speech.

'When shall we go to Peshawar?' he asked, changing the subject.

'As soon as I hear the car is ready,' she replied. 'You can go to see it at any time.'

'Certainly,' he replied. 'But, obviously, the sooner, the better.'

He paused for a moment, then decided to tell her about his unease. Maybe he was taking her into his confidence

79

because they were both doctors and could keep their own counsel over whatever they were told; or maybe it was for some other reason, which he could not quite identify. She seemed so relaxed, so sensible, she invited confidences.

'When I arrived at Islamabad,' Love went on, 'various people were waiting for arriving passengers. One carried a card with the name Glover on it. When I checked in here, the clerk informed me I had no booking, but there was a booking for this man Glover who, he had just heard, had been killed in a road accident on his way from the airport.'

'Fast work, to phone the hotel so quickly.'

'I thought so, too.'

'And a shock for you?'

'Worse for him, poor fellow. Fatal. Anyhow, Richard Parkington has someone looking into it. The local agent.'

'Agent?'

Stevie's voice sounded sharp.

'Insurance fellow, I mean. Not a secret agent, that sort of thing.'

'I see.'

Stevie Khan finished her coffee and stood up.

'I know where to find you.'

'Good.'

Love watched her walk away across the grass – and suddenly, surprisingly, wished he was walking with her, or that she was staying with him. After Maureen had gone, he had firmly adjusted his outlook to being on his own; now, for the first time since then, his resolve began to thaw. What had Stevie said about the value of a moment of love?

Colonel Vorbachov pushed forward the safety catch on his Heckler and Koch VP70 as he waited outside the mortuary in Ramzak for the four orderlies to carry out the body of the long-dead traveller. He felt uneasy, unsure of himself. He did not trust these scientists. He felt they had been unnecessarily vague – perhaps deliberately – about what had been written in the dead man's diary, and on the piece of skin in his pouch. But if they were holding something back from him, he was not being entirely open with them. The message from Moscow had only suggested the propaganda ploy as a cover. He sensed there must be something else about this body, or in the diary or on that skin, of far greater importance. But Moscow had not told him what it might be: no one trusted anyone else entirely. Trust was a luxury they could not afford.

The orderlies were inside the room for at least ten minutes, trying to transfer the unwieldy load on to a stretcher without damaging the corpse in any way. Now they appeared in the doorway, their breath hanging like white fog around their mouths.

'The truck is over here,' Vorbachov called to them. They knew this already, of course, but to say anything was better than to stand in silence with a frozen corpse between them. Sometimes speech could break the mask of unease that characterized so many of his assignments. This time, curiously, it did not. He wanted to shout, to run away, to be anywhere but where he was, and he fought down rising panic that forced bile from his stomach up into his throat. He swallowed; he must be growing soft. Or he had been in this accursed place for too long. That was it. The strains here of a violently hostile people, in the harshest climate he had ever encountered, told on everyone after a time. Now, a ten minute drive to the airfield and this macabre scene would be over. The body would be on its way to Moscow and what propaganda or other value they could extract from it there would, thankfully, be out of his hands.

The men started to march in step, bent with the unexpected weight of their burden. The tailgate of the truck was down and the driver stood ready to help them slide the stretcher inside. The colonel saw the scene etched in his mind clearly under the floodlight. Then, as he stood, revolver in his hand, he heard a faint high-pitched whistle, as of an express train, miles away, entering a distant tunnel. And he knew instinctively with terrible clarity that this tunnel opened only on to the unknown, unthinkable wastes of the eternal dark.

'Down!' he yelled and dropped flat on the earth.

As he fell, the mortar shell landed on top of the truck tarpaulin. For a fleeting fraction of a second Vorbachov saw the cruel, unbearable blaze of light that surrounded the explosion, felt the roaring rush of air, and gasped for breath that would never come again.

Up in the hill, outside the camp, the four Mujahideen who had carried their mortar from the camp where Ahmed found them, were already dismantling the weapon with the controlled haste of constant practice. One carried the tripod, another the barrel, the others a spare bomb each, in case they had missed with the first. But watching through their night glasses, they could see they had scored a direct hit. The truck had disintegrated. So had the orderlies, an officer, a driver and most important of all – the stretcher with the frozen body.

It was far too risky to attempt a second shot now on any other target, because already the Russians must have calculated the direction of the firing, and within minutes patrols with dogs would be out after them. They could hear the faint frantic clang of alarm bells thinned by distance and freezing air as the guard was turned out. Within seconds, they were on their way, moving with the desperate, tireless energy and urgency of men who know their lives depend on their speed, but with light hearts; they had achieved their intention with a single shot. Allah had guided their weapon; blessed be his name always.

PART FOUR

Mr Hossein was an ambitious man. He was thirty years old and, before he was thirty-one, he was determined to be senior representative of the Midland Widows for all Pakistan. At present, he was only in charge of the Rawalpindi office. He had the very strong feeling that if he helped this Mr Parkington successfully, then Mr Parkington, in return, would doubtless be willing to help him realize this ambition.

It was not often that he had the opportunity to meet anyone from head office, and so clearly this was a chance not to be missed. Mr Hossein had taken a correspondence course designed to make him more successful in what the course called The Psychology of Selling. Each chapter had a heading in capital letters, from the first, Recognizing a Prospect, to the last, the climax, to which all else was but a prolonged prelude, Closing the Deal. Mr Hossein now tended to think in such phrases. He was therefore determined to Recognize the Prospect of promotion that he believed helping Parkington could offer.

He drove to the office, told the secretary she could take the afternoon off, and then sat down at a telephone with his small address book of contacts. He knew people he did not wish her to know he knew, because as the course had wisely pointed out, it was not *what* you knew but *who* you knew, and his contacts were many and various. For the gift of an envelope of rupee notes it always surprised him how much information one could find. He telephoned an inspector of police.

'I am asking you one small thing,' he said.

'Again?' asked the inspector warily.

'Just this once more, my friend. Have there been any motor accidents involving Europeans today? I heard someone called Mr Glover had been hurt.'

'You've insured him or something?'

'Not to my knowledge. But you know nothing?'

'Nothing yet. But this morning's traffic reports are not in yet. There may be some news in an hour or so.'

Hossein then telephoned a contact at the airport, an old man who marshalled taxis and took a few rupees from drivers for this service. He had the use of a telephone in one of the hotel booths.

'Did you see anyone holding a notice for an Englishman, a Mr Glover?' Hossein asked him.

'Many Englishmen coming in today,' the man replied defensively, not wishing to admit he had not seen the notice in case this could affect any largesse from Mr Hossein.

'Any accidents you've heard of today with taxis?'

'Not taxis, but these rickshaws that undercut the taxis. One got in the way of a truck on the Murree Road.'

'Who was in the rickshaw?'

'The driver, poor fellow. May Allah the all-merciful have mercy on him. May he walk tonight in paradise.'

'I hope so. And the passenger?'

'He was European. An unbeliever. Killed, too. I am saying it is bad for tourism, if this sort of thing happens.'

'Where's his body?'

'Hospital, mortuary. Who can say?'

'I am asking you to say. Find out and ring me back.'

'This is a difficult time of day. Offices are closed, people are taking their rest.'

'You can rest more easily with thirty rupees in your hand.'

'I am just now agreeing about that. I will ring you back.'

He did so within ten minutes.

'The city mortuary,' he said briefly.

Hossein drove down to the mortuary. A watchman at the door was not one of his contacts.

'Who do you want?' he asked sullenly. 'It is closed.'

'I am asking you just now to open it.'

'On what basis should I open that which is closed?'

Hossein produced a twenty rupee note.

'On the basis that it is written that in time of need we should help each other.'

'If I am seen, I can help myself to the loss of my job.'

'I will see you are not seen,' Hossein promised.

The man glanced around cautiously.

'Come with me,' he said, and led Hossein into an anteroom.

'I cannot show you the bodies,' he said. 'I have not the lock for the room, otherwise I would.'

'I believe you.'

'We have a list of people who've died today. It has many names. One of the buses from Peshawar overturned in a nullah and caught fire. Sixteen were trapped inside. Very bad thing.'

'Let me see the whole list.'

Hossein skimmed through it. The bus casualties did not concern him, but beneath them was the name he sought: Mr Erasmus Glover. Occupation: Business. Home address: Leeds, England. Age, 35.

'Who's been told?'

'The police. But they are slow. They know nothing more than what you read here.'

'Anyone else?'

'Perhaps the police will tell the British Embassy. Who can say?'

'Who was in the truck?'

'Only the driver. There were no witnesses. The driver was wise. He did not stop.'

Hossein went back to Bowker's Hotel, knocked respectfully on the door of Parkington's room.

'Come in,' Parkington told him. He was sitting in an easy chair opposite Love.

'What did you find?' he asked.

Hossein told them.

'Do you think it was an accident?' Love asked him.

'Why should it not be?' asked Hossein. 'In the early hours there are many accidents. Drivers are sleepy.'

The explanation seemed so reasonable, but even so, Love felt the metallic taste of unease grow on his tongue. Someone had telephoned this hotel to say he was dead and would not need his room. When they discovered they were wrong on both counts – what then? Parkington opened a folder.

'A routine check,' he explained. 'All I had to go on was that a fellow called Glover had been involved in an accident. I sent a telex to London to see if we'd insured him.'

'And?'

'We had. He was a bachelor, holding a life policy for ten thousand pounds.'

'What did he do for a living?'

'Salesman with a Japanese electronics firm. Fairly specialized line of country. These Japs have factories in Scotland, England and Wales to qualify for EEC quotas.'

'What did Glover sell? TV sets?'

'No. Bits and pieces for defence systems. Radar, early warning systems, surveillance, directional microphones, sonar, that sort of gear.'

'There's a market for that out here?' Love asked him.

'There's a market everywhere for better and cheaper ways to kill people by blowing them out of the sky or out of their skins. And consequently as big a market for gadgets to stop that sort of thing happening. You've been living in the country too long, doctor.'

'Perhaps not long enough,' retorted Love. 'What do you say to the theory that Glover was murdered?'

'Why should he have been?'

'Perhaps he knew too much – or too little. Perhaps he was getting above himself, selling on his own behalf – maybe even buying on his own behalf, for someone else? There are all sorts of permutations, and no computer to put them through.'

'With you around, we don't seem to need one. Keep talking,' said Parkington.

'Find the truck driver,' said Love. 'He'll do the talking.'

Parkington turned to Hossein.

'You heard all that?'

'I am just now listening with much interest,' Hossein admitted.

'Good. Well, listen to this with even more interest. You find that truck driver and help us generally during our stay here, and I will recommend you for promotion. You know there is going to be a vacancy shortly for a deputy general manager in Pakistan?'

'You are now telling me something I did not know,' said Hossein, not altogether truthfully.

'Now I'm telling you something you may like to know. That vacancy can be filled if you help us – quickly.'

'Who will be filling it?'

'I am saying you will be filling it, Hossein. Now get the hell out of here, and let's have some action. Like the chapters in that salesmanship book you keep telling me about – Go for your Goal!'

Mr Albert Sherriff, like Mr Hossein, was ambitious. But unlike Mr Hossein, he was much older, infinitely richer and so his ambitions were more complex. He sat now at his desk in his house thirty odd miles north west of Peshawar, examining, not for the first time, his British passport; in times of concern, he always drew a certain comfort from the splendid if dated declaration in the inside cover: 'Her Britannic Majesty's Principal Secretary of State for Foreign Affairs requests and requires in the name of Her Majesty all those who it may concern to allow the Bearer to pass freely without let or hindrance and to afford the Bearer such assistance and protection as may be necessary'.

Mr Sherriff had never in fact invoked such protection, but then he had never been a British subject. This passport described him as a merchant, which was correct. His place of birth given as Leicester, England, which was not. And in a safe to which he alone knew the combination, he kept French, Canadian and American passports for use in any dire emergency. They had all been stolen, of course, and the details forged.

His real name was Alwar Sharif. His father had been a Muslim clerk from Bombay, his mother a half-caste Portuguese housemaid, and he had been born in the basement of a rooming house in Marmagao, the capital of Goa, then a Portuguese colony on the west coast of India. His father died in the last year of the Second World War, when Alwar was ten. His mother took him to Bombay, where she hoped to find another husband. She did not find one and no one offered her employment as a maid. After drifting for weeks, begging in the streets and sleeping rough on a pavement, she found unhappy lodgings in Grant Road, a long narrow street of brothels.

Here, every day, women like her, without money or hope, caked their faces with make-up to conceal the ravages of time, tiredness and frequently disease, and took their places on wooden chairs in open-fronted rooms. Here they sat like caged, docile animals behind strong vertical iron bars, facing the street.

Sailors from ships; soldiers, civilians – Indians, British, Americans, Australians – would venture into Grant Road by taxi, rickshaw, tonga, on foot, and pass slowly by these cages, viewing the women within. Sometimes they stopped. Mostly they went on.

During these early years, Alwar lodged with his mother in a hut made of sheets of unwanted enamelled metal advertisements, wattle and strips of canvas stolen from an army camp, on the road from Santa Cruz, Bombay's airport. His main memory of those lonely times was of a continually weary woman whose face, when he saw her in the cruel

88

early morning light on her return, crawling into the rags with which they wrapped themselves for sleep, became increasingly the face of a stranger.

He could not understand why it was painted with what to him were such terrible colours. He did not realize then how, if these generally unattractive and dark-skinned women wished to attract American and European customers, who would pay more than Indians, they had to lighten their skin in the hope that in the dim light they might pass as French, Italian, Spanish.

One day Alwar woke late and instinctively put out a hand where his mother slept. Her place was empty. Years later, when he made enough money, he employed an investigator to try and trace his mother but he had no address for her, not even a definite name. He assumed it was Sharif, but he had no proof his father and mother had ever married. He never found her; she had simply vanished.

Left on his own, Sharif was employed by a homosexual professional beggar whose legs were swollen by elephantiasis to grotesque proportions, as thick as a healthy man's waist. One of Sharif's duties was to push this creature on a wooden trolley into the path of European visitors, and hold out a copper bowl for alms.

This task barely paid for his food and he resented having to submit to the gross sexual assaults of such a foul and mutilated man. He decided he could do better on his own, and drifted into Grant Road, running alongside taxis as they slowed, to open their doors. He had to doss down on pavements, sometimes, in the early hours, when the women went home, in their empty cages.

He stole all he could, robbing drunken soldiers, tourists, anyone. Sometimes he joined with other older boys to knife them if they put up a fight. He saved money, wrapping the notes carefully in a rag which he wore like a belt under his trousers. When he had made enough, he returned to Marmagao. Here he led sailors from the foreign ships to the dockside brothels, and after several Goanese rums, while they slept, snoring, stupefied with lust and alcohol, often laced with laudanum, which was very easy to obtain, he would empty their pockets. He stole passports, cigarette cases, watches, small packets of drugs sailors had smuggled ashore. Gradually, he accumulated enough money to open a deposit in the Imperial Bank of Goa.

After India became independent, Sharif noticed that increasing numbers of Indians visiting Goa would buy quantities of gold ornaments, earrings, tiepins, necklaces. For generations, Indian women had worn gold bangles, rings, and stars in their pierced nostrils. They did not trust banks, but preferred to carry their capital with them, and every bride's dowry had to contain some gold. This demand meant that gold in India was always more expensive than gold in other countries. After Independence, a rupee's worth of gold in Goa would fetch at least five rupees in Bombay.

Sharif advanced money to sailors from Europe and the United States, whose ships made regular runs, to bring back gold ornaments and trinkets. Some sailors took money and brought nothing in return. There would then be short, sharp fierce engagements in back alleys and on darkened water-fronts. Bodies would be found next morning, floating, face down in the oily water of the harbour.

Because India was in the sterling area, Sharif could legally transfer money to the Bahamas. Here, by sleight of financial hand, pounds could be transformed into US dollars.

When the post-war Socialist government in Britain devalued the pound, he bought pounds with these dollars and trebled his savings overnight, moving back the pounds to Bombay, then to the Bahamas in a lucrative circuit. Then in the 1960s, Indian troops invaded Goa.

Pandit Nehru, the Indian Prime Minister, declared that this would eradicate unwelcome Portuguese colonial influence from India – an excuse which the United States would approve, with their pathological dislike and misunderstanding of any colonization, unless it was their own.

But Sharif realized that an infinitely more important economic reason outweighed this noble claim. Several German sailors had been interned in Goa during the Second World War, and afterwards had no wish to return to their homes in what was now East Germany. They therefore married local girls and raised families in Goa. One was a geologist, who pointed out to influential Goanese and Indians that the soil of Goa was virtually pure iron ore. Indian traders extracted from the Portuguese governor the right to dig for any minerals, and Goa speedily became one of the world's largest suppliers of iron ore. The Indian government then decided that these new and seemingly endless riches could be better employed in their own country, hence the invasion: a theft on a national scale, under the cloak of honour. Sharif took note of this. If a nation could conceal an act of aggression so satisfactorily, an individual could do likewise much more easily.

Now that Goa was part of India, the price of gold there was the same as in Bombay: his main source of income had disappeared overnight. This was an unpleasant discovery. Another was that Muslims were not generally welcomed in the commercial exploitation of Goa. In a predominantly Hindu society, Muslims felt unwanted. So, taking his passports with him, Sharif left for Pakistan and bought a property close to the Afghan border. With the entrepreneurial antennae of the born dealer, he sensed that the West, which in a previous century had forced China to buy opium the Chinese government strongly wished to ban, would soon offer a huge market for the forbidden drugs from the East.

From his house near the foothills, he took a percentage of the traffic that passed regularly south in polythene bags from the wild poppy-strewn fields of Afghanistan. Within years Sharif was immensely rich, but wealth made in this way brought envy, and envy meant enemies and enemies meant danger, possibly even death, so he found he had to maintain a sizeable number of bodyguards.

To keep these men in work, and cover costs, for he was

known as a very frugal man, Sharif ran a trucking business. After the style of the country, his lorries were elaborately painted red and blue, their high sides decorated with brightly-coloured likenesses of lions, tigers, elephants and flying horses. Above the driver's cab on each one was a huge open structure, shaped with sides like a Roman chariot. Here, passengers could be carried standing up, thigh to thigh, body to body, while goods, animals, any merchandise whatever, was transported behind them.

Mr Sharif also owned a number of equally brightly-painted tanker lorries, like the trucks masterpieces of the art of the bizarre. They were draped with metal strips, rods, steel mesh and hung with bright metal nets, hooks, chains, hub caps from other vehicles. Drivers vied with each other to have the most spectacular vehicle; a harmless pastime, of which Mr Sharif approved, because with vehicles so grotesquely decorated, it was difficult to describe one accurately, if it should be involved in an accident, and no one had taken its number. Since Mr Sharif paid his drivers by results and not by hours of work, they were all encouraged to drive as fast as possible. Accidents were frequent on the long, narrow roads with deep ditches or nullahs on either side.

For years, before the Russians invaded Afghanistan, his tankers carried kerosene, petrol and cooking oil from Rawalpindi or Peshawar across the Afghan border. The interior of each tank was then swilled out, and behind high walls where no prying eye could see, Sharif's men packed them with polythene bags of heroin and cocaine. Down the Khyber Road these tankers trundled, into another yard at Peshawar, where a constant stream of private cars and taxis carried off their quotas in boxes, suitcases, parcels.

When this trade was becoming so profitable that it seemed even better than printing his own money, Mr Sharif faced difficulties of another kind: the Russians entered Afghanistan. They soon realized the foreign currency inflow represented by the wide acres of poppies, stretching in vast red and white squares like the chequer boards of giants, and demanded their share of the spoils from Sharif and others who controlled the trade.

Sharif could, of course, have retired to any country and lived like a king, but he would have been a king in exile, without power. The money which he had sought so assiduously for so long, for which he had helped to corrupt a generation – for which he had regularly bribed, maimed and even murdered – now exerted its own peculiar pressure on him. In theory, he was free to leave. His money was banked and invested and earning interest in a dozen countries. There was nothing now to hold him here in this bleak, barren outpost – baked by a vertical sun for much of the year, swamped by rain, chill as an open grave for the rest – within sight of a ragged frontier.

Here, every man carried a gun and some two or three, with bandoliers of ammunition over their shoulders and grenades stuck into their belts. Here, the only real rule of law was the rule of the bullet: he who shot first won his case. Sharif could easily afford to leave all this behind him – but he could not bear to go. He realized the truth a drunken sea captain in a Goa whorehouse had once uttered: 'A man either has no money – or he can never have enough.' Mr Sharif had become permanently infected with the need for more; he could never have enough.

Now he sat looking at his passport, that described him as Albert Sherriff, wondering if perhaps at last he should go, but knowing, deep down, that his avarice would never allow him to leave. Yet events were happening around him which he did not understand, let alone control. He felt like a man in a coracle who starts to row down a wide, calm, peaceful and slow-flowing river – and then suddenly the current increases to a torrent, and his coracle is being swept along relentlessly, despite all his frantic efforts, towards unknown rapids and perhaps oblivion. The Russians were leaving, for one thing. Who would seize power when – if – they all did return to their homeland? The Mujahideen were divided;

sects and parties could not agree on a common policy, and with instability, his enterprises could suffer. Afghanistan was thick with arms; it was impossible yet to prophesy which of seven political groups would come out on top – or whether a left-wing government would invite the Russians to return. He was not surprised at the hostility the Russians had aroused among the mass of the population. Who could warm to individuals who could give children little boxes of bonbons, with one in every twenty sweets containing a tiny explosive device concealed in the candy? The warmth of a child's hands unwrapping the paper would set it off. Children had lost their hands, their sight, even their lives.

Now, apparently, a group of Mujahideen had blown up a truck and a building – some said a mortuary – at Ramzak, and a cargo plane on the runway. There were reports of bodies everywhere – among them Colonel Vorbachov's.

Sharif had invested a lot of time – and, more important, money – in making sure that Vorbachov was his ally. Now he would have to start all over again with the Colonel's replacement. It was neither easy nor safe to offer bribes. The process was slow, a hint here, a vague suggestion there, over a period of weeks, or even months.

Also, the Pakistan authorities, increasingly concerned at the presence of around three million Afghan refugees already in their country, had instituted new customs checkpoints and police posts along the roads. Keen young men could still carry bags of drugs overland on their backs, but it would need an army of such couriers to equal what one tanker lorry could move. Now even the tankers would not be making the journey for much longer. Pakistani police had stopped several going south and banged the tanks with rods. When they sounded hollow, the driver was allowed to proceed, but too often, they boomed like giant, dulled gongs, and then it was only a matter of minutes before the lids were off and torches showed they contained a fortune in drugs.

Sharif accepted that nothing, not life itself, possibly not even the world, could last for ever, but it was always sad to see one source of revenue close unless another opened. Then he had discovered the Cord. He knew its significance, and here he would make a profit – and then possibly, just possibly, retire.

A movement on one of the three monitor screens across the room caught his eye. Instantly, he put away his passport, peered intently at the screen. He saw a man approach the house across the compound that surrounded it, press the front door bell. Sharif recognized one of his own people, touched a button. This activated a buzzer in an anteroom where guards waited, day and night, and gave them permission to open the door to the visitor. He came straight to Sharif's study, bowed deeply.

'I have two things to report,' he began, eyes downcast, as befitted one who accepted his total inferiority to Sharif. 'First, the Englishman, Glover, has been dealt with.'

'How?'

'A motor accident outside Islamabad. A truck hit the motor rickshaw in which he was travelling.'

'One of my trucks?'

The man bowed assent.

'With no rear lights and carrying false numbers,' he explained hastily. 'The driver had a scarf around his face. No one could recognize him. There were no witnesses in any case.'

'Did he get what was needed?'

'Yes. That has been taken care of.'

'Anything else?' Sharif asked.

'One thing, sir. The insurance man, Parkington, has arrived with an English physician, Dr Jason Love.'

'Who is he?'

'He appears to be an expert on Cord cars.'

'So he has been asked to examine this one?'

'That is so. He was surprised to find his booking at Bowker's Hotel had been cancelled. Of course, it was the booking for Mr Glover that had been cancelled. The clerk there is a fool and got the names mixed up. He has done this before, so I am told.'

'Is this Dr Love suspicious of anything?'

'Wary, I would say, sir. He has been making enquiries about Glover.'

'Then we will deal with him before he puts his nose in anywhere else. But I want to see him first. Here. Understood?'

'Understood, sir.'

The man bowed and left the room. Sharif lit a long, thin Burmese cheroot and brooded on what he had heard. Then he took out the British passport and looked at it again. With this deal finalized, it might at last be the moment to leave his past behind him and become Albert Sherriff of England forever – or again, it might not. At least, not yet. Soon, no doubt; but later, a little bit later.

Shaven priests in a Burmese temple were beating a golden gong with oiled leather thongs.

Love stirred uneasily in his dream – and then was instantly awake. Years of receiving emergency calls at night had given him immediate reaction to unexpected noises. The bedside telephone was pealing impatiently. He picked up the receiver.

A man's voice said: 'It is Dr Love I am seeking.'

'It is Dr Love you have found. Who are you?'

'I am just now speaking for Dr Khan.'

'Which Dr Khan?'

'Lady Dr Khan.'

'Who are you? Where is she?'

'I am in reception at Pink's Hotel, Peshawar.'

'What does she want?'

'Just now telling you.'

There was a click of switches. Stevie came on the line.

'Sorry to wake you at this God-awful hour. I've been trying for ages to reach you, but the line was busy – or there is something wrong with the telephone.'

'There usually is,' Love agreed. 'What news of Glocka-morra or anything else – like the Cord?'

'That's why I'm calling. It's here in Peshawar and so am I. When can you come and see it?'

'Today,' said Love. 'Are you staying in Pink's Hotel?'

'No, I have a house, but no phone. So I am using the hotel telephone.'

'Then please book rooms for Parkington and me,' Love told her, before realizing he was speaking on a dead line. He jiggled the receiver up and down impatiently. Bowker's hotel operator answered sleepily.

'Please get me Pink's Hotel in Peshawar. I was cut off.'

'I will ring you,' said the man. Love lay back on his bed, switched on the bed light and for the first time in years wished he had not given up smoking. A Gitane or a Gauloise would have soothed his impatience. He checked the time: twenty-five minutes to three o'clock in the morning. An odd time, surely, for Stevie to ring, even if she had been trying to reach him for some time? But then women always tended to exaggerate delays involving telephones. It gave their messages a false importance which they seemed to value. ('Your number's been engaged *all* day. I've been ringing it for *hours*!')

Had the Cord just arrived in Peshawar – or had Stevie just arrived there? And if either or both suppositions were true, where had the Cord been until now – and how did she hear about it?

After ten minutes of turning over possibilities, he picked up the receiver.

'Any luck?'

'I am just now trying, but while that person at the number is speaking to me I am not speaking to him.'

'What do you mean, exactly?'

'I can hear them. They cannot hear me. We have not got connection.'

'Well, can you get connection? Please do your best.'

Love heard other voices whisper faintly on the line, like

97

spirits murmuring, but not to him. He replaced the receiver, waited another ten minutes, picked it up again. This was spoiling his sleep.

'Any luck?' he asked again.

'My God, man, I am doing my best!' cried the hotel operator angrily. He also resented his loss of sleep, and he had drunk a bottle of vodka a former tourist had given him instead of a tip. The spirit pounded in his head like a piston.

'I am trying all the time, trying to get plugs fitting in holes and not getting any answer. But I can hear them. As I am telling you. But they cannot hear me. What to do?'

'Please, would you have one last try? I'm in Room 51. If you could give me a bell, either way, win or lose, I'd appreciate it.'

For the third time, Love replaced the receiver. The room felt unseasonably chilly. He lit the gas fire. Blue flames hissed and crackled, and the tin surround creaked and groaned with the sudden unexpected heat. Ten minutes, eleven, twelve minutes passed. Love picked up the receiver. As he did so, he heard the telephone ring in the room next door through the thin walls. It stopped as the operator asked him sharply: 'Yes?'

'Any luck with my call?'

'I have just got it, but you are not answering. Your phone is ringing. Why are you now speaking to me?'

'Because there's no one else to speak to. I haven't had a call.'

'But I've just rung 52. Is that not you altogether?'

'No, not altogether,' said Love and replaced the receiver for the fourth time. He switched off the bedside light, turned out the fire and lay watching the elements glow red and then die. He was thinking about the Cord, about difficulties of communication between different cities, different people, about Stevie; mostly about her.

It was a curious fact about what he always called the chemistry of attraction, that out of a hundred people, one or two could be drawn to each other, simply by sight. What invisible antennae of the mind sent and received these secret and important signals? This was as remarkable to Love as it was to Sir Thomas Browne, 'the common wonder of all men, how among so many millions of faces, there should be none alike.'

Something in the way Stevie Khan walked, talked; the slightly crooked smile when she bent forward to make a point, moved Love in a disturbing way. He wondered how long she had been married, what her husband had been like. For the first time in years, he found himself pondering the idea of a woman sharing his life, and he tried to imagine how Stevie would fit into a West Country village. She might even like to practise medicine there. Or, she might not; in that case, perhaps they could move to the States. But such a possibility assumed a long, stable relationship, the word for which was marriage. He had seen too many marriages between his friends falter and fail and then fall apart, and had witnessed the sadness and heartache and sense of rejection that such breakdowns could bring.

That day he had seen a car with a sticker pasted on the rear window: *Reach out and love someone.* It could be good advice . . . couldn't it? He was still pondering the matter when he fell asleep.

Love awoke early, shaved and was dressed and packed by half past seven. At breakfast he told Parkington of Stevie's call.

'We will take Hossein with us,' said Parkington at once. 'He's very useful as a translator or a gofor. Also, he has a car.'

'I couldn't book rooms,' Love explained. 'The line's impossible.'

'So's life. But it's not the tourist season. We'll find something.'

They set off in Hossein's Toyota, travelling at the only speed at which everyone seemed to drive – flat out. Love sat in the back. The sun was shining, but not hot. Men walking along the road were still wrapped in blankets. Dust hung in clouds above unmade earth verges. Villages through which they sped, horn blaring, were simply clusters of houses. Flags with Muslim crescents hung listlessly on flat roofs as though too tired to flutter. In the far distance, atop a thin long spine of hills, stood rows of spindly trees, like wisps of hair on an old man's scalp.

Birds fluttered overhead, waiting for some animal to die; a withered goat, a thin-shanked calf, a tiny donkey. Buffaloes scratched the green scum from powdery rocks for food. Red, green and black flags on sticks hammered into the earth marked the graves of holy men. The graves of the less holy were simply long mounds of earth with a large stone at the head and a smaller one at the foot. 'Dead bones,' as Sir Thomas Browne had written, 'quietly rested under the drums and tramplings of three conquests.'

Country buses overtook their car with an angry blare of horns – and then stopped abruptly in the centre of the road to let down some passengers and take others aboard. Tongas came jogging steadily towards them against the oncoming traffic. Small cars surged past on either side, festooned with foreign plaques – Union Jacks, the blue and white cross of Scotland, AA and RAC badges, GB plates – without any association with these countries or organizations. A bus carried a black inscription on its back: SUPER DE LUXE. The letters U R D and U were painted in bright yellow.

Everywhere, Love noticed curiously unchanged artefacts from the British Raj: army barracks, with a tank splendidly painted in front of the officers' mess; guidons with red and white flags were stacked neatly like tripods on either side. An Army Medical Corps base had a poster: Health is Wealth. Half a mile further on, a man sat on a wooden chair at the edge of the road, reading a newspaper. To one side stood a pile of lemonade bottles, each filled with honey, and six beehives, while above them was a handwritten notice: English Pure Honey.

They came into Peshawar past the old fort, the head-quarters of the Frontier Force regiment, threading their way through a clotted mass of traffic: rickshaws, tongas, men heaving giant barrows laden with metal tubes, horses pulling crates of sugar cane. Then they were into wider double-tracked roads with a stern notice repeated at intervals: No horn. Silence is golden.

Past an ice factory, a military tailor's, a Catholic church, a mosque, and they reached the front drive of Pink's Hotel. Parkington had been right; the hotel was nearly empty. They were given three rooms in an annexe behind the main building. Love's room was divided by a bamboo partition, with a bed on one side, a desk on the other. The chimney piece was covered in bamboo slats above an antique gas fire, the bath carved out of a solid block of stone. The place felt very damp and smelled faintly, like a pond that has just been emptied. Parkington appeared in the doorway, and sniffed the chilly air disapprovingly.

'My room's as bad as yours,' he said. 'But at least there's a letter for you, which is more than I've got. They have mixed up our rooms apparently.'

Love opened the envelope. The note was from Stevie: 'Am at the camp all day. Will see you outside the hotel at seven this evening.'

'What camp?' asked Love.

'Refugees,' said Parkington. 'There are nearly three million here. She works there. Well . . . I'm off to the Permit Room. Medicinal purposes, doctor. Alcohol drives out germs – if you drink enough of it.'

Against the amplified evening call to prayer for the faithful, dusk was falling gently from the air. Not darkly, but as a grey mist that gradually shrouded the far mountains, and crept like a slow, seeping tide through the trees towards Love.

Beyond the hoarse cries of the city, necklaces of sharp bright lights began to glitter out on dusty foothills. From

101

the tops of higher buildings, red bulbs winked a warning for aircraft. At street level, shops lit up all at once as though on cue. Above open fronts, they spelled out their names in plastic letters, Khan Medical House; Computer Academy; First Class Garage.

Birds flew in a thankful frenzy through the suddenly cool air, perching briefly on top of piles of sand, on wheelbarrows and bins which workmen had left on unfinished flat roofs. Drivers in the long lines of traffic hooted mechanically and constantly, without any hope or faith that this would gain them a place in the queue, but because a finger on the button gave them something positive to do. They could feel they were still taking part in their journey, not just sitting passively, impotent among unnumbered others.

Love stood at the crossroads outside Pink's Hotel. On the far side of the road, half a dozen three-wheeled motor rickshaws waited. In little blue cabins their drivers sat astride their saddles, ready for trade. A water buffalo came slowly down the road with two children riding on its back. A man hurried along pushing two empty invalid chairs. Was he going to collect customers, or had he deposited them somewhere? Love wondered. And all the time, country buses kept coming in from the frontier, packed with passengers wrapped in blankets, or huddled up behind the blue-tinted windows. Who were they? Refugees from Afghanistan? Tourists? Office-workers going home?

A woman's voice broke into Love's thoughts.

'Waiting for someone?'

'You,' Love told Stevie. 'But why we have to meet out here, I don't know. We could have taken a taxi from the hotel front door.'

'There's no need to. We can walk. But I'll go ahead. You follow. I don't want us to be seen together too much.'

'But why ever not? One can't have too much of a good thing.'

'This may not be a good thing. Now, please follow me, and keep about 20 paces behind. Other people may also be

102

interested in the Cord and we don't want them to know we are.'

Love shrugged; she was clearly not in a mood to answer questions.

Stevie started to walk quickly along the pavement, under fluorescent strips of light hanging from concrete posts. Some paving slabs were missing, and the pavement stood a good foot above the level of the road. On the other side, it sank away for several feet to a ditch. Here and there in the dusk, backs modestly to the fluorescent tubes, men squatted, urinating. They passed a row of shabby cars with palm trees behind them and a flickering neon sign: 'Motor Palace'. One car had a purple spotlight fixed on its radiator to glare the driver's annoyance at anyone who might cut in or brake too suddenly in front of him.

They walked for possibly four hundred yards before Stevie paused, looked over her shoulder as though to check they were not being followed, then turned off the road into an alleyway. This was barely wide enough for one person. Love took out his pocket torch, for the nullah had suddenly degenerated into an open sewer that reeked of putrefaction. He could see the floating bodies of dogs, bloated with gas and decay.

In about twenty yards, the alley branched into a larger road, with high walls, trees. Shops lined one side, shuttered now, and opposite them was a row of garages. Stevie paused outside a wide metal door. A goat charged away almost from under their feet.

'Walk on by,' Stevie told Love sharply.

As he passed her, Stevie took a key from the pocket of her trousers. He sensed rather than saw she was turning it in an oiled lock.

'Now come back.'

She pushed against the door that slid sideways on oiled rollers. She motioned Love inside the garage, followed him and shut the door carefully behind them.

103

'Stand still till I put on the light,' she warned. 'There's not much space.'

She flicked a switch and in the low ceiling three fluorescent tubes flickered into pale green life. Beneath them, boot facing the door, and so large that it virtually filled the garage, stood the Cord Love had come so far to see. He shone his torch on the silvery paintwork, walked around it, opened the doors, looked inside critically. The leather looked original and was in such good condition it might never have been sat on. The carpets appeared equally new. He looked at the speedometer; the mileage reading was less than 700 miles.

Standing so close to the car, it was not easy to appreciate the magnificently classic lines of a vehicle that had been built against the clock in a last desperate attempt to stave off bankruptcy. Errett Lobban Cord had founded a commercial empire embracing the manufacture of aircraft, engines, cars and taxicabs, but each company was closely interlocked with the others, and all were losing money. To solve the problem, or at least to arrest decline, he needed what nowadays would be called a market leader, a car to attract people into their showrooms, to start them talking, and so begin to steer the business around from loss into profit.

He instructed his designer, Gordon Buehrig, who had previously worked for General Motors and Stutz, to design a car that would encapsulate the age – but on a shoestring budget. Buehrig reacted brilliantly. He had studied Le Corbusier's architecture and produced a car that followed his philosophy of design. It looked like no other car in the world; and this was its attraction. Hinges did not stick out from the doors, there were no running boards, no visible headlights. But before it could be exhibited at the 1935 New York Automobile Show – essential for publicity purposes – fifty had to be built. They were, but there was not time to produce the complex front wheel drive and transmission system to test it to destruction. Deliveries were late. Dealers for more orthodox makes put in the boot. Enthusiasm for what was new and radical dwindled. Every difficulty could have been solved, and the Cord empire saved, if only there had been more time. But as Love knew full well, 'If only' are the two saddest words in every language.

Now he lifted the bonnet, shone his torch beneath its great alligator mouth, read the engine and chassis numbers stamped on a metal plate with the maker's name: Cord. Front Wheel Drive, mfd by Auburn Automobile Co, Auburn, Indiana, USA under US patents. Above this was a second, much smaller plate with the body number.

He would have to drive the car, of course, but certainly it appeared to be in remarkably good condition. He felt the tyre treads with his thumbnail; they were like new. He pointed the torch under the wings. Even they were polished; he could see no trace of mud or dirt.

'Well?' Stevie asked him impatiently. 'What's your verdict?'

'In wonderful condition,' Love told her. 'Magnificent. In fact, I've never seen a better Cord. But I have to be absolutely honest. There's still no way this car can be worth ten million pounds.'

'And *you* must say it is worth that, before it can be insured?'

'That's why the insurance company got me here. If I didn't approve its value and you paid the premium, if there was a claim you would only receive a proportion of whatever you asked for. If something is thought to be under-insured or over-insured, you never receive the value *you* set on it.'

'This car is worth every penny,' she insisted confidently. 'Every cent, every anna. I know it.'

'Who says so?'

'I do. You admit it is in terrific condition. And it will easily find a buyer.'

'But not at that price.'

'You are absolutely certain?'

Love nodded. He could see disappointment in her eyes, in the downturn of her lips; and something else in her face, too, an emotion about which he was not quite sure. Was it determination, insistence – or fear? Why was it so important to this young American doctor that an old car, manufactured years before she was born, should suddenly be so valuable?

'Who set this price on it, anyhow?' Love asked her.

'It gives a great leeway to do some good,' she replied, not answering his question.

'To whom?'

'To the refugees. People like you and me, with qualifications, as well as those without. They have fled here from Afghanistan with only what they can carry. If I can get the price for this, some goes immediately to help them. There but for the grace of God, and so on. You must come and see for yourself how they live. Then maybe you'll think again.'

'I know how you feel,' said Love sympathetically. 'But this is like giving a second medical opinion. We unfortunately can't always tell patients what they want to hear. You *may* get your price from some grossly rich collector, and good luck if you do. But why must it be insured for so much? Exactly whose car is it? Yours?'

Stevie looked at him gravely, not answering any of the questions.

'Why are you so certain the car *isn't* worth ten million pounds?' she asked.

Love took a small cloth covered book from his jacket pocket, opened it at a well-thumbed page. Over his shoulder, Stevie saw that it contained columns of numbers and dates.

'Here are all the chassis and engine numbers of every Cord ever made,' he explained. 'And the date each one left the factory in Auburn, Indiana. The numbers are stamped on this plate screwed under the bonnet. And above the plate there is this smaller one, with the body number.'

He pointed these out to her, and handed her the book.

'See for yourself,' he told her. 'None of the numbers on this car tally with the official list.'

'So what does that mean?'

'It means that according to factory records, this car was never made there. It doesn't exist. To be absolutely blunt, Stevie, the car is a total fake.'

PART FIVE

Ahmed came through the gorge, leaving the snow-covered hills behind him, and paused for a minute like some prophet of the past, surveying the promised land. To him, Pakistan was that and more: it held out the hope of a recovery of his dignity – and a repository for the knowledge he carried in his mind, and which he kept repeating lest he forget.

A wide empty plain lay ahead, littered with grey and brown rocks, wrinkled and dry as an elephant's scrotum. He sat down on a round stone to gather his strength for the last, possibly most hazardous, part of his journey. If he failed now, all would have been in vain.

This vast emptiness, bare of trees and bushes, was without cover save for these huge odd shaped outcrops, and here and there a cluster of rushes around some brackish pool.

He gathered his blanket around him, chewed a piece of the salted goat's flesh they had given him at his last halting place, and waited for the sun to slide down the sky. It would be unwise to venture across this dry and arid place in daylight. Nothing moved on its face, and a man on his own could be seen from a dozen miles away – and he could not doubt that others would be out looking for him. He would wait until dark and then attempt the journey; and if he could not see very far ahead when the sun went down, then any pursuers would be equally handicapped.

Ahmed shivered and turned his mind to the past, as old

men do. He thought of students whose careers he had helped, of others who had sunk out of sight, but never out of his memory. He remembered them all for something they had said or done, or not done. And if he had his life again he would still choose to be a teacher. Was it not written, a teacher labours not for himself alone but also for all those who seek knowledge?

Dwelling on these thoughts, Ahmed's head nodded and he slept. When he awoke, he felt stiff and his joints had locked with the evening chill, for the sun was already sinking behind the rim of the distant hills. Within seconds it would be dusk, and then dark. He had no time to lose. He stood up, spat out the remains of the goat meat, and taking a bearing on the abandoned ruin of a turreted fort a mile away, and as far again behind that, the withered, stunted trunk of a leafless tree, struck by lightning, naked of leaves, he set off.

Even after the sun had gone down he could still make out the landmarks dimly. He walked with the unhurried steps of a man born in the mountains. Now and then he paused and looked back, holding his breath in the hope that if he could not see anyone following him, he might at least hear them. But there was nothing except the empty sough of the lonely wind, and the beating of his own heart.

Ahmed reached the base of the foothills in the early hours of the following morning, and lay down in a cave which would give him cover when the sun came up. He should have been relieved now, relaxed, but instead he felt on edge, his nerves raw. He sensed he was not alone; that he had been followed, although he had neither heard nor seen anyone behind him.

Perhaps they wanted to see which of the 300 or so unguarded passes into Pakistan he would choose? They were allowing him to lead them on, using him as a guide.

He came out of the inner part of the cave and stood in its mouth, listening. Water was running somewhere – a roaring, rushing stream he could hear but could not see. Then he heard a faint tinkling, as of a distant temple bell. So he was right. Someone *was* down below him, nearer the water. Probably more than one person, who had disturbed some small stones. Now they were climbing up towards him. He had no weapon, nothing with which to defend himself, and he was old, while almost certainly his follower, or followers, would be young and fit and ruthless. Perhaps they planned to kill him here? They must be pretty certain by now which pass he would use – there were few in this particular area of the hills – and once they knew this, maybe he was of no further value to them? He could not know and he did not care; all that mattered was to escape them, to confound them. The hunted must become the hunter – but how?

Like a trapped animal, Ahmed retreated carefully into the depths of the cave, moving backwards very slowly so as not to make any noise. After a few paces, he bent down to feel the surface of the ground. It was covered with small, polished pebbles; there must have been water running through the cave at some time. Instinctively, his academic mind wondered when this could have been – tens or hundred of thousands of years ago? The thought was totally irrelevant, but instantly led to another, which was not. He had ammunition all around him.

He picked up a handful of stones, feeling in the darkness for the roundest ones; an oval stone could not be aimed with anything like the same accuracy. Then he undid the elastic strap from his waist that had secured the bundle of chapattis and crouched down on the ground. He bent the metal hooks at each end of the elastic around the finger and thumb of his right hand, pulled back the strap carefully to test the strength of this rudimentary sling. Now he was no longer without a weapon.

He heard more sounds outside, a soft, stealthy whisper, a faint rattle of stones. Despite their obvious caution, whoever was out there had dislodged more stones. They were hurrying. The sky was growing lighter now, and through the gaping mouth of the cave, jagged with spikes of rocks like teeth, he could see the sky turn amber, then pink with dawn. He might be hiding in the belly of a great fish, a shark, a whale, peering out through its throat. For some reason, this analogy cheered him. Had not a man named Jonah in the Christian Holy Book been swallowed by such a great fish, and survived? That must be a good omen; he would do the same. Allah, the all and ever merciful, had delivered his enemies into his hands, blessed be his name for evermore.

He saw a man in brief silhouette against the sky. He was crouching at the entrance to the cave, to afford the smallest possible target; and then he saw a second man near him. Ahmed slipped a stone into the centre of his sling, drew back the elastic until he felt his finger and thumb would break with the strain. He held his breath as he took careful aim. Then he released the elastic.

The round stone hit the first man on the forehead. He fell forwards on his face, arms spread out on the rocks. His colleague seized him by the shoulder, thinking he had slipped. There had been no sound, no warning.

Ahmed put the second stone into his sling, fired at this man as he bent forward over the body of his companion. His soft, circular Afghan hat took the main force of the stone. He cried out in rage and pain, pulled a revolver from his belt and began to fire wildly, furiously into the depths of the cave.

Bullets flicked sharp splinters of stone all around Ahmed, who dropped flat on the floor. The crack of the shots echoed and re-echoed like circus whips in the long labyrinth behind him and finally died away. The man reloaded and began to come on into the cave, crawling on hands and knees, unsure who or what had hit him. He could hear nothing, see nothing ahead. Had that stone dropped from the roof or was there an enemy within, firing out at him?

Ahmed let him come to within 20 feet, and then fired two stones in quick succession. He heard a grunt of pain, and the metallic clatter as the revolver fell from his target's hands. Then Ahmed was out past the two bodies, running like a stag across the rocks, now tinged pink as coral by the rising sun.

Ahmed did not stop until he had reached the pass and then he paused briefly, resting thankfully against a rock, gasping for breath, his heart pounding like a drum against his ribs. He could see no one behind him now, no one following him, but he could not assume that his pursuers were dead. It would take more to kill them than stones fired from a home-made sling.

When he was satisfied there was no one in pursuit, he went on through the narrow pass. Sandstone dripped on either side; water oozed from cracks and fissures and stained the rocks. The air felt dank, sharp with mineral salts contained in the water, soaking up from the heart of the hills.

Then he was through, over the border, and coming down on the other side of the mountain range. Although the land appeared much the same – dry and featureless and inhospitable – the air did not. Here, for the first time in years, he was breathing the air of freedom.

He felt safer now, but safety was only relative; it could never be absolute. No one on the run could ever be truly safe until the chase was abandoned or the pursuers overwhelmed. Ahmed wanted to reach Peshawar, because he knew someone there who would help him, who could save his life, probably the only person in the world who could – if only he could find them.

He had no doubt that although he had temporarily put off two of his pursuers, others would soon take their place. All that mattered was to stay free until he could pass on the message he still kept repeating to himself as he walked.

He was aiming first for a town on the Peshawar road that no tourist or foreigner was allowed to visit: Darra. The name meant simply, A Pass in the Hills, but the town was much more than a pass. Here, in the street of the armourers, a shabby half-paved thoroughfare maybe a mile in length,

111

local craftsmen could copy any weapon of war made in any country in the world – and from any period of history. All that they needed was a sample of the original. No drawings, no measurements, only a metal weapon they could re-create.

They made accurate telescopic sights, pistols, revolvers, shotguns, machine guns, anti-aircraft guns, bullets, shells. They could produce a 17th-century American dog-lock musket, a 19th-century Turkish long-arm rifle, an English blunderbuss, as readily as a Russian missile launcher, and Dutch, Italian and Belgian shotguns with beautifully chased barrels and polished stocks. The price of an English Lee-Enfield rifle, now obsolete but still much in demand, was roughly 5000 rupees, £150; a Kalashnikov machine gun would cost ten times as much. To copy a Lee-Enfield, complete with a fictitious number, took a week; a Kalashnikov, rather longer.

The countryside through which Ahmed was now passing seemed featureless, almost a moonscape of dried-up rivers and dusty earth, dotted by groups of primitive hutments roofed with bamboo rattan and reddish mud. He passed a brick kiln, with a big cone-shaped chimney and mountains of discarded broken red bricks. Ahead, he could see, at a Pakistan police checkpoint, a red-and-white metal barrier balanced on a weight blocking the road. Half a dozen vehicles waited in line behind it. Drivers lounged against the wall of the police post, out of the wind, basking in the tepid sunshine.

Ahmed had to avoid all such police or customs checks: he had no passport or papers or card of identity. He walked behind the brick kiln, keeping his head down in an effort to appear anonymous, only one of many rootless people on the move, harmless, old, minding their own business. The policemen did not see him, or if they did, they did not stop him. He breathed more easily and pressed on past houses with small towers pierced by holes. This was tribal country; one tribe against another. Within minutes, at any approach of strangers, these holes, that now looked as harmless as open windows, could bristle with guns. This was no place to linger: a bullet solved many disputes and afterwards no one ever remembered who had fired the shot, or why. That way, they did not get shot themselves.

The road was smoother now. Some men were walking along it, women actually working on it. On their heads, they carried wooden trays and baskets filled with stones. Mountains beyond and behind him shimmered in the growing heat of morning. Dust, like yellow fog blown on the endless wind, swirled around him and made him cough.

Buffaloes scratched green weeds in a dried-up waterway as he approached Darra. The road broadened suddenly, almost unexpectedly, to become a main street, each side lined with open-fronted shops or booths. They displayed painted signs above their doors, illustrating the weapons in which the owner of the hut specialized: machine guns, shotguns, revolvers, pistols, bandoliers of ammunition and unusual weapons for unusual purposes; a walking stick that fired bullets like a rifle, a fountain pen with a single bullet beneath its nib. All had corrugated iron doors, or strong trellises, now slid to one side. The air rang with the tapping of craftsmen's hammers on hot bright metal. In the background Ahmed heard a constant crackle of gunfire from rifles, machine guns and revolvers being tested behind the huts by firing them at targets against the side of a hill.

Between gun-shops, squeezed into small, narrow spaces, because in a town of arms, anything associated with peaceful goods must be of secondary importance, other booths displayed piles of Russian refrigerators, radios, TV sets. How these had crossed the frontier in such numbers, only men like Sharif could say, and they kept silent.

Little boys ran from shop to shop, carrying trays of metal cups of tea, crossing and recrossing the road almost under the wheels of hooting trucks and buses. Others moved importantly about with rods of bare metal, each an inch thick, on their shoulders. These would then be bored through by primitive power drills, rifled and assembled.

A continual stream of traffic threaded through the rutted, pot-holed street. Little trucks, covered by canopies, decorated with metal stars cut from tin cans, animal pictures, lengths of chromium plated chain; buses with round bodies, like huge barrels and deep blue windows, and several radio aerials, each flying a pennant or a Pakistan flag. Old men sat on benches watching them. Their shoulders slung with arms and bandoliers, they drank tea or sucked stumps of green sugar cane. Other, younger men, wearing flak jackets beneath their shirts, who had just come from Afghanistan to have weapons repaired, or were about to return with new weapons, waited in groups, smoking cigarettes, talking in low voices.

Here, in this one street, as many arms were being made as in many a Western arsenal – and much more efficiently. It had been like this, Ahmed knew, for a century and a half; even the British had bought arms here when they guarded the Khyber Pass. Darra appeared an undistinguished town, dirty, with unmade roads, open drains, telegraph and electric cables drooping from shop to shop, but it was rich beyond accounting. From it, or through it, weapons went north, drugs went south, and money in both directions. The men who owned the shops, who squatted out of the light of the sun, legs crossed, tapping with hammers, scraping with files as their fathers and their fathers' fathers had done before them might be multi-millionaires, their wealth measured in blood and death and mutilation, but there was no outward evidence of money. There was nothing about them, except perhaps a certain hardness of eye, a dignity of bearing, to distinguish them from young employees, who sat on mats in the mouths of the shops, their feet in holes in the floor, vices between their knees to grip rifle barrels and bolts on which they worked tirelessly.

Ahmed knew the address of the man he needed to see, a man he knew he could trust, a kinsman by blood. He went up a narrow alley, where walls on either side leaned towards each other as though to discourage pedestrians walking two

114

abreast. This led, behind pylons supporting electric power lines stretching across the road, towards the base of the hill where marksmen constantly tested newly made guns. A goat charged away at Ahmed's approach; a dog, scavenging on a pile of rubbish, bared yellow teeth at him.

The buildings here were larger than those on the road, and from inside them, as he passed, Ahmed could hear the hum and whine of lathes, and the chatter of electric motors driving other equipment. Here and there, too, sunshine caught the blue paint on a sophisticated German milling machine or on men wearing violet coloured goggles as they brazed and welded some complex weapon.

He stopped at the shop of the armourer he sought. This was like a concrete cell, thirty feet square, its front open to the alleyway. In the back, rows of rifles and shotguns stood neatly, chained for safety in wooden racks. In the fore-ground, two men sat on a mat, holes cut through the floor for their feet. Their knees gripped strong vices in which they held rifle barrels ready for assembly, blued and oiled to give a satiny effect.

'Salaam,' said Ahmed softly. The man nearest to the door looked up, frowning at the interruption. Then he recognized Ahmed, extended his right hand in greeting, but did not stand up. Nothing should stop the task of a professional armourer: there was so much skilled work to be done, so much money to be made – so many buyers to supply.

'Salaam Aleikum,' he said shortly. 'What brings you here?'

'A job for you.'

'A gun?'

'No, something else. But I will wait until you finish.'

The man nodded and went back to his task. In his left hand he held a small chisel, no longer than half a pencil. In his right, he grasped a lightweight hammer. He tapped the chisel constantly, turning the blade this way and that with each hammer stroke. When he had finished, he rubbed an oily rag over the barrel, handed it up to Ahmed.

115

'You work very quickly,' said Ahmed admiringly. He always enjoyed seeing an expert at work.

'Each to his own trade,' the young man replied. 'I could not translate a line of your Sanskrit in a hundred years. Now, what can I do for you?'

Ahmed squatted down on the ground beside him. This was business not for other ears, and there were many in Darra. A little boy brought a tray of teacups without handles. Ahmed drank the sweet tea gratefully. He had not realized how thirsty he was. Then he picked up a pencil from the floor, and a folded newspaper, and wrote something in the margin.

'I want you to tap that out for me,' he said.

'Where? On a gun barrel?'

Ahmed shook his head. He drew an outline on the newspaper. The man looked at it for a moment, said something to the boy who had brought the tea. He ran off into the alley, came back with a thin, narrow strip of metal, about four inches long.

'The right thickness?' he asked. Ahmed nodded.

'Cut it as in my drawing,' he told him, and drank another cup of tea as he watched his kinsman work. In five minutes, the man handed the metal back to Ahmed.

'Is that what you want?' he asked.

'Perfect. How much will that be?'

'Nothing. It is my pleasure to help you, as you in the past have so often helped my family.'

He paused and for a moment he looked at Ahmed quizzically.

'You are going back over the border?'

'No. On to Peshawar.'

'By bus?'

'No. I will walk and hope to get a lift on the way.'

'It is a dangerous road on one's own. That is why most people prefer the buses. And even if they have a car, they do not drive alone. It is most unwise to walk.'

116

'I have no money,' Ahmed explained simply. 'A man without money cannot buy a seat in a bus.'

'That is so. I can give you some – not lend you – give you.'

'You are very kind, but you have already given me this example of your work. I will walk.'

'Tell me, are you armed? You have a knife, a pistol?'

'No,' Ahmed replied. 'But who would wish to attack an old man who carries nothing worth stealing?'

'Some people kill because they love to kill,' the other man replied grimly. 'Times are not as they were. But I have devised a little weapon to dissuade them.'

He opened a wall cupboard, took out a black fountain pen, handed this to Ahmed. He examined it. The pen felt slightly heavier than any pen he had previously used. He looked at the nib. Beneath it protruded the pointed nose of a small calibre bullet.

'A fountain pen pistol,' said Ahmed. 'I have seen such things. But how would that protect me? One shot at an attacker, and it is useless. And I might miss him.'

'Impossible,' the young man assured him. 'Look more closely, my friend.'

Ahmed held the pen under the shadeless bulb that hung above the vice, fingered the pocket clip. By pressing this, he would fire the pistol, but now he saw that the end of the pen away from the nib and the bullet was not made of hard black metal like the rest. It appeared to be plugged by some soft substance like putty, but the same colour as the pen.

'It fires in reverse,' the young man explained. 'My own idea. You are attacked. Someone seizes the pen, aims it at you – to shoot you with your own weapon. He fires – and it backfires – and kills him.'

'But the bullet is in the nib?'

'A dummy,' said his kinsman, grinning, showing yellow teeth like a wolf. 'The real bullet is in the other end of the pen. I give this to you, my friend, and may Allah guide your steps into the ways of peace. And if that is not his will, may this present protect you from all attack.'

Stevie could not bring herself to accept that Love's verdict on the Cord was final. She had appealed to Parkington, who referred her back to Love.

'I know nothing about the value of old cars,' he explained. 'The doctor does and he is an expert on this particular make. My company has to accept what he says. That, after all, is why they have paid him to come and look at it.'

'But how do you account for other cars going for nearly as much at auctions, without any dispute as to their value?'

'I can never account for the ways of the wealthy,' Parkington admitted. 'But although I sympathize with you, I am sorry there is really nothing I can do.'

Stevie feared that Love and Parkington would now either insure the car at Love's valuation or fly back to London, to advise the Midland Widows to decline the business altogether. She felt it was imperative to keep them here while she did all she could to persuade Love to change his mind. So, on the impulse, she suggested she take them to the camp where she worked. Then they could see for themselves how much any infusion of money could help the refugees.

Crammed shoulder to shoulder in the rear seat of a Morris Minor taxi, Love and Parkington drove with Stevie from Peshawar out on the Khyber Road towards the refugee camp. As the little car droned on, rain began to fall, out of season and quite out of time, but somehow symbolizing Stevie's gloomy feelings. How could this stranger say that the car, on which so much more depended than he could ever imagine, was overvalued? What did it matter to him? And did he suspect who owned it – and why she was involved? Surely, he must have made a mistake?

The monsoon was not due for two months yet, and the rain was gentle, misty, foggy. It seemed more like an early afternoon in a New England October than a Pakistan morning in March. They passed through a military area with notices in English: Unit Lines, Garrison Engineer. Against the heat of dry seasons, a nineteenth-century military barracks wore hoods like heavy wooden eyelids over its windows. Outside the building, on barbed wire fences, dozens of pairs of khaki trousers had been draped to dry when the rain stopped. Tethered goats along the roadside nibbled at grass, and tonga ponies waited, heads down, sleeping on their feet, under a thin line of trees. All the outlines seemed merged, a living aquatint, as subdued as Stevie's thoughts.

Despite the rain, the dust felt sharp as sandpaper on Love's throat, and the morning was unusually chilly. They passed cyclists wrapped in blankets which virtually covered their entire bodies, even their heads. Beneath these blankets their thin cotton pantaloons and sockless feet shone with rain as they pedalled.

Stevie broke the uneasy silence in the car:

'I can't believe what you said, Jason. That the Cord is a fake. How can it be? Who could possibly construct such a thing out here? But even if it is – which I doubt – can't it have extra value just by being a replica or whatever you call it?'

'Not ten million pounds extra value,' replied Love soberly. 'No way.'

'I'll ask for a second opinion on that,' said Stevie. 'I've seen in the papers what old cars go for at auctions. Fantastic sums.'

She paused abruptly, as though she was about to say more, but then thought better of it. With an obvious effort, she attempted to change the subject.

'When we reach the camp you can see for yourselves just how much any money would mean to these poor wretched people. They have been there for years, most of them. Children are growing up never having known any other life.'

119

'But as the Russians are leaving Afghanistan, won't they all go home?'

'To what? In many cases their houses have been destroyed, their belongings seized, their businesses ruined. And what sort of government will be in power there then? There are seven different political groups vying for power in Afghanistan, all of them armed by the West – or the Russians. Each group feels that at last they have a chance to gain power – and the right to it – and the pro-Communist government in command won't relinquish control easily. These refugees fled here to escape Communism. Do they go back to be jailed or killed? Most, I think, will want to wait and see. Even the conditions they are in now could be better than what they'd return to.'

As the car splashed through muddy puddles, Love was thinking of all the armies which had marched along this road. Twenty-five centuries earlier, Alexander the Great's legions had been held up for forty days by local tribesmen who hated the invader.

The emperor Babur had also marched along this road in the sixteenth century to conquer south Asia and set up a Mogul empire. He had noted in his memoirs that the whole plain was ablaze with flowers. Indeed, Peshawar took its name from the Sanskrit *pushpapura*, which meant The City of Flowers. Now the flowers had gone in wreaths for unnumbered dead, for many armies had marched up this road – and some down again, among them the British when they had attempted – and failed – to subdue Afghanistan by force early in the nineteenth century.

Now the only army coming from Afghanistan was of bedraggled refugees on foot, on the backs of weary donkeys, in tongas, or crammed into trucks and country buses. This road, which had once seen emperors, with teams of war elephants pulling giant, gold-mouthed cannon, now ran between shacks and hutments, all glory gone before.

Behind these shacks stretched patches of open swamp, green with stagnant water, pocked now with rain. Peshawar

120

was still a frontier town. Men loafed around wearing loose grey shirts and baggy trousers. Bandoliers, crammed with brightly polished bullets, hung across their chests; they wore pistols at their belts, and rifles or Kalashnikovs slung over their shoulders. These men were fighting soldiers off duty. They had neither uniforms nor need of them; their trade was total war. The frontier, so far as they were concerned, was simply a line drawn on a map, without real significance. They crossed it as easily as others would cross a road, without passports or papers. The only law they observed was their own: the law of the gun and the sword. No insult, real, imagined, even totally unintentional, would ever go unreturned. An eye for an eye, a life for a life, a death for a death, sometimes from one generation to another, was the rule by which they lived. No wonder then, Love thought, that the whole area seemed abrasive, raw, ready to be set alight by the wrong remark, a hasty answer.

Through the open window of the car, he inhaled the smell peculiar to the city: over-ripe fruit, tobacco smoke, roasted, burning meat, and red hot metal being hammered into the shape of gun barrels, bayonets, sword blades, in a hundred roadside smithies. On either side as they drove, in the hutments, the shacks open-fronted towards the road, he saw other craftsmen hammering leather, carving wood, seemingly oblivious of all that was going on outside. The West seeks a profit, the East, a destiny, he thought as he explored two back teeth with the tip of his tongue. Every day, the only item on the hotel menu was curried chicken. A small sliver of chicken had wedged itself between these two teeth and he could not dislodge it. Stevie's hand on his arm brought him back to reality.

'When we are in the camp,' she said quietly, 'do not buy anything, whatever they may offer you.'

'Is it likely I'd want to?'

'I don't know, but remember you are strangers, foreigners, and they may want to sell you something. This can cause trouble with locals who feel they're losing trade to the Afghans – who, to them, are also strangers.'

More and more houses now began to appear on either side of the road, without windows, all made of mud, dark under the rain. Suddenly, the road led through the centre of a mud hut city, brown, featureless, without names or numbers to differentiate one windowless mud dwelling from ten thousand like it. Long-legged chickens pecked hopefully in damp grit. Children looked up with bright eyes, sharp with curiosity, as the car slowed and stopped.

Stevie climbed out and led the way across a makeshift bridge, past stalls behind which Afghans squatted on stools looking at them over pyramids of oranges, mounds of stained wooden carvings, and they were inside the perimeter wall.

Love had not known quite what to expect, but he had not expected this. To his comfortable Western mind, a refugee camp must surely mean neat tents in lines of a size that could be easily controlled. Refugees to him were people he remembered vaguely from boyhood – not this – a city of despair and destitution.

'Where do you want to start?' Stevie asked Love. 'It runs for several miles along this road and back across the desert for maybe ten miles.'

Walls boxed them in like a maze. Each one was about eight feet high, rounded on top and surrounding homes that, close to, looked like giant ant-hills. These had all been built by hand, by human ants, by men and women and children driven out of their own homes, only able to bring their basic skills, their pride in independence, their memories, and what few belongings they could carry, over bleak, desolate and dangerous passes. Between these walls were small alleys, damp and narrow, barely wide enough for two people to walk side by side. Rain was punching dimples into long purple puddles of brackish water which would not drain away. Three chickens sheltered under a stretched cloth over a wooden bed frame, keeping out of the rain, staying alive to be killed another day.

Stevie led Love and Parkington into the nearest house. Mud walls supported a crude roof of tarpaulin stretched over bamboo rafters, but inside all was clean, neat; the air of pride stronger than the air of poverty. A man bowed and extended his hand. He said something. She translated:

'He was a carpenter in a village outside Kabul. He and his brother joined the Mujahideen. The brother was killed. He didn't die quickly. Both his eyes were blown out by the blast of the bomb, and there was no medical aid. The Russians wanted to question this man. He realized there was no future for him in his home village, so he gathered what tools he could, a few chisels and saws, and with his wife and two children, they came here.'

'How long ago?' asked Love.

'Six years.'

'So what's he doing here? Does he work at all?'

'Oh, sure. Further up the road you will see tree trunks, spruce and larch, cut down, planed and fashioned to make things – furniture, poles for these huts. That's his work. Every man does what he can to make a living. They weave carpets, beat metal poles. Anything they can sell.'

Resignation, the acceptance of seemingly endless exile and despair, hung like a sad miasma over the camp. Narrow tracks twisted and turned between the high windowless walls. Men trudged through mud and puddles, heads down, minds miles away, without even looking at them. There were no women, only men and children. This was a Pathan world, dominated by men; women might be there, behind these walls, in dark airless recesses of the huts, but not outside, never on view.

Stevie led them down the alley past other houses, into a building larger than the rest, still mud-walled, covered with a crude wooden roof. A number of men were lying on *charpoys* – rough bed frames with rope mattresses – the name came from the fact that they stood on four legs. They were wrapped in dirty blankets, shawls, odd pieces of cloth. Some started up nervously as the newcomers came into the

123

room. There was a smell of tired, unwashed bodies, a smell of fear.

'If any of them don't want to be examined by a woman,' said Love, 'I'll be pleased to stand in for you.'

'Thanks,' Stevie replied. 'Since they're Pathans, women have a very subsidiary role. But they seem to trust me. To them, I'm not a woman, but a doctor. Also, I'm American, which is something else again.'

Love and Parkington followed her into another wider room. Here women, some all in black with only their eyes visible, other less encumbered, with heads and faces free, held sickly babies. Children sat quietly on backless benches, bare feet not quite reaching the mud floor, wriggling their toes.

'My out-patients department for women and children,' Stevie explained.

As fast as she gave one patient pills in a twist of paper or a bottle of medicine, with directions written in Urdu script, another patient took their place. Men were coming in as the women left and Love noticed that several times Stevie glanced towards the doorway as though she was expecting someone who did not arrive – or had noticed someone briefly in the outer room, and wanted to see them again.

Finally, the last patient left, and they were on their own. Love saw her face suddenly tighten. She was looking towards the doorway; he followed her gaze. The light was dim in the windowless room. Naked bulbs throbbed brightly with the heartbeat of a generator, casting trembling shadows on the walls.

In the doorway stood a man Love could scarcely see. The eyes were bright and piercing; the eyes of someone running a high fever. He saw high cheek bones, an aquiline nose – and a brief flicker of surprise and recognition the man could not conceal, before he turned away. And then, behind him, Love saw another man, younger, with a sharp, vulpine face. He was also watching them, his eyes narrowed as though trying to impress their faces on his mind, so he could recognize them again quickly.

Were these two men patients, reluctant to admit their malady to a woman doctor, simply because she was a woman? Was it shyness – or something else that made them both flit away into the darkness with the silence and speed of shadows when a lamp is moved?

'Come in!' Love called to them. '*Idhar*', remembering the word from Urdu learned in the army years ago.

But the figures had gone as quickly as they had arrived. Love crossed the room. Somehow he felt that it was important to find the first man; he was obviously ill. He looked down the dark passage outside. In the distance a light burned, but there was no one in sight. A dog slunk along, baring teeth, eyes green in the gloom.

'They've gone,' said Love.

'It is nothing,' said Stevie firmly. 'Nothing. We sometimes get people who just look in.'

'Sort of Peeping Toms?'

'I guess you could say that,' she replied.

But Love had not said that, and nor had she. There was something strange, almost desperate, about this old man who lacked the courage to enter that had worried, distressed, unnerved her – and something sinister and dangerous about the younger man's cruel, predatory appearance. However, this was not his business. Everyone had a part of their lives they needed to keep private. Perhaps this was a part of Stevie's?

No one spoke as they drove back to Peshawar. Stevie dropped Love and Parkington at the gate of Pink's Hotel, went on to her rented house.

'If you've no better social engagements,' said Parkington when they were on their own, 'come and have a glass of Aftershave with me.'

'Thanks. I will.'

First, Love went into his own room, picked up a plastic

125

container of dental floss and removed the morsel of chicken that had been irritating him. It was tiny, but as with a piece of grit in an eye, had seemed of enormous proportions, until he examined it closely. Would the mystery behind the Cord also come down to size if he applied more concentration to it?

When Love returned, Parkington locked the door, motioned him to take a seat, and poured out two whiskies.

'You saw that old man in the camp?' said Love. 'He looked very ill to me – and much sharper than the others.'

'He is.'

'You know him, then?'

'Yes. Only briefly, in a professional way, and that was years ago. He was Professor of Oriental Languages at Kabul University until the Russians came.'

'I didn't know you were a student there,' said Love. 'I thought you graduated from the University of Life. In Experience.'

'So I did. With honours. But he belongs to the old firm.'

'You mean, Intelligence? Colonel MacGillivray's lot?'

'The same. And his father before him. Ever heard of Subhas Chandra Bose, in India, in the Second World War?'

'Of course. An Indian Nationalist agitator from Calcutta. A Bengal lawyer with a Cambridge degree. Felt that he and a few other intellectuals and politicians would have a better future if they could kick out the British. So he applied himself vigorously to that task.'

'Right,' agreed Parkington. 'Well, the Bengal Special Branch had him under observation in his house in Calcutta in 1942. The Japs were sweeping on towards India then. Many rich Bengalis had already packed their goods and fled east. After years of shouting to get the British out, now they wished they'd stay. They were almost giving away houses and shops and cars and furniture, remember?'

'I remember,' Love assured him. 'I also remember that Bose gave the police the slip. He escaped from his house, disguised as a Muslim – and they were looking for a Hindu.

126

I remember reading about it. Not too bright on the part of the plod, I thought.'

'Actually, it was,' Parkington replied. 'The authorities wanted to be rid of the man, so they turned a Nelson eye. Bose went on to Kabul, then on to Russia, which wasn't on the Allied side then, but had a pact with Germany. Bose wanted Russian help to kick out the British. Ironically, the Russians thought he must be a British plant, and sent him on his way smartly. Bose got a German visa and travelled to Berlin to try his luck there.

'Hitler personally interviewed him and decided the Germans could use him as a figurehead. So they put Bose in a submarine and back he went to Rangoon, where, from a safe distance, he led what he called the Indian National Army – poor wretched sepoys who had been captured in Singapore and Burma. He died in an air crash, just before the war ended, fleeing to Tokyo.'

'So what has Bose got to do with this former professor in the camp?' asked Love.

'He lodged with the professor's father in Kabul, that's what. Bose thought he was also an anti-British agitator. He never guessed the old man was a British agent! The professor has also been very useful to us. I must have a private word with him. I will help him if I can.'

'You can't get into the camp on your own.'

'I'll get a permit. They'll let me in.'

'Why don't you ask Stevie to help you? We both went into the camp with her, and no hassle at all.'

'I'll manage on my own.'

'Now?'

'No. Later. Possibly tomorrow morning. In the meantime, I have something to show you that may give you a reason for not involving the lady doctor too closely in my business.'

Parkington took from his briefcase a thin black folder marked 'Insurance Claims', shook out a dozen black and white photographs. Love picked them up.

'These are of my room in Bowker's Hotel in 'Pindi,' he said in surprise. 'Why, there's Stevie.'

'Who else? Keep looking.'

'She's going through my things. What the hell is this?'

'I thought you'd be interested,' said Parkington. He scooped up the photographs, slipped them back into the folder.

'How did you get these?' Love asked him.

'I set up a special camera on top of a cupboard in your room with an automatic gadget that works on body heat, like a burglar alarm.'

'You bastard. I might have been screwing the girl!'

'I wouldn't have shown you these if you had, so you'd never have known. The camera cannot lie – but sometimes it is silent.'

'But why do this to me?'

'I didn't mean to. I never expected you to be in that room in the first place.'

'But it was my room. You must have known that.'

'No. It was booked for the late Mr Glover.'

'By whom?'

'By me.'

'But you booked *me* into the hotel.'

'I checked they had an extra room first, for when you came along. There's always room for Love. But the clerk is an idiot.'

'How do you know this man Glover? You never said, when I told you about his accident.'

'Why should I? You never asked me. And in my trade it's never wise to give answers to questions you've not been asked.'

'Your trade? You mean insurance?'

'That. And the old firm.'

'MacGillivray again? MI6?'

'Call it that. Or the circus, the firm, the club, anything you like, but not Intelligence. That's something we don't boast about.'

'Understandably.'

'You see, *I* wanted to meet Glover. He was bad news.'

'In what way? Insurance-wise?'

'No, national-wise. He was selling secrets.'

'To whom?'

'The highest bidder. Gaddafi in Libya, for one. Rumania, for another. We knew he was also dealing with the top, the heart of the three-ring circus – Moscow. And the easiest way for him was through Pakistan – he frequently came out here for his firm. Then over the border into Afghanistan, and he'd done another deal. We knew he wanted to make a final killing, three hundred thousand cash, half a million. And then he would pull out. Or so he thought. He didn't realize that they'd never let go of him – and he would be in no position to argue the toss over that. So the only killing he made was his own.'

'What sort of secrets was he selling?'

'Electronics. Underwater listening equipment mainly. That's what they're after. That's what we lead the world in. So they say.'

'Why didn't you get him before? Was this like Bose, deliberately letting him go?'

'For a time, because often it's better to give these guys a bit of rope. We wanted to see where he'd lead us – and to whom.'

'Did you kill him – or have him killed?'

'No. We wanted him alive so we could find exactly who he was dealing with. But someone else had other ideas. Either Mr Glover had outrun his usefulness, or someone feared we were on to him and might make him talk. Or there was another reason altogether. So they chopped him. I'd like to know who – and why.'

'On behalf of the Midland Widows?'

'Since he's insured with them, yes. But chiefly on behalf of my other employer, MacGillivray.'

'You knew Glover was coming here?'

'Of course. And after we discovered that, the Midland

Widows' indefatigable employee, Mr Hossein, sent word about the Cord's unusually high value and asked for further instructions.'

'So you suspected that the two things could be linked?'

'We thought it was just possible. No more. But certainly no less. Maybe the car was to be his pay-off – ten million pounds in solid metal. Put a torch to it or run it over a cliff and the money's his.'

'Is that a tenable theory?'

'That's what we're going to find out. In my business you learn to suspect everything – and everyone. It seemed odd, such a big price *and* Mr Glover. Together. Here. Same time. Same place. And I wanted you here, Doctor, because I thought you'd say the car was too pricey – but you might come up with a genuine reason for this. Which you haven't done – yet.

'When people pay millions for old cars that can't even drag their weight over a manhole cover, real values don't count for much. But there's still time. As the old man said to his young wife, the night is still young.'

'And you think the Cord's somehow involved with Glover – and his death?'

'I don't know. But I have to find out – and fast. If Glover was trading, someone else will now be in his place, and we don't know who.'

'What about Stevie?'

'I don't know about her. But I thought I'd show you these pictures. Just in case you got too close. Remember, in this business, trust no one.'

'I'm not in this business,' Love pointed out.

'You are now, like it or not. An honest man has hair in the palm of his hand. And I've not see too much hair around here so far on the people I shake hands with.'

'I'll keep looking,' Love promised.

'And while you do, keep your head down. And here are a few little bits and pieces to help you.'

'Oh, you mean MacGillivray's gadgets? Sort of James Bond things?'

'These are of rather older ancestry. You know why so many British and Allied prisoners-of-war escaped in the last war? Because they took into the camps with them what I call the keys of freedom. For example, the top button on every pilot's uniform contained a compass. He unscrewed the front to read it. When the Germans discovered this, our people simply gave it a left hand thread. All razor blades made during that war were magnetized. Hang one on a thread and it would point north – a simple compass. And so on.'

'So what have you got for me now?'

'Knowing your obsession with the Cord car, I have bought you a belt with a special Cord buckle.'

He opened a drawer, took out a supple black leather belt with a huge brass buckle showing a Cord head on, blunt coffin nose bonnet, raked screen, covers closed over the headlights like eyelids.

'Beautiful,' said Love admiringly. 'But what does it do?'

'Gets you out of a really tight spot – if ever you're unwise enough to get into one. To activate it, bring your left hand across the front of the buckle. This will flick open the cover on the left headlamp, and breaks the seal on a flat pressurized bladder of anti-riot gas built into the leather. The jet will reach about ten feet. If you jump back, and hold your breath, you should just save yourself from its effects. But the gas will temporarily knock out anyone facing you.'

'What if I can't get my hand across it?'

'That's been thought of, my friend. Say you're standing with your hands in the air. They've got you – so they think. But if you can just lower your hands so that your elbows touch the sides of the belt, then bring 'em in sharply – together. There are two release buttons built into the leather. They do the same thing. But don't ever let the gas go in a confined space unless you've a gas mask handy. It's pretty concentrated.'

'How about refills?' asked Love.

'None. This is strictly a one-off affair. If you need refills – you don't deserve them. You haven't done the job with the first one.'

'Here's something else,' added Parkington. He put a pair of shoelaces on the table between them. Love picked them up. They felt more springy than any laces he had ever used.

'They've got surgeon's trepanning saws inside them,' Parkington explained. 'Again, a Second World War idea, issued to RAF aircrew. Stone walls would not a prison make nor iron bars a cage – if you could saw through the bars with these.'

'Clever,' admitted Love. 'But these gadgets are really not for me.'

Parkington shrugged, replaced the belt in the suitcase, put the laces in his pocket.

'Never say we didn't make you a good offer,' he said.

'I won't,' Love promised. 'But why show them to me in any case?'

'Because they could be useful. I believe we are now both in a situation that has become potentially very dangerous.'

'You never told me this when you asked me to fly out here.'

'Of course I didn't – in case it put you off. I always work on the principle of need-to-know. I only tell anyone how much *I* think they need to know. Then they can only give away so much if they get caught. Like the old ocean-going queens – the ships, I mean, not the sailors – we like lots of water-tight compartments. If there is a leak in one, it can be closed off immediately. The *Titanic* hadn't got those. It is a lesson to be learned.'

'But why now especially?' persisted Love.

'That refugee camp,' said Parkington. 'That old man. I can't figure out why he's there. But I sensed he could be in danger.'

'You also saw the rat-faced young man watching him – and us?'

'Of course. So when I go back, I'm going back armed.'

He took a nine-millimetre Browning High Power pistol from his bag, checked the gun was loaded.

'How did you get that through airport security?' Love asked him.

'With ease. Have *you* ever watched suitcases go through the X-ray machines at airports?'

'Often. They stand them up on end. They have to, so that the operators can see what's inside, in silhouette.'

'Exactly. So I break this gun, and put it in my case, facing from top to bottom. The X-ray then picks up an end-on view of the barrel. It shows up like a coin or a collar stud. The handle is plastic, so that doesn't show at all. Next question. None? Right. I suggest you take a very close look at the Cord again. A much more thorough examination than you gave it with Stevie. See if there is anything fitted to it that could increase its value phenomenally – or hidden in it. The Midland Widows don't want to lose the business. Understandably. Equally, if there's any risk of a swindle, they don't *want* the business. And if there's a tie-up with Mr Glover, my other employer wants to know. Now, where exactly is this bloody car?'

'Locked in a garage.'

'At that value, I would hope so,' said Parkington. 'Have you got the key?'

'No. Stevie has that.'

Parkington took a penknife from his pocket. Instead of gadgets for removing stones from horses' hoofs and opening beer bottles, Love saw three sharp pieces of metal, each with a small hook.

'They'll pick any lock,' Parkington said confidently, giving it to Love. 'Now try your luck. Take my torch, too. It's got a halogen bulb, the nearest thing to a searchlight.'

Parkington climbed into the motor rickshaw; there was no taxi in sight.

'Where to, sahib?' the driver asked him.

'Permit Office.'

'Very good. Just now going.'

They drove through crowded streets. The city seemed full of people and shouts, hoarse cries, imprecations, and the constant braying background of car horns. Men padded past, grunting beneath the gross weight of enormous bundles of bright green maize on their backs. Eventually, the driver stopped outside a long building with a vaguely Victorian appearance.

'Here is office, sir.'

'What time does it open?'

'Just now, nine o'clock.'

'Well, it's ten,' said Parkington, checking his watch. 'We should be lucky.'

'You got lucky face, sir. I tell you, you got lucky face.'

'Then it's the only part of me that is,' Parkington told him. 'I've been married three times. Unlucky in love, you might say.'

'I'm not saying any such thing. Any children you have, sir? On three wives?'

'No. Not on or under, before or behind any of them.'

'Ah! I got four children on *one* wife,' said the taxi driver proudly.

'Then you're a better man than I am,' Parkington told him. He felt like adding 'Gunga Din', but thought better of it; hadn't Gunga Din been a Hindu?

'Just now asking at the door,' said the driver. He led Parkington across the street. They climbed two steps to a building like a ticket office in a 1930s railway station in the shires. Three cubby holes were protected by wire netting screens; all were closed. Above them were notices in Urdu script. A man squatting on his haunches contemplated the ground in front of him.

'When opening?' asked Parkington, falling unconsciously into the local clipped way of speaking.

'Just now closed,' said the man. 'Much trouble. Students marching.'

'Where to?'

'Main office.'

'Where's the main office?'

'Up the road.'

Parkington walked up the road. Half a dozen policemen with rifles watched him without interest. A hundred paces on, he saw the tail end of a great crowd, mostly young men: no girls, no women. Were there no women students, no demonstrators in favour of Women's Lib, or crèches for lesbian one-parent families, or whatever the feminine cause of the moment might be? This was a man's country, all right, male-oriented, male-dominated. He could drink to that – if drink was the right word. Double iron gates were chained and padlocked. Policemen behind these gates held sub-machine guns.

'I want a permit,' Parkington told the crowd in general. A man approached the gates from the other side. He faced Parkington with the metal bars between them.

'It is now closed,' he explained. 'There is much trouble. Students are demonstrating. You can see for yourself.'

'But why here? What's that got to do with me?'

'They have been cheating in their examinations. They have all been failed. Now they are saying that it is unfair, because *everyone* cheats in examinations. They have been buying and selling question papers the day before. But the price asked was too high, so all students could not buy. That is unfair – so they are demonstrating.'

'This is madness,' said Parkington. 'All I need is a permit to visit a refugee camp.'

'Come back tomorrow.'

'What time?'

'Opening nine o'clock.'

'If I get here at ten, like today?'

'Wait a minute. Perhaps *not* opening tomorrow. That is special day.'

'What sort of special day?'

'Holiday.'

'So when will it open?'

'Who can say? Maybe day after tomorrow. Chief permit officer is very busy man.'

'So am I. It's terribly important I get a permit.'

'I am sorry, cannot help you. If you would come in here, you could see someone in the office.'

'Well, let me in.'

'Have you got a pass?'

'Of course I haven't a pass. I want a permit. I didn't know I needed a pass to get a permit. But I've got my passport, my American Express card, to prove who I am.'

'That's not good enough. Not doing so nicely here, thank you, eh? I am sorry to say you have to get pass first.'

'But where from?'

'From the office.'

'But it's closed, you say.'

'That is so. So you cannot get pass.'

'Well, thanks for telling me,' said Parkington.

'No problem, sir. My pleasure to help visitors.'

Parkington walked back down the road.

'You got *unlucky* face, sir?' the taxi driver asked him.

'I have indeed,' said Parkington. 'No luckier here than in love. I can't get a permit.'

'Who needs permit? What for?'

'To visit a refugee camp.'

'Ah, so now you are telling me.'

He pulled a ten rupee note from an inner pocket.

'That's good permit. Twenty rupee note better permit. That is how we can get through checkpoints, sir, on the way. I know the policemen on the road. They are of my people, Afridi. We will go together.'

'I should have known you years ago,' said Parkington. 'You've got a great future.'

'I know. I have no lucky face, but I have a lucky life. I am asking you, which is the more important?'

'And I am telling you, you already know the answer.'

* * *

Love went out through a back door of the hotel that evening, past the line of waiting motor rickshaws, along the uneven pavement down the side street. Outside the garage door, he paused. Parkington had not lied: the prongs opened the lock as easily as a key.

Love slid open the door on its oiled rollers, closed it carefully behind him, and then shone the torch on the car. It seemed safer to do this than to put on the main light, and he could not work in the gloom of a windowless room.

He examined the Cord methodically from front to rear bumper. The engine was standard, the interior seemed totally original; only the engine and chassis numbers were false. But why have such obviously bogus numbers that could so easily be checked and found wanting? How many more questions would he have to ask about this car before he found the right answer – or, indeed, any answers?

He examined the Cord's huge luggage boot, walked around the car several times, puzzled why Stevie should be so certain it must be worth the sum she claimed – and why she had been searching his room. There was nothing about this roadster that warranted such a high value and, so far as he could tell, nothing concealed on it or in it; neither jewels, drugs, nor contraband. Love switched off the torch and stood, pondering the problem. There *must* be an answer, and possibly a simple one, but he could not think what it might be.

Then, as he stood, he heard a faint noise outside; a careful intake of breath, a stealthy movement. Slowly, inch by cautious inch, the door began to slide open. Someone was coming inside; not Parkington, surely, for he would have opened the door quickly, knowing that Love was already inside. This was someone who did not wish to be seen or heard, who might even have been surprised to find the door unlocked, and wished to take immediate advantage of such an unexpected and fortunate discovery. A casual thief, possibly, after a car radio, a set of tools, anything he could sell easily to one of the open-fronted shops that specialized in second-hand spares and accessories?

Love retreated into the depths of the garage, where he could see but not be seen. He felt in his pockets for anything he could use as a weapon – wishing now he had accepted Parkington's offer of the belt. All he could find was the small square plastic container of dental floss.

He searched the bench for a spanner, a screwdriver, but there was only a tin of engine oil. He moved this to the edge of the bench, tied one end of his floss to the handle, paid out several metres of thread from its container, and tied the other end to the belt loop on his trousers. Then, holding the waxed cotton, he crouched down between the bonnet and the wall on its left, so that he would not be seen if a light was flashed on the car. He heard the door close, and then saw the thin pale beam of a pencil torch directed on one of the Cord's wings, and the rough whitewashed concrete of the garage wall behind it. Whoever was inside the garage with him was now on the other side of the car.

The driver's door was opened carefully. Love heard a faint creak of springs as someone sat in the driver's seat, then faint metallic sounds, as though the intruder was trying to unscrew something on the dashboard. Springs squeaked again. The door opened and closed. The pencil beam played on the ceiling, the walls; its owner was now out of the car and appeared, like Love, to be looking for something, to judge by the constantly moving ray of light. Could that 'something' be a secret worth £10,000,000?

Again, Love heard the sound of metal scratching metal, and then a faint ping from the rear of the car. He knew from experience of his own Cord that this was the sound made when one of the two large rear light lenses was removed. Each was held in place by a circular piece of sprung metal that had to be prised away with a screwdriver – and usually sprang into the air as soon as it was released. It was time to announce himself, before the intruder could find what was sought and be away through the door into the safety of the dark.

Love moved silently, shoulders hunched, between the wall and the side of the car, paying out the floss with each slow step. When he was within feet of the intruder, but still with the bulk of the car between them, he stood up, and pressed the switch button on Parkington's halogen torch.

The garage erupted into a brilliant, eye-aching blaze of light. Love heard a man curse in surprise and fear, and the clatter of a screwdriver on the floor. A dark-skinned man, blinking dazedly in the sudden glare, stood up slowly, eyes narrowed against the sudden dazzling intensity of the torch beam.

PART SIX

The older Colonel Douglas MacGillivray grew, the less enthusiasm he felt for work – especially on a warm, spring day. He was not sure – nor did he care greatly – whether this was simply a matter of age, whether the nature of his duties as the deputy service head of British Secret Intelligence Service disenchanted him or, again, whether everyone felt the same about their jobs.

He felt very conscious of an ever increasing sense of *déjà vu*. He had been here before: sometimes it seemed that he had been everywhere before, and many times. Like Roman gladiators who had to face new lions every day in the arena, his problems continually presented themselves in a new guise, but basically remained the same. Who was betraying or deceiving whom, or what country, and why? Once, the motives had been relatively easy to discover: sex, money, blackmail. Now they were more subtle, concealed beneath layers of idealism, sexism, and self-delusion – and therefore infinitely more difficult to detect and isolate.

His office Rover dropped him at the house in Museum Street, Bloomsbury, which for the past three months had been his office, and which would cease to be his office within as many weeks. While the headquarters of MI5 and MI6 by the very nature of their size remained static in office blocks, many of their more sensitive departments moved continually and erratically around London and the inner suburbs, to confuse, if only temporarily, pursuit from intelligence agencies of unfriendly nations. The polished brass plate on the front door of this elegant house, divided, like many in the area, into offices, declared that it was the Citrus Development Division of Beechwood Nominees Ltd. The word citrus had a certain acidic tang about it that amused MacGillivray; it sounded redolent of bitter lemon, wormwood, gall and the taste of death, all appropriate for his calling.

He climbed the stairs, glanced briefly upwards to give the hidden spy camera a chance of registering his arrival, then tapped out the code to open the electronic lock of his private office. This complex lock typified the increasing complication of life at every level now, and especially his own. Years ago, if he needed some information from, say, Cairo, he might approach a surgeon or a businessman attending a seminar in the Nile Hilton and ask whether they could, in the course of their ordinary duties (and naturally as cheaply as possible) find out whatever facts he needed. If they succeeded, and most did, they did not receive a fee for their trouble, and if they were arrested on a charge of espionage, then that was their affair, not MacGillivray's. Win or lose, they were on their own.

Nowadays, such simple and inexpensive arrangements were not so easy to organize. People were less willing to put their freedom or their lives at risk under what MacGillivray could only call 'the old pals act', without hope of reward, recompense – or rescue if things went wrong.

Also, this was the age of the specialist: the gentlemen had long since abdicated in favour of the players. What might, until quite recently, have taken months to discover, now could be found without even sending out an agent, professional or amateur. Radio transmissions were constantly broken into as easily as a safe without a lock. Satellites perpetually revolved around the earth like man-made suns, bristling with electronic eyes and ears. These were so powerful they could pick up the digits on a number plate of a car parked in Connaught Place, in Delhi, or overhear an

141

assignation being agreed between two lovers in Los Angeles who might be unwise enough to use a cordless telephone.

Indeed, they saw and overheard so much that it was virtually impossible to monitor more than a fraction of their gleanings. Ships carrying illegal arms to terrorist organizations in another country would be loaded at night, when there was less chance of being seen from outer space. Decoy ships might even be loaded at another dock in the early morning when the satellite could observe them more clearly, and so produce false information to waste the time and energies of experts in half a dozen countries. Machines were overtaking the brains of men who had made them; a computer could be ready with a dozen possible answers before the operator had finished phrasing the question.

Inside his office, MacGillivray left the outside world on the other side of his door. His was now a realm of dark corners where were hidden so many secrets, so many discreditable truths that sometimes he despaired of human nature. Had it always been so venal, so susceptible to bribery, corruption, treachery? And always, as he asked himself this question, he realized he already knew the answer.

His middle-aged secretary, Miss Jenkins, had already made the cup of strong black coffee with which he started every morning. It was waiting for him on his desk, next to the two telephones, one red, one green.

'Anything special?' he asked her, as he always did: it made a change from 'Good morning'.

'Sir Robert's been on the green telephone,' she replied. 'Twice.'

MacGillivray nodded. Sir Robert was head of the SIS. He liked being on the green telephone; he could pass the buck more quickly then. His career was like a long and successful session of political musical chairs; he always managed to be safely seated when the music stopped.

'Anything else?'

'That business in Damascus. Our man there is three hours behind with his routine transmission.'

'I see.'

This could mean trouble. The fellow was totally reliable. Was? MacGillivray found himself unconsciously using the past tense, as though he had already written him off.

'Any *good* news?'

'Not really. Some new satellite pictures from Afghanistan. More Russians are moving out. And Professor Harbottle wants to see you.'

'About them?'

'About some of them, yes.'

'Where is he?'

'In the waiting-room.'

'Well, don't let him wait. Send him in.'

'We were waiting until *you* arrived, Colonel,' replied Miss Jenkins tartly. She opened another door. Harbottle came into the room; a tall, thin, prematurely bald man. He walked with oddly uncoordinated movements, and wore a shabby suit and a cream nylon shirt. MacGillivray looked at him with disfavour. The professor's shoes were scuffed: he even had odd laces. Perhaps that was a mark of genius – the absent-minded professor? Or maybe his mind could not concern itself with such unimportant, everyday matters.

'Sorry to keep you,' MacGillivray said, not altogether truthfully. 'Coffee?'

'I don't drink the stuff. It's bad for you,' replied Harbottle sharply. He had a north country accent.

'Tea? Something stronger?'

'No, nothing, thank you. You haven't had a chance to examine these photos yet, have you, Colonel?'

MacGillivray shook his head. Harbottle picked up two large pieces of cardboard tied with pink tape which had been placed on end against a wall. He undid the tape, spread out a dozen blown up black-and-white photographs on the desk. MacGillivray looked at them without much enthusiasm. In his time, he had examined many aerial photographs and still

143

thought privately how much alike they all looked. At certain times of day, the Weald of Kent could appear not unlike some sections of the Sahara. He never understood how anyone could deduce what all the tiny dots and shadows really were. People? Animals? Vehicles? And did it matter? The photos showed where they had been hours or even days previously. Where they were now was what really mattered.

'This one,' said Harbottle. He slid one out from the bottom of the pile, handed MacGillivray a magnifying glass. The picture seemed cloudy; it showed an undulating surface covered by snow. One part was almost entirely obscured by white cloud.

'What is it, and where is it?' MacGillivray asked.

'Afghanistan. West of Kabul. Not too far from the Russian base at Razmak.'

'Yes,' said MacGillivray, as though he had really known this all along.

'They have been blowing up the hills.'

'The Russians, you mean?'

'Of course, who else?'

'Why? To block the roads as they leave?'

'No, they are still looking for minerals – as they have been for the past nine years. But now more desperately than ever as time is short. Afghanistan is pretty well virgin territory for such explorers. They have never exactly welcomed prospecting parties, you know.'

'We found that out long ago,' MacGillivray agreed, thinking of a British punitive force a hundred-and-fifty-odd years ago when 21,000 men and horse were despatched from India to subdue Kabul. They had succeeded, but then, as the weather grew colder, the Afghans laid siege to the city and the British garrison was forced to capitulate on the humiliating promise of a safe escort back to India. This promise was not kept. The Afghans massacred every man in that retreating column – except for one, a medical officer, Dr Brydon, who somehow survived to tell this story of ineptitude, treachery and revenge. As a boy, a print of Dr Brydon riding home, called 'The Remnants of an Army', had hung above MacGillivray's bed. He remembered it well, just as he recalled Napoleon's declaration that one spy was equal to twenty thousand men. On that basis, one agent could have saved the whole army – if he was listened to, which, of course, was always doubtful.

'These other photographs show what they found in one of these explosions,' Harbottle continued. 'A block of ice, apparently. With a man's body entombed inside. Here is a close-up.'

'A recent death? The body seems to be well preserved. Rather odd clothes, though, eh?'

'It is rather difficult to make out exactly, because the ice must be a couple of feet thick, and the camera's 20 miles up, but our feeling is that he was an explorer, perhaps several hundred years ago. About the time the East India Company was making its early profits, in the seventeenth century, various merchant adventurers tried to find a competing overland route to the East, as opposed to going by sea. They went through Afghanistan, for the Amir was relatively friendly.'

'Did they do any trade there?'

'Yes. Afghan silk, sheepskins, rubies, gold, iron and zinc, exchanged for our sugar, woollen goods, tea. Anyway, the Russians took this body to Razmak – the satellite photographed its passage in a truck – and put it in a building used as a mortuary. Then the Mujahideen blew up the building – and the body. A cargo plane was on the runway and they destroyed that, too.'

'Nothing else?' asked MacGillivray thoughtfully.

'Nothing. Except for several human casualties, of course. From these pictures, it looks as though someone had told them that the body wasn't simply an ordinary corpse, but had some special significance or importance. Maybe the Russians wanted to transport it somewhere in a hurry and the Mujahideen were determined to prevent them – while they had the chance. Once it was airborne, they could do

145

nothing about it. Have you heard anything from your sources, Colonel?'

'Not a dicky bird,' MacGillivray admitted. 'Perhaps there was something on the body? Some papers, samples of minerals?'

'That is my opinion. But what?'

'Impossible to say, of course. Do you scientific people know anything about the area around Razmak – say over a fifty-mile radius?'

'Not a lot. Refugees have brought out bits and pieces of rock, stone, fossilized shells and so on, and we always examine these samples as far as we can. There have been a few traces further east of a rare element, suddenly very much in demand. Rhodium.'

'What's that?'

'A chemical element, Rh, a member of the platinum group of metals. Atomic number is 45, atomic weight, 102.905. It is less ductile than platinum or palladium, but more ductile than any of the other platinum metals. It was discovered and named in Britain in 1803 by two scientists, Wollaston and Tennant, working in partnership. They isolated pure platinum and revealed four additional elements as constituents of a native platinum from Spanish America. They called this one rhodium, from the Greek, *rhodos*, meaning a rose, because of the red colour of the chloride solution in which they first isolated it.'

'I see,' said MacGillivray. It always surprised him how vocal even dull experts could become, when describing their own subject.

'Rhodium is very, very rare, and consequently extremely valuable. Of all the platinum deposits in Canada and Russia and South Africa, only four parts in every hundred are rhodium. And when you consider that one ounce of platinum fetches $500, you can see how valuable rhodium is.'

'What's it used for?'

'Up to now, largely to harden and strengthen platinum. It is a catalyst, used in the hydrogenation of benzene to cyclohexane and the oxidization of primary alcohols to aldehydes. With the increasing international campaign to go over to lead-free petrol for biological reasons, it has become possibly the most sought after metal in the world – and there's so little of it.

'South Africa has deposits, but the political problems there rather limit overseas sales. Canada has some – but they use all they produce. Russia also has deposits, but the rumour is that perhaps the largest undiscovered deposits anywhere are in Afghanistan.

'There have been legends and references to a rose-red river – rhodium is insoluble in water – and the Russians have obviously been very anxious to find this source. But it is difficult – almost impossible – in the terrible weather conditions out there and faced with relentless hostility from the locals. If they could locate deposits in any quantity, they would immediately solve all their foreign currency problems. That is how important it is to them – and to every other country, too.'

'And you think this body might have contained a clue as to its whereabouts?'

'It is just possible. But what, I have no idea. Remember, the Russians have only a limited time left to carry out their search because they are leaving. A description of a site, even a vague clue to its position, could help them enormously.'

'Would the locals have known about rhodium hundreds of years ago – when, presumably, this traveller was in Afghanistan?'

'Not as rhodium, obviously. But they might have used it for treating metals, perhaps. Sword blades, spears, that type of thing. I can't say. It is only a possibility.'

'Thank you, Professor. Anything else?'

'I think that's enough for one day, Colonel.'

'I agree. We'll act on this at once. Let me see any more pictures that come in.'

He showed the professor to the door, went back to his

desk, studied all the photographs and pressed the bell for Miss Jenkins.

'Is Parkington still in Peshawar?'

'Yes. That sonar business. He reported that the courier was killed in a motor accident on the way to his hotel from Islamabad airport.'

'Convenient for someone,' said MacGillivray. 'If not for Mr Glover.'

'Mr Parkington is also out there for the Midland Widows Insurance company. They have paid his fare, so it doesn't come out of our budget.'

'That's a help,' said MacGillivray approvingly. 'Can we reach him urgently – and securely?'

'Yes. Through the insurance people. We have agreed a code about annuities, premiums, bonuses, that sort of thing. For urgent signals only.'

'Then make an urgent signal to him.'

MacGillivray began to dictate as he sipped his coffee. It was already cold, but his interest now was warming. He had left his distaste for work on the other side of his front door.

Love faced the intruder in the Cord's garage.

'What the hell are you doing here?' he asked him, keeping the torch focused on the man's eyes.

'I was going to ask you that,' the man replied in a quiet, cultured voice. He might be Pakistani, but he spoke without any accent.

'This garage belongs to my family. We own it, and seeing the door was open just now, I came inside to admire the car more closely. A beautiful machine.'

'So why dismantle the rear light – if all you wanted was to look at the car?'

'Because I saw the lens was loose. I was trying to secure it. Unfortunately, your very bright torch dazzled me and I dropped the glass. I regret that it is broken beyond repair.'

His explanation sounded so reasonable, so plausible that it could almost be true – but what was truth? If Pilate had not known, how could Dr Love? He moved along the side of the car, paying out the thread of dental floss as he did so.

'This *is* rather ridiculous, holding my hands up in my own garage,' said the intruder gently. 'You must see that, Doctor.'

In the harsh glare of the torch, Love suddenly saw naked hate glitter in the man's eyes, red as the broken tail-light lens. And how did he know he was a doctor?

'Please, that light. It is hurting me.'

The man drew one hand across his face, shielding his eyes. For a second, surprised at the courteousness of the request, which was totally at odds with the sullen anger in his eyes, Love deflected the torch. In that brief fraction of a second, the man's other hand dropped. When Love swung back the torch on to the man's face, it also shone on the blued barrel of a snub-nosed Smith and Wesson .38.

'Hands up, Dr Love!' the man ordered roughly. 'Now!'

Love slowly raised his hands, wondering how this stranger not only knew his profession, but his name.

'And since you won't take that torch out of my eyes, I'll do it for you.'

His gun moved. The whip crack of a shot echoed and re-echoed from the whitewashed concrete walls. The torch shattered. Love let the twisted metal drop to the floor.

'Next time,' the man warned him in the darkness, 'that will be your hand, or your head. Now, what the hell are *you* doing here?'

'Examining a car on behalf of an insurance company.'

'I heard about that.'

His hand scratched the inside of the wall until it reached the light switch. A fluorescent tube throbbed into reluctant life in the ceiling. Love came round the side of the car; he needed to be nearer his adversary.

'Don't try anything,' said the man warningly.

'I don't *try* things,' replied Love quietly. 'I do things. And sometimes people.'

He was closer to the man now.

'I haven't all night to hang around. Just what are you looking for here, Doctor?'

'Like all of us, the secret of eternal life,' said Love. He took another half step forward, lowering his arms slightly. Then he tugged on the thread. From the far end of the garage, the oil tin fell noisily, striking the car's bonnet like a huge gong. The man's aim wavered as he glanced involuntarily towards the sound.

In that split second, Love brought up his right knee into the man's groin. As his head came forward with a gasp of unexpected agony, still choking for breath, Love brought down both his hands locked together on the back of his head. Under the terrible blow, the man collapsed on the floor. Love turned him over with his foot, took the revolver out of his hand, broke it, slipped the cartridges into his pocket. Then he leaned against the wall, spinning the empty gun on its trigger guard, while the intruder struggled to stand up. Love let him stand, then frisked him in case he had another gun. He seemed clean.

'Now,' he said, 'give me the truth, what are *you* looking for in this car? And why is it said to be worth so much money?'

The man moved his head weakly to shake the pain away.

'A cigarette, Doctor?' he asked hoarsely.

'I don't smoke,' said Love. 'It is damn bad for you. It can be fatal.'

'Yes.'

The man felt in his pocket for a packet of cigarettes, extracted one, put it in his mouth. Suddenly, he bit hard on the cork tip and chewed, forcing himself to swallow. His eyes bulged suddenly, unnaturally, like onions, in his head. Veins stood out on his forehead and his neck like blue serpents writhing beneath the skin. He began to choke, to retch, and clapped one hand in front of his mouth to stop himself being sick. A little yellow vomit seeped out between his fingers and down his shirt front. The garage was filled with the sweet smell of over-ripe apricots. Cyanide. He was killing himself. Love wrenched the cigarette from the man's mouth, but it was too late.

The man crumpled up slowly, sagging like a sawdust doll. As he fell, his head struck a rear wing of the Cord. The metal boomed like a bell. Then he fell on the stained concrete, arms and legs outstretched at preposterously unnatural angles. Love knelt by him, loosened his collar, felt for his pulse. There was no beat to feel; his heart was still. Love rolled up one of the man's eyelids. The eye stared out unfocused and sightlessly, as though fixed on the swirling mists of eternity. Love remembered the ironic words of Sir Thomas Browne: 'We all labour against our own cure, for death is the cure for all diseases.'

This unknown intruder had certainly cured himself, but in doing so had left behind him more questions which Love could not answer. Who the devil was he? What was he doing here – and what was Love going to do now?

There was only one thing he *should* do, of course; tell the police, explain that the stranger had drawn a gun on him. But what police force in the world would accept such an explanation without asking *why* he had drawn a gun?

The death of a stranger was only part of a larger, unsolved equation. A more important part was that he had killed himself rather than risk having the real reason he was there forced out of him. Death had seemed an easier option than to admit failure – but to whom, and what sort of failure?

Love glanced towards the half-open door. A face appeared briefly on the other side, peering in from the darkness. Love pulled the door fully open. Stevie stepped inside.

'Why are *you* here?' he asked her.

'I come here every night to check that the garage is locked up.'

Then she saw the man on the ground, and sniffed.

'Apricots,' she said in surprise.

'Cyanide,' Love explained. 'He pulled a gun on me and I hit him. Then he said he wanted a cigarette, and must have

151

had a death pill concealed in the cork tip. Did you know him?'

Stevie shook her head.

'No. Never seen him before.'

Love told her how the man had claimed his family owned the garage.

'Garbage!' she said at once. 'An old widow owns it. Her husband left her three in his will. They are her only source of livelihood.'

'It isn't going to increase the value of her investment having a body found here,' said Love.

'That depends how it's found. And by whom.'

'What do you mean? We're both doctors. We have to report this to the police. Don't we?'

'Sure we do,' she said. 'But I'll leave it to you to decide how much – or how little – we tell them.'

'In that case,' said Love, 'close the door.'

He untied the end of the dental floss from the tin of oil, put the cotton thread in his pocket, then hunted around the garage, found a pile of cleaning rags and a bucket, filled this from a tap used when hosing down cars. With a damp rag, he carefully wiped all traces of cyanide from the dead man's mouth, sprinkled a little water over his face.

'So we can say we tried to revive him.'

'You've done this before?' Stevie said, looking at Love quizzically. 'This can't be usual among country doctors in England, surely?'

'Not usual. Shall we say, occasional? I have been involved in odd situations before, yes.'

'With Parkington?' she asked.

He nodded.

'I guessed as much.'

'Why?'

'I don't know. You didn't appear to be particularly fazed by having someone aiming a gun at you. Not usual, again, I imagine, in a country practice.'

'Your imagination does you credit,' Love replied. 'But I

was brought up in a hard school. You must be able to defend yourself, for no one else will. If you want a helping hand, there's one at the end of your own right arm.'

'Spare me the philosophy,' she said, and smiled. 'Now, if you've finished smartening up this character, I'll ring the police from the hotel. I have got better contacts here than you. You wait here for them. And forget I ever called in.'

The police arrived in a dark blue van without any side windows. A radio aerial quivered like a long fishing rod on its roof. Two men in uniform and one wearing a check shirt and grey worsted trousers, picking his teeth with the sharpened end of a match, came into the garage.

'Dr Love?' he asked. 'Tourist?'

'Yes.'

'Your passport, please.'

The man looked at it, spoke into a pocket tape recorder, giving its number, where it was issued, Love's description, and a brief description of the garage and the corpse.

'Just checking,' he said.

'Of course.'

'What happened, Doctor? In your own words.'

'I can't use anyone else's. I was in the garage and this man came in. He'd seen the light shine on the back of this car, and wanted to have a closer look. It's quite an unusual vehicle.'

'So I can see. And then?'

'Then we had a little chat, and suddenly he collapsed.'

'You had an argument?'

'No. A discussion.'

'Well, I am sorry this should happen to you on a visit to our country. Tourism is very important. The more we see how others live, the better. I was in your country last year. Where do you come from in England?'

'Near Salisbury,' said Love.

'Ah, I was staying with my brother in Kingsbury, in London. Not far away, eh?'

'Not really. England is a small country.'

'So it is. We had a very good time there. Very pleasant. I hope you have the same here.'

The two uniformed policemen brought a stretcher from the van. They put the body on the stretcher, slid it into the back of the van and locked the doors.

'I'm at Pink's, if you want me,' said Love. 'Room 51.'

'It may not be necessary to ask any more questions. I am not a medical man, but I have seen men die of heart attacks before. I assume that is what he had?'

'Certainly, his heart stopped beating very soon after he fell down. I could not feel any pulse.'

'So. Dr Khan has given us great help in many ways. This is a wild country, Doctor, not a small one, as you say, like England. Many people die here every day. There is violence. Accidents. Disasters on a big scale. We have a flood, and thousands die. Nobody seems to bother much. It is very sad. What is one more among so many?'

'A good philosophical point,' agreed Love, 'so long as you are not the one.'

'Ah,' the plain-clothes man smiled, shook hands. 'I see you have humour.'

'Thank you.'

'Goodbye, Doctor. I cannot say, as in America, have a nice day, for the day is long past. But have a nice night, eh?'

He grinned and winked.

Love watched the van drive away, locked up the garage, walked back to Pink's Hotel. The stars seemed very bright, like a myriad unwinking eyes staring down at him. He wondered uneasily what other eyes were watching him closer at hand. And whether – or when – and how – they would react to whatever they saw.

Stevie let herself into the front door of her rented house, locked and bolted it behind her, and then stood with her back against the still-warm wood. She could think more clearly in the dark, away from the distractions of radio, TV, and where there was a telephone, the endless arrogant summons of the bell.

She passed one hand in front of her eyes as though to wipe away the memory of the suicide on the garage floor and then stood, listening to the old house breathing. The hall smelled of furniture polish, with a faint and not unpleasant scent of curry from the kitchen.

Through the uncurtained window a street light lit the brass face of a Japanese carving, leaving its eyes in shadow. She sometimes had the feeling that they were watching her, following her movements about the room; but not tonight. Tonight, she was watching them. She had just connived with another doctor to conceal what elsewhere would be considered vital evidence, but here, in a world of crime, murder, cruelty, it seemed of relatively little account, except to the man who had taken his own life rather than admit – what? Discovery? Failure to shoot an expert engaged to value the car? Or was there some other reason altogether, born of fear and despair? Stevie went upstairs, drew the curtains in her bedroom and sat down thankfully on an easy chair.

That morning she had received a letter from her widowed mother. She switched on a reading light, looked at the postmark, Waldport, Oregon, opened the letter. Her mother was not a great correspondent: just two pages filled with her large round handwriting, describing in the briefest detail a lonely life of small nothings. Her Siamese cat Anna had died. The veterinarian had been unable to save her, and thought she must have been poisoned He had wanted to do a post-mortem but she had refused. Nothing could bring back Anna now. The weather was good, and the roads were much more crowded because the tourist season was starting. What a lot of strangers were in town. And when was she going to see Stevie again?

There was no mention of Stevie's husband, but then there never was. She could not understand how her daughter could have had an affair with a Pakistani doctor doing postgraduate work in Portland, and then, amazingly, marry him. It was not a question that he was Pakistani; just that her mother could not understand *any* American girl, least of all her only daughter, marrying a foreigner, whoever he was.

Weren't there plenty of nice American boys around? There were, of course, Stevie agreed. Plenty. But she had not met one who had attracted her like her husband. But her mother had not been entirely wrong. This attraction waned. Their backgrounds were as different as their outlooks. In bed, they might become one person, but out of bed, it often seemed that their differences were irreconcilable. They had so many petty disagreements about trivial things, unimportant to her, of the utmost importance to him. He was a Muslim and would not drink alcohol. She said that if whatever gods there were had intended people not to drink alcohol, they would not have put grapes into the world. He could not accept that. Similarly, for religious reasons, he would not eat pork. Stevie had frequently tried to explain that surely this ruling stemmed from the time when it had been unwise – indeed, sometimes fatal – to eat pork or shellfish in hot climates, long before refrigeration had been invented. The most efficient way then to stop people in a hot country being poisoned by bad food was to make it a sin to eat items most likely to go bad – or as they would say now, with a short shelf life.

Her husband could accept the logic of this, but that was all; he still believed what he had been brought up to believe. And then he had volunteered for what she privately thought was a quixotic mission in Afghanistan. Surely he could have done far more good for his cause with his medical and surgical training, treating wounded fighters?

She looked again at the stamp on the letter, thought of the little town with its strange moonscape beaches off Highway 101, where she had been brought up. The river was usually muddy, its banks littered with redwood logs, bleached grey by wind and weather. She recalled the sign many visitors remarked on outside the town, 'Waldport, Population 999, Drive Carefully'.

The last figure was on a small plate that could be removed when a new member of the population arrived or another citizen died. It was not always kept strictly up to date; a birth could so easily cancel a death, and why add a number if it was to be subtracted, perhaps within hours? She remembered the yellow revolving ball advertising Ball Realty, the red, white and blue Chevron of the local gas station: Big Wheel Drive-in, Burgers to Go, signs for charbroiled burgers, Homes in a Tree, Drive a Train through a Tree. At evening, all these bright neon signs grew misty with the haze from the ocean that rolled and thundered only yards away. That was more than a part of a new world; it was a different world altogether. How could she explain to anyone there, any Rotarian, any Veteran of Foreign Wars, as they held their meetings with flags and regalia, what it was like to be out here in *this* foreign war?

People everywhere were gullible. Most believed what they wanted to believe, what was easiest to accept, the account of events that made fewest demands on their minds and consciences. And now she wanted to believe she could sell this Cord, which seemed to mean so much to so many people, for a huge sum.

The front doorbell rang, cutting into her thoughts with the harsh urgency of a fire alarm. Stevie jumped out of the chair, heart racing, and glanced instinctively at her watch. Half past midnight.

Who could be calling at this hour? The bell clanged again. She went out to the landing, down the stairs, turning on lights as she went. She did not like the dark; she had seen one dead man in darkness that night, and although she was accustomed to death in many forms, the sight had disturbed her more than she cared to admit: not so much because he was dead, but for the unknown reason for his suicide.

The hall, usually friendly, now seemed hostile. The eyes of the Japanese idol gleamed balefully under the bright

157

shadeless bulb in the ceiling. She shot the bolts of the door, opened it. A uniformed policeman and a colleague in shirt and grey worsted trousers were standing on the step. The plain-clothes man showed her a pass in a cellophane cover. She opened the door to let them into the hall.

'I was going to visit you tomorrow,' he explained, 'to tell you that after your call to the West cantonment police station, we went to the garage and found the body of the man on the floor. We have removed the body.'

'Who was he?'

'A man with a long record of violence. Extortion. Beating up people who wouldn't – or couldn't – pay protection money. Not on his own account, though. He always worked for someone else.'

'Who?'

'A man we have been after for some time, but without any success. He is too rich, too cunning, has too many powerful friends. He lives near Darra and keeps a stranglehold on lots of things – and people. Name of Sharif.'

'But why come here at this hour? Why not wait until tomorrow, as you said?'

'Because we have just had a report that someone has been trying to break into this house.'

'A report from whom?'

'A passer-by. He said he saw a man trying the front door here, and then going round the windows. You've found nothing missing?'

'I haven't been through the place,' Stevie admitted. 'I only rent it. It is not my furniture. If I do find anything has gone, I will report it tomorrow.'

'Would you like us to check through the house for you, now?'

'No,' Stevie replied. 'It is not necessary. But thank you.'

She watched them walk down the road, in step, not looking back. Then she closed the door. Who could be trying to get into her house? Could it be Love or Parkington? Surely not. She stood, turning the problem over in her mind, uneasy and fearful, very conscious of the fact she was on her own and vulnerable in a strange country, an alien land seething with ancient hatreds.

She heard a faint tapping from a window on the other side of the room, and her heart contracted at the sound. Why had she not allowed the policemen to look round the house? At least she would not be on her own. She waited for a moment to compose herself, then crossed the room, pulled the curtain. A dark face was pressed against the glass, a hand gesticulated towards a side door. She opened the door. Ahmed came into the house.

'I saw you in the camp,' he said.

'I know. I was going there again tomorrow to see you.'

'I couldn't wait that long,' said Ahmed. 'I am not well and I was followed over the border. I shook off two men, but I know there is another in the camp, a young man. And probably others as well.'

'Will they harm you?'

'If they get the chance, yes. Fatally. That is why I had to see you – now. I have something I want to give you. Something of value. I've wrapped it up.'

He passed over a folded handkerchief, knotted at the corners. She felt a thin strip of metal inside it.

'What is it?' she asked.

'A coded message. I have had it stamped on metal so that it cannot be rubbed out. I walked over the mountains to deliver it.'

'To whom?'

'I did not know, but I had faith, and Allah, the all-wise, blessed be his name always, has come to my aid.'

'How?'

'By showing me a man who can help me.'

'Who is he?'

'One of the two with you in the camp. We recognized each other at once, although we have not met for years. Richard Mass Parkington.'

'He works for an insurance company.'

'Does he? When I last saw him he worked for the British government. An agent.'

'Insurance?'

'No. Intelligence.'

'You are sure of this?'

'Certain.'

'A man killed himself today. In the garage I rent for the Cord.'

'So that car is here?'

'Yes. This man was looking at it and Dr Love – the other person who came to the camp today – disturbed him.'

'Do you know who he was?'

'The police say he is a bad man, a *budmarsh*, working for Sharif.'

Ahmed's face clouded.

'Sharif is the worst of all. He would sell his own mother for an anna profit. He is a man without the faith, without honour.'

'I know. Anyhow, the police have just left. They said someone had reported a man trying my front door and examining the windows. Was that you?'

'No. I have just arrived.'

'We can't talk here, anyhow. Someone may have seen you come in.'

She picked up a key.

'Down the road, on the left, first right, left again,' she told him. 'A lock-up garage. This is the key. Go in, shut the door, and don't turn on the light. I'll join you in five minutes. Before I come in, I'll tap on the door, the only Morse I know. V for victory, three dots and a dash.'

Ahmed's hand closed over the key. She could feel his flesh hot and dry; he was running a high fever. Stevie went to the side door, opened it, looked out cautiously; the street appeared deserted. She let Ahmed out, locked the door behind him. Then she went upstairs, changed into jeans and a sweater, for the night was cold. She left the bedroom light

160

on, and another in the hall. She did not wish to advertise her departure.

She hurried along the road, carefully stepping over the sunken manhole covers in the uneven pavement. The smell of rotting vegetation and sewage from the open drains seemed sharper after the rain. Hungry dogs prowled around piles of mangoes on street corners.

Stevie reached the garage, saw the padlock hanging loose, went inside, and closed the door carefully behind her. Ahmed was waiting near the front of the car. He came towards her.

'That message,' she said. 'Can you tell me about it as well as giving me the metal tag it's written on?'

'No,' he replied. 'I have changed my mind. It is not right to involve you in all this. You are not really one of us.'

'I married your son.'

'May he walk tonight in Paradise, brave believer.'

'Marrying him makes me of your family, surely?'

'It does, but not of our faith. Our battles are not yours. It is not fair to involve you like this, to inflict risks on you, about which you can know nothing – and do nothing to avoid. This is not women's work.'

'That is the Pathan speaking,' Stevie retorted angrily. 'In my country, men and women are equal.'

'But this is not your country. Here, we take a different view. But I did not cross the mountains, always at most only a few miles ahead of my pursuers, to argue with you '

'You are not well,' Stevie said, instantly sympathetic. In the gloom and dimness of the garage, lit only by her pencil torch, she could see Ahmed's eyes glitter with fever. His flesh was drawn as tightly over his cheekbones as the skin on a drum.

'I have some illness,' he admitted. 'Yes. These past few years have not been easy. And it is difficult for an old man to cope with the high altitude and the cold.'

'You were relatively safe in Ramzak,' she said. 'Why did

161

you risk your life by coming over the mountains? And now the Russians are leaving in any case.'

'Some are. Some will remain. I discovered something. That is why I had to leave – with my message. The Russians were dynamiting part of a hillside, and a body was blown out of a crevasse. It was of a European, apparently one of a group of travellers hundreds of years ago. There was some writing on a piece of parchment in his pouch. These scientists asked me to translate.'

'And did you?'

'Not to them. That is what I brought here. But it may not be safe for you to see Mr Parkington with it. I may have been followed here, right to this place. It would be folly to allow you to be the bearer of this message. And more than folly, death – for you. So I have made other arrangements. I – .'

'Quiet!' Stevie whispered, interrupting him sharply. She had heard faint footsteps outside. Could these be the police returning?

'There is a back way out of this garage, under the bench,' she said urgently. 'A small door. The owner usually puts rubbish through it, but it is just big enough for a man to crawl through.'

'Now?'

'No. Get into the back of the car, in the boot.'

She opened the lid. Ahmed climbed inside. He seemed very small in its cavernous space.

'I will try and keep them out of the garage, whoever they are. But as soon as they've gone, you go. I will see you at the camp tomorrow.'

'What if they open the boot? They will see me.'

'Not necessarily. A vertical leather sheet divides the boot from the front compartment, just behind the seats. If you hear them begin to open the boot, move the sheet and go through to the front. The sheet is stiff and will conceal you. But if you hear they are going to look in front of it, stay in the back. They cannot look into both hiding places at once.'

162

'May Allah keep you in his care,' said Ahmed. 'And me.'

Stevie lowered the lid silently, went out of the garage, locked the padlock. The policemen were standing on the other side of the road.

'Hello!' said the plain-clothes man easily. 'What brings you out so late, Doctor?'

'Your visit to me,' she said. 'I thought I would check that my car is okay.'

'And is it?'

'Yes.'

'Mind if we have a look round it?'

'Feel free.' Stevie fiddled with the padlock, putting in the key upside down, turning it the wrong way to give Ahmed time to make his decisions. Then she switched on the garage light and waited, heart thumping, by the door as they walked round the Cord, tapping the heavy tear shaped front wings.

'What's in the boot?'

'A small box of tools, that's all.'

'Can we have a look? Just a check?'

'Of course. But the locks are old and a bit tricky. Let me open it for you.'

She lifted the two handles. The lid swung up.

'As you say,' said the plain-clothes man, shining a torch inside. 'Quite empty. Now we'll escort you home, Doctor. It is not good for a woman to be out late at night on her own, even for a Western woman – and a doctor.'

'This is a man's country,' agreed Stevie, turning off the garage light. She followed them out into the street.

'It is a man's *world*,' the plain-clothes man corrected her gently.

The go-between was a round, small man with a cheerful appearance. In his wrinkled linen suit, he looked rather like the Michelin man in the tyre advertisements, or a latter-day Mr Pickwick, all creases and smiles and folds and bulges. Only his eyes, hard as olive stones, hinted at another side to

163

his character. He sat now opposite Sharif, crossing and uncrossing his short legs, folding his fingers together, cracking the joints, running one hand through his thick, dark, oily hair.

He appeared supremely ill-at-ease, unsure of himself, like an applicant desperate for a job he felt he could not possibly be given. This was a ploy that had helped to make him successful as an intermediary between groups of people who might not wish or could not risk to be seen together, or, through political disagreements or man-made frontiers, could never be seen together. The go-between's anxiety to please all parties, all the time, put them at their ease – and himself at perpetual profit.

'I wasn't expecting you,' Sharif told him shortly.

'I know,' the go-between explained contritely. 'It is most unfortunate, I was not intending to come here either. I had meant to be elsewhere. I have an appointment in Damascus next week. And then on to London.'

'Your daughter is in hospital there, I hear?'

'Yes. She is by no means well. But I live in hope she will make a complete recovery. Eventually.'

'But unfortunately time is not always on our side?'

'Exactly,' the go-between agreed. 'Which is why I am here. My people are concerned that they have not yet received what was promised. Time is not on their side, either. They are leaving Afghanistan. It is important that this item is delivered promptly.'

'I know,' Sharif replied, frowning. 'I am concerned, too. There have been difficulties. I felt it wise for the car to be insured.'

'For a very large sum, I am told,' said the go-between innocently, glancing at his short, bitten fingernails. There was still a bit left to nibble off the left index finger. 'Why did you set the value so high?'

'It is a rare car, and should it meet with an accident, I would not wish to be out of pocket. I approached the company through which I have insured so many things, and

164

to my surprise they said an expert had to come out from England to value it. This turned out to be a doctor, one Jason Love.'

'And what did he say?'

'He did not think it could be worth ten million pounds.'

'So you have persuaded him to change his mind?'

'That is easier to say than to do.'

'Not for you, Mr Sharif. Look what you have done already.'

'You are very kind,' said Sharif, warming to the praise. He knew the go-between by reputation, but he had no idea of his real identity, or where he had been born. Perhaps, as in his own case, the go-between's climb upwards had been dictated by a humble, even a cruel start? Some said he was Estonian; others, Armenian. But what did nationality of such a country mean? They had lost their names, their independence, long ago: they were only small footnotes in forgotten history books.

'I don't give a damn about the doctor or the insurance,' the go-between said, his voice now hard and sharp, like the edge of a sword. 'We just want your side of the deal to be kept. Otherwise . . .'

He paused, licked the index finger. There was still a millimetre of nail to chew. This was like money in the bank. Something he could come back to, something to be savoured for another time.

'Otherwise what?' asked Sharif.

'There will be difficulties, I fear, about the heroin. You know that Colonel Vorbachov was killed. A mortar shell. There will be changes, and change, in my experience, usually means delay. Of course, nothing really satisfies these people. Nothing.'

'The Afghans are a very warlike race,' Sharif agreed, stating a fact, not giving an excuse. He wished he belonged to that race; life could have been simpler lived on parallel lines, by simple rules, reward or revenge, not in the convolutions of money-making, always in illegal, convoluted, desperate deals.

'How long have we got?'

'Days,' said the go-between. 'This has been going on for quite a time already, you know.'

'We had to arrange with some Western person who could negotiate the sale of the car. That took weeks. Then we came to an arrangement with a Dr Khan, an American, who would do this. Now we run into these totally unexpected troubles.'

'Troubles should be foreseen,' said the go-between sternly. 'They should never be unexpected. Like a storm, you see a small cloud first. Then you take appropriate action.'

Sharif shrugged. He did not wish to argue the point. This man was too powerful; he held the key to too much money, he knew too many people of importance.

'I give you my word,' he said earnestly. 'Your people will have what is theirs by the end of this week.'

'It is now Tuesday. That means Saturday?'

'Or Sunday. The Holy Day here is Friday.'

'I will tell my principals that. They may not be pleased, but I can probably persuade them to wait that long. But not for an hour longer.'

The go-between's cold eyes did not reveal any inkling of his thoughts; no one ever really knew his private opinions. He was assessing Mr Sharif's situation, and how he could best benefit from it. Sharif was without a Russian protector now Colonel Vorbachov was dead. He would not have time to build any real relationship with his successor, so he was probably planning on one big coup before the Russians left Afghanistan entirely; that could account for his valuation of this old car. Ten million pounds sterling was not a killing, but it could be part of one.

The Russians would not all leave, of course. Key people would remain as advisers, diplomats, engineers, whatever their real purpose might be, and then Sharif would be vulnerable. He could possibly be building bridges elsewhere against this contingency. And in pondering this, the go-between thought of the only person in the world for whom he reserved any real feeling, his daughter, now lying in London's most expensive private clinic, a heroin addict. It was ironic – more, almost unbearable – to think that this man Sharif had possibly – no, probably – taken his percentage as the drug travelled south from Afghanistan in one of his trucks or petrol tankers. The thought was not new, but each time the go-between considered it, the more his anger against Sharif and his kind increased. He swallowed lest his voice should betray his emotion.

'I will bid you good-day,' he said softly.

They did not shake hands. Sharif could smell a strong scent of lavender from the go-between's hair oil. He disliked the man, but more than that, he feared him. He would have felt even more uneasy if he had known that the go-between had already decided on a course of action.

Once, as a child, the go-between had stood on a beach and watched an attendant hoist a red flag for danger. The sea was calm, the sun was shining, but the man knew, without benefit of barometers, meteorological balloons, radar checks, that a storm was due. The bathers must be warned: they had no idea of the approaching danger.

'How do *you* know?' the go-between had asked the beach guard curiously. Even as a boy he was inquisitive; early on, he had realized that knowledge was power.

The old man smiled.

'I can tell it in my bones, boy. They start to ache. I have lived all my life by the sea. I can read its moods. The clouds and the way the wind blows. They all have messages for me.'

'How is it that others cannot do that?'

'They haven't the gift, boy. They haven't the gift.'

The go-between possessed this gift in another dimension. He had not survived so many political and military coups, revolutions, assassinations, uprisings, and profited by them all, without some inner sense, some antenna of the mind that could warn him in advance of approaching danger. He knew by instinct who he should back, and who he should abandon.

Sitting opposite Sharif, he had sensed that the man's power was waning. Sand was running out through the glass; the storm flag was up. It was time for him to change sides to protect his own interests, and in a cruelly oblique way, to strike at the man who had made a fortune from a traffic that had all but killed his only daughter.

PART SEVEN

Parkington sat in the cramped and scented darkness of the little motor rickshaw. Its single front wheel bumped up and down on the rough surface of the Khyber Road going west out of Peshawar. A strong smell of jasmine lotion from the driver's thick black hair, and petrol from a bad connection on the carburettor, pervaded the tiny vehicle.

Parkington braced his feet against the corners of the compartment; the ride was unexceptional, but a rickshaw was less likely to be remembered than a taxi. They all puttered about like identical blue beetles, hung with strips of polished metal, doors lined in bright red plastic, curtains on either side decorated with animals, birds, strange fish. The driver spoke a little English, which was useful as Parkington spoke no Urdu.

'Where to now, sir?' the driver asked.

'Straight ahead,' Parkington told him. 'I'll tell you when to stop, and then I want you to wait off the road till I come back.'

'You pay me first, sir?'

'Of course, and double pay if you wait for me, so you don't lose, either way. A double-headed penny.'

'Double-headed anna, sir,' the man replied cheerfully, and laughed at his own wit.

They began to come into the area of the refugee camp. Against scudding clouds and a pale moon, Parkington could see a row of spindly trees like telegraph poles with ragmop dusters of leaves forty feet up, then the featureless mud walls of the camp. A fire was burning by the roadside; three men cooked a meal on a wide, flat plate, near a pile of logs shaped with sharpened ends, waiting to be collected in the morning. There were no shops, no cafés, nothing here but a windowless city of the dark at the edge of the road.

'Pull in now,' Parkington said. The driver switched off his feeble headlight, swung the handlebars over to the left, stopped the engine.

'How much?'

'Agreed price, ten rupees.'

'Here's fifteen,' said Parkington. 'Now wait for me.' He patted the midget mobile telephone he carried in his right pocket and the Browning High Power pistol in its holster under his left armpit to reassure himself both were in place. Then he walked back along the road, scarf around his neck and face.

Buses and trucks roared past him, their headlamps carving tunnels of light through the dust and darkness. He was not sure exactly how he would find Ahmed, but he had stopped as near as he could to the opening he and Jason Love had walked through with Stevie earlier in the day. Looking for a man he had known years ago, name of Ahmed, must be like looking for a Mr Smith in the back streets of Birmingham or Brixton. However, if he was there he would find him.

He left the road, walked down the narrow alley. The puddles of water had shrunk, and the mud walls gave off an unpleasant smell as they cooled. He walked past openings on either side, caught brief glimpses of families around a guttering fire. Some were reading, others sewing, others just sitting. They paid no attention to him.

He could not ask anyone where Ahmed was. There could be a hundred Ahmeds, and only a few of the people he asked would speak English. But he believed that somewhere in this labyrinth of hutments, he could find a vital part of the

170

mosaic that so far had eluded him. If he could only locate Ahmed, he might begin to see a picture of the whole.

He walked down one alley, up another, into a third. Then he saw the headlights of cars and trucks; he had come full circle, and was back on the Khyber Road about a hundred yards farther south. He had found nothing, and he was no nearer the solution than when he had started. And then, in a doorway, he saw two men sitting in front of a charcoal fire. One had the face of a wolf – or a rat: the man he had seen behind Ahmed at the surgery door.

Parkington walked on, turned into the first alley, and waited. After about a quarter of an hour, this man came out of the door, walked past him towards the road. Then he stopped in the shadow of a hut; he was clearly expecting someone. Parkington decided he might as well see who this might be.

Two hundred yards down the road to Peshawar, caught briefly in the lights of an oncoming truck, he saw Ahmed, walking slowly. He looked very old and weary, as though it was all he could do to keep on walking. The man with the wolf's features also saw him, and stepped back more deeply into the shadows. Parkington took a pace nearer the main alleyway. He could not risk a shot here – if any shooting was needed. He would be overcome, disarmed and probably lynched in seconds. The crack of a revolver would instantly bring out every able-bodied man: to them the sound of a shot meant death.

Ahmed coughed wearily, turned into the alleyway. The man waited until he had passed him and then jumped on the old man's back, twisted his arms behind him, brought him down. Ahmed shouted in pain and surprise, but no one paid any attention. Perhaps, in their huts, they did not hear him. Anyhow, if they had heard his cries, what business was it of anyone if there was a fight by the roadside? Fights took place almost every night; they were a means of relieving tension.

Parkington jumped out, put his right wrist under the

man's neck, brought it back with all his strength. Bones snapped like dry twigs. He had used too much force; he had killed the man, who rolled like a heavy sack to the ground. Parkington knelt by his side, went through his pockets. He found a small .25 pistol, a clip of rounds, but nothing else: no papers, not even a comb. He put the pistol and rounds in his own pocket, crossed to Ahmed. The old man was unconscious and breathing heavily. It was impossible to examine him where he lay and possibly wrong to move him in case he had broken any bones – yet move him he must. Parkington went to the doorway of the nearest hut. Two men and an old woman looked out at him enquiringly.

'Can you help me?' he asked. 'Someone has been hurt.'

They nodded; so they understood English, he thought with relief. They came out of the hut, and the three of them carried Ahmed inside. Then Parkington took out his mobile phone, punched out the number of Pink's Hotel and waited impatiently until the receptionist answered.

The beating on Love's door, frantic as a madman on a drum, was splintered by the shrill ringing of the telephone in his ear.

Love swung himself out of bed, switched on the light, picked up the receiver. From long habit as a doctor, a telephone call always seemed to be more imperative than a visitor. He could reach whoever was outside the door in a matter of seconds, but whoever was telephoning must be some distance away. Parkington spoke urgently in his ear.

'I'm out at the camp,' he said brusquely. 'In a hut near the entrance we stopped at. That old man, Ahmed – he's in a bad way. There's another complication. Someone tried to hurt him, and has left us – permanently. Get out here as soon as you can. And bring your medical kit. And *hurry!*'

The line went dead.

The beating on the door continued. Love crossed the room, opened the door. Stevie was standing in the porch.

'You must come,' she said. 'At once.'

172

'Where to?'

'The camp. There's been trouble.'

'I know,' said Love. 'Parkington's just told me.'

'What's he doing out there?' she asked in surprise.

'He's with Ahmed. Have you a car?'

'Yes, outside.'

'Good.'

Love picked up a few basic instruments, with antibiotic tablets, bandages, pushed them all into his airline bag. He had no idea what he might want, and in any case he had brought very little out from England with him. But, in an emergency, any medical kit would be better than none. Within minutes, they were on their way. Even at this hour, the road seemed unexpectedly crowded, mostly with cyclists, riding without lights and heavily wrapped up against the chill night air. Stevie threaded her way expertly between them all.

'Who told you about this?' Love asked her.

'A helper in the camp.'

'But how did they reach you so quickly? Parkington was phoning as you arrived – and you haven't a telephone in your house.'

'I have a mobile phone. Many of us do. For emergencies.'

'Like this?'

'Yes. And other things.'

'Did your helper say what had happened?'

'Not exactly. Just that Ahmed was injured.'

They passed the camp entrance they had used that morning. Stevie stopped the car a hundred yards further on, led Love into the camp through a different way. Chickens roosting on boxes clucked disapprovingly as they stepped over puddles. They reached an open doorway leading into a room without windows. A hurricane lamp burned smokily on a chair. On a truckle bed Ahmed lay in his underpants and a vest, stained with blood. His face was drawn and shrunken. Parkington sat on a box by the bed, watching him. The room contained no other furniture.

'What happened?' Love asked him.

Parkington explained.

'What about the other man?'

'I have no idea. I took his gun in case, like Lazarus, he came back from the dead. Here, you had better have it. Take mine, too. If I'm to be questioned, I'd rather be clean.'

He handed the two pistols to Love and then nodded towards Ahmed.

'How is he?'

'Bad. Does he speak English?'

'Yes.'

Love knelt down by the bed, felt the old man's pulse. Ahmed opened his eyes. At first he looked at Love vacantly, unable to comprehend who he was, why they were all crammed into the tiny, dim-lit room. Then he recognized Stevie, and smiled thankfully. One hand moved out towards her. She took his cold, wasted fingers in her own.

'What happened?' Love asked him gently.

The old man's lips moved. He swallowed, groping for words, but the effort was too much; he could not find them. He shook his head slightly. The fingers of his other hand clenched and unclenched.

'He wants something to write with,' said Stevie.

Love took a ballpoint pen from his pocket. Stevie handed a piece of paper to Ahmed. The old man could not move his body, only his wrist. He began to scrawl indecipherably on the paper, then lay back, exhausted by the attempt. Love held the paper up for him to see. Ahmed shook his head, irritation at his own feebleness in his eyes. Again, he tried to write, more deliberately this time, slowly, gasping for breath at the enormous effort and concentration it took to propel a pen across the paper.

Then his hand went limp, turned upwards. The pen rolled out on to the bed, then to the floor. The paper fluttered down beside it. Love and Stevie had been at too many bedsides not to know that Ahmed was dead. She released his hand; Love closed the old man's eyelids. He had

174

only managed to write – or draw – three small vertical lines on the paper. The woman who had been almost out of sight in the darkness of the room brought a sheet, and covered his body with it.

'Any idea who did this?' Love asked his companions.

'I don't know,' Stevie answered. 'He told me someone was after him.'

'Where from? Why?'

'Over the border. Afghanistan. He knew something important. He wanted to tell me, but I did not want to hear. It is dangerous to become involved. Then I said I would, but he had changed his mind. He said he would make other arrangements. Now, he never will.'

'Have you any idea what he knew?'

'None. Only that the communists feared he knew too much.'

Love nodded, remembering the young man with the vulpine face. Had he also known too much – or was he simply over-confident, possibly knowing he was not alone, while believing that Ahmed was totally on his own? Now, like Ahmed, he was dead. Who remained alive to revenge his killing?

'Where did you see him? Here?'

'Yes. With you both, today. Only hours ago, and yet it seems like years. Then he came to see me this evening.'

'Why?'

'He was my father-in-law.'

'Your father-in-law? What was he doing in this camp? Why wasn't he staying with you?'

'He'd only just arrived. I didn't even know he was in the country until I saw him here. I planned to come back here in the morning. I would have taken him home with me then. But he came to me first. He knew time was running out. He used to be Professor of Oriental Languages at Kabul University. When the Russians came, he lost his job. He became a sort of messenger, anything to earn the price of a meal.'

'And your husband . . . ?'

'His only son.'

'He knew where you were?'

'No. My home is in 'Pindi. But it's easy to find me. They all know the American lady doctor. There aren't too many of us here. Not nearly enough.'

Stevie picked up Ahmed's jacket, went through the pockets. There was nothing to give anyone his name; no wallet, or letters, not even a rupee note. But in a side pocket she found a small screwdriver. This had a polished metal blade set in a black wooden handle. Into the end of this, a design had been stamped. Love recognized the Cord crest, three hearts, three arrows. Could Ahmed's three pencil lines be an attempt to draw this? But if so – why?

'There's also this pen,' said Stevie, and handed Love a thick-barrelled fountain pen.

'Watch that,' warned Parkington sharply. 'It's a pen pistol. You press the clip hard, and Bob's your uncle.'

'I'll watch it,' said Love. He examined the pen closely. 'Most ingenious,' he added, admiringly.

'Let's go, then,' suggested Parkington.

'What about the other dead man?' Love asked him.

'I'll have a word with Hossein about that,' he replied. 'He'll know who to see, what to do. Fights here are fairly common – even to the death. There is so much misery, so much tension. Don't worry about that.'

Parkington walked to his motor rickshaw. Stevie and Love climbed into her car. As they drove back to Peshawar, some items began to settle in Love's mind like shaken flakes in a child's kaleidoscope. He could see a clearer picture of events; perhaps not the complete picture, maybe not even the right one. But where previously there had only been a hazy fog of seemingly unconnected events, now, suddenly, he began to glimpse a possible relationship between a screwdriver bearing the Cord crest and a man killed because he knew too much.

'Stop the car,' Love told Stevie suddenly. 'I want to talk to you – here. Where there's no one else in earshot.'

To his surprise, Stevie did not demur, but swung the car on to the dusty strip alongside the tarmac, switched off the engine.

'Now,' he said firmly, 'tell me the truth about the *whole* business. We are both doctors. We have both heard patients give us all kinds of vague and specious explanations of aches and pains which we know aren't the truth, or at least, not all the truth. I want to help you. So does Parkington. But first we must know what *exactly* is happening here. How could an old man like that cross the mountains on his own?'

'Because he's tough, a Pathan.'

'And why?'

'Because he believed that what he had discovered – whatever it was – could be so important he could not live with himself a moment longer if he did not attempt to bring out the message.'

'And he succeeded – and then failed to deliver it to anyone?'

'Yes. But at least he had achieved the physical part. That is very important to a Pathan. First, he must always conduct himself like a man and live – and if necessary die – by his own strict code of honour. This is nothing to do with the laws other men may make, but what he personally feels is the law of his own honour.

'Let me tell you a story, and you'll understand what I mean. A Pathan had two sons. The elder was a spendthrift, the younger worked hard and saved his money. The elder discovered that he kept this money he saved in a pot, buried in the ground behind his house. One night he dug this up and spent all the money himself. His younger brother found that he'd stolen his entire savings over years. They had a fight – and he killed his elder brother.

'Of course, he could have been brought to trial, but Pathans have their own way of settling things. The elders called the father to them.

177

'"Do you wish that *we* punish your young son, a life for a life, or hand him over to the authorities? Then, he will be tried and, since he admits his guilt, he will be sentenced to death."

'"No," the father replied. "Do not do that. If a man has only one eye, it is better he keeps that, even if it is dim, rather than to be totally blind. If he dies, I will have no son. So let him live. God never owes anyone a debt."

'The young man got married, and had two sons himself. As his father grew very old, he went to live with his son and his wife and family.

'One day, the old man sat his elder grandson, who was then about twelve, in front of the fire, and told him the story I am telling you, but not as though it had ever happened, more like a parable. The little boy was moved by it, and asked whether the killer had ever been punished.

'"Not yet," his grandfather admitted. "But now he will be."

'Then he took out a pistol – and killed his grandson. Of course, the police came at once.

'"Why have you done this?" they asked him. "You have already had one tragedy in your family. Why did you cause another?"

'And the old man replied simply: "I wanted to show my son what it felt like to lose *his* firstborn."'

'Sounds like an Old Testament story,' said Love.

'But it isn't. Ahmed was the younger son. He felt *he* had a debt of honour to pay back. He wanted to prove to himself – and to everyone – that, old as he was, he still was a Pathan, still a fighter.'

'Is your husband like that?' Love asked her.

'I would rather not talk about him. We were not married for very long.'

'You came back here with him, meaning to practise?' Love persisted.

'I came here with him,' Stevie corrected him. 'The fact that I could help some people in the camps was a bonus.

178

And he was like old Professor Ahmed in his courage. Yes, he was like him in many ways.'

'Now,' said Love, 'that Cord. Why do *you* think it is worth so much? Who really owns it? What is its history?'

Stevie turned towards him, and looked him in the eyes, as though making up her mind.

'I will tell you what I know,' she said at last. 'I owe you that.'

At that moment, a truck swerved off the road behind them, skidded in the dust into the back of their car, and knocked it forward over the edge of a nullah. The car fell for six feet and then, overturning in the ditch, burst into flames.

For a second, the shock of the collision temporarily stunned Love. He heard a roar as the petrol tank took fire, saw Stevie on her side jammed in behind the steering wheel, her face pale in the sudden orange glow of the flames. She had hit her head on the roof, was unconscious.

He struggled with his door; it had jammed and was impossible to open. He leaned over Stevie's inert body. The front door on her side was in the air. He forced it open and up, crawled out and pulled her out after him. He dragged her clear, carried her up the bank, laid her down in the dust by the roadside and went back to the inferno. He had seen a fire extinguisher fastened beneath her seat. He undid the clip, smashed the nozzle to break the seal and directed the stream of foaming chemical at the seat of the fire.

Plastic was burning now, and a front tyre exploded, but gradually, as the petrol burned itself out, he brought the fire under control. He threw away the empty fire extinguisher, went up the slope to Stevie. She was coming round, slowly.

'You're all right,' he told her. 'No bones broken. You'll have a headache for a time, but nothing worse.'

'What happened?' she asked weakly.

'That's what we want to know,' said a voice behind him. Love stood up, turned to face the police inspector he had last seen in the garage with the dead man between them.

'We have met before,' said the officer in surprise.

'Yes,' said Love. 'We don't seem to be too lucky for each other. We were run into by this truck.'

'There's no one in the truck now,' the officer told him.

'Were they thrown clear?'

Before he could reply, another policeman came up, with a young man pushing a bicycle. The youth looked nervously from Love to the inspector, then at the ground.

'He says he saw the driver jump clear seconds before he hit you.'

'What happened to him?' asked Love. 'Was he hurt?'

'I don't think so,' said the inspector. 'He ran away.'

'You mean, he drove deliberately at us?'

'It appears so. The truck is empty, it is in second gear and there's a brick on the accelerator to keep the engine running fast. If you hadn't moved very quickly, you could both have been burned to death.'

Love helped Stevie to her feet.

'Why, it is Dr Khan,' said the inspector. 'We saw *you* quite recently, too. What an odd thing. We warned her someone had been seen outside her house, trying to break in, apparently. And we found you, Doctor, with a man dead between us. And you say *we* are not lucky.'

'I am lucky to be alive,' said Love.

A motor rickshaw came past with a feeble wail from its horn, and then stopped. Parkington jumped out.

'What's going on?' he asked in amazement. 'Are you all right?'

'Only just.'

'You know this man?' asked the inspector.

'Indeed I do.'

Love introduced them.

'We'll have to take statements.'

'Another day,' said Love. 'It's been a long, long day for me, even worse for Dr Khan.'

'Can we give you a lift back to her house?'

'Please do. I would be very grateful. You can find me at Pink's, if you want me.'

'We know that already, Dr Love.'

Love helped Stevie into the back of a police car.

'See you tomorrow,' he told Parkington. The car accelerated away, blue light flashing. It stopped outside Stevie's rented house.

'Shall I take you on, Doctor?' the inspector asked Love.

'No, I'll walk. Thanks very much for the lift.'

Stevie took out her key.

'Come in,' she said.

'I intend to,' said Love. 'You don't look too good.'

'Let's both have a drink and I'll feel better.'

She poured two whiskies; they drank them neat. Colour began to return to Stevie's face.

'You *really* think they wanted to kill us?' she asked.

'I don't know who *they* are,' replied Love, 'but someone certainly had a good try.'

'That means they must have followed us to the camp.'

'Not necessarily.'

'Well, from the camp, then.'

'Yes,' he said. 'You're probably right. Before we were so rudely interrupted, you were going to tell me what you knew about the Cord.'

'Oh, the car. I had almost forgotten that. Yes. Of course.'

She paused, as though grouping her thoughts.

'As you know, my husband was killed in Afghanistan. I was told this by someone who said he fought with him with the Mujahideen. He showed me letters that I had written to my husband and which had been in his pocket. This man said he had been with him when he died.'

'And you doubted he had?'

'No,' she said, looking at Love in surprise. 'Why should I?'

'Because it is in a doctor's suspicious nature to doubt. At least, it is in mine.'

'There was no reason here. Then I had a call from a man

181

called Sharif near the frontier. He said he knew about my work in the camp. Sharif offered me ten per cent from the sale of this car, which he claimed was worth ten million pounds. A million pounds, Jason, a fortune.'

'But why you?'

'He said the Cord was American – and so was I. An American collector would have more money to spend – and might trust another American more than a foreigner. It made sense.'

'Go on.'

'That sort of money could do so much good among the refugees. Buy medical equipment for them, drugs, instruments, pay to train theatre staff. You have not seen the terrible wounds I have to treat – people with jaws, hands, feet blown off by mines or booby traps. Eyes right out of their skulls. And they've still travelled a hundred miles, perhaps carried by their friends if they can't walk, or strapped on the backs of mules. As many die as reach us because they simply didn't have the drugs, the equipment.

'Most could have been cured in the West, but not here in the primitive hospitals, crammed with ten times the patients they are ever designed to treat. I wanted that money. I told Sharif I'd sell the car as though it was mine.'

'But why did he choose you? He could have found other Americans here, surely?'

'That's what I told him. Maybe even a genuine Cord buff – like you. Sharif said my husband had done him a good turn. He didn't say what – he wouldn't be drawn on that. But he said he wanted to pay it back, and this was his way.'

Love said nothing, but doubt showed on his face. He remembered Sir Thomas Browne's words, 'To be nameless in worthy deeds exceeds an infamous history.' Had this man Sharif experienced a sudden rush of blood to his conscience?

'Did he say why it was so valuable?' Love asked her.

'No. I had read that old cars were now worth ludicrous sums of money. Millions seemed to mean nothing in that world of rich collectors, and I believed him.'

'Ever met him?'

'Yes, he came down to see me when he brought the car.'

'It wasn't driven?'

'No. It came in the back of one of his trucks.'

'Like the one that ran into us?'

'Yes. There are dozens – hundreds – like that. They are all the same. They take people and goods.'

Her voice began to fade.

'I don't really feel very well,' she said weakly. 'And I'm afraid in this house. I don't know why, there's something evil here. Someone tried to kill us tonight. My father-in-law was murdered. That other man committed suicide in the garage. I just don't understand it.'

'Don't try,' said Love, as she fainted. He picked her up and carried her up the stairs to the bedroom, lit the bed light, laid her on the bed. She looked absurdly small and defenceless, dark hair spread out like a fan on the pillow. She opened her eyes, smiled up at him.

'Come to bed, too,' she whispered, already half asleep.

Love undressed her, then himself, climbed into the wide bed with its scented satin sheets. They lay for a moment, side by side, and then drawn by mutual instinct, rolled together. He kissed her gently at first, stroking her firm breasts as she cried on his shoulder. He felt her tears wet on his face, salt on his lips. That they should make love seemed as inevitable as death, as though this moment had been foretold from the time he had first seen her sitting in his chair in Room 51.

Afterwards, they lay clasped in each other's arms. She told him about growing up in Oregon, walking the strange empty moonscape beaches. She explained how her father had died suddenly, how her mother had struggled to bring her up on her own. She had won scholarships and bursaries, for she had always wanted to be a doctor. She had just qualified when she met Jemshir Khan, who was doing post-graduate work at the same hospital.

'I thought it was love,' she admitted frankly. 'But it was

only attraction, the attraction of opposites. The old world to the new, brown skin to fair, one culture to another.'

'Magnetism of two poles, positive, negative,' said Love. 'Put a filament between them, and you have a bright light . . .'

'The battery can run down,' Stevie pointed out. 'And ours did. I came here, not really knowing what to expect. I felt that if I knew my husband's background, his family, his country, then I might know him better.'

'And did you?'

'No. I like the people, I like the place and I am desperately sorry for all the refugees, but I am not the missionary type. I didn't want to make my life here. A part of my life, yes, okay, but not all my life.'

'Did your husband know that?'

She nodded.

'We were married according to the Muslim creed and then, really to please my mother, we had a service in St Paul's church in Rawalpindi.'

Love remembered the church; it was near Bowker's Hotel. Once it had been a splendid building with a high storm porch and two wide drives to take the carriages of the congregation. Now one entrance was chained shut and the other led to a garden centre, with hundreds of potted plants for sale. He had walked into the church, deserted now, and seen in yellow, amber and green robes, Matthew, Mark, Luke and John look down from stained glass windows across a smashed altar, a vandalized organ with the keys, like teeth, crammed together.

He had read the brass wall plates commemorating men of the garrison battalion of the Gordon Highlanders who had died in the service of an empire vanished away. Who now remembered the sacrifices of those who bore old Scottish names like Hamilton, Macleod, Macdonald and Macbean? He thought that Sir Thomas Browne must also have experienced the sadness of such little memorials when he wrote: 'Time, which antiquates antiquities, and hath an art to make dust of all things, hath yet spared these minor monuments . . .'

Love turned towards Stevie, moved the bedlight so that he could see her face more clearly. He looked at her closely, as though storing up the memory of her eyes, her mouth, in his mind, as a sunflower stores up the warmth and light of a summer day for the winter when there will be no sunshine.

'I'll be leaving in a few days,' he told her. 'Come back to England with me.'

'No,' she said. 'I cannot. I have things to finish here. I have to stay for the time being.'

'How long is the time being?'

'Until I get the money for that car, and put it towards helping my patients – and the patients who'll come after me when I've gone.'

'So you might come?'

'I hardly know you,' she said.

'I don't make love to every lovely woman I hardly know,' he told her.

'I am glad to hear that.'

'Only every other one.'

'That's a pretty high average.'

'A pretty goddamn high average,' he agreed.

'You know something?' she asked, biting his ear, running her fingers gently down his back.

'What, in particular?'

'I'm glad I'm the other one.'

They made love again.

Love let himself out of Stevie's house just before dawn; he did not want to embarrass Stevie by leaving later with her. In a Muslim country, there were strict rules to abide by, and he knew the displeasure that could come from breaking them.

He walked back to his hotel through almost deserted streets. Flocks of tiny birds fluttered around the tops of the chinar trees outside Pink's, filling the sky with song. Within an hour, when the sun came up, they would fall silent until the brief tropical dusk, when once more they would serenade the welcome coolness.

As Love turned the key in the door of his room, he sensed rather than saw a movement in the shadows to one side. Instantly, he tensed. A woman's voice asked him tentatively, nervously, in English: 'Are you Dr Jason Love?'

'I am,' he said. 'And you?'

'Mrs Lambourn.'

'Do I know you?'

'Not under that name, Doctor. But in your practice in the West Country, do you remember Ruth Clarke?'

The name rang a distant bell of memory.

'Of course,' Love said with more certainty than he felt. He had employed Ruth Clarke briefly to help Mrs Hunter, his housekeeper. She had left under a cloud – Love could not now recall what had caused this, but Mrs Hunter had told him firmly that if Ruth Clarke did not leave, she would, and as she had worked for Love since he had taken over the practice, there could only be one answer to that. He remembered vaguely that Ruth had married an Army sergeant, and there had been a divorce. But Lambourn had not been her married name.

'You remember me then?' she said hopefully.

Love nodded.

'But I can't remember a Mrs Lambourn.'

'My second husband,' she explained. 'Could I come in and speak to you privately?'

'Certainly.'

She came into his room.

'Now,' he said, 'what happened to the Army sergeant?'

'He went off with someone else. I married again. Jack Lambourn. That didn't work out, either. He drank.'

'I'm sorry,' said Love. 'But what brings you out here to Peshawar, the other side of the world?'

'I have a job here, looking after the children of an engineer on a big construction project, about 20 miles north.'

186

'I see. And what do you want to see me about? Are you in some sort of trouble?'

As a doctor, Love was resigned to the fact that people seemed seldom to seek him out for social or friendly reasons; they came when they were in trouble, when they wanted help, advice, reassurance. Usually they wanted to be told that some symptom was not serious, that their debt to God was not about to be called in.

'I saw a bit about you in the paper,' Mrs Lambourn said hesitantly. 'You had come out here to look at a Cord car. I thought there must only be one Dr Jason Love who had a Cord car. You still have it?'

She allowed herself a smile as though remembering a happier time.

'Yes,' he said. 'But what brings you to see me now? If you are unwell, there must be plenty of excellent doctors in Peshawar. I am only here for a few days.'

'I'm not ill,' she said, 'I am just unhappy.'

'That goes for most of the human race,' he told her. 'Believe me, you have many to keep you company. But please sit down. I can't offer you a drink here, but I can ring for a coffee or tea or cakes or something.'

'No,' she said. 'Just to talk to you is enough.'

She sat down.

'Do you mind if I smoke?'

He did, but he did not say so. He picked up a box of matches by the side of the emergency candle, lit her cigarette. She inhaled deeply two or three times. She was obviously strung up, nervous, embarrassed. He waited.

'I was going to get married again for the third time,' she began, 'but my fiancé has been killed.'

'I'm sorry to hear that,' said Love. 'Where did this happen?'

'On the way from Islamabad airport. He was in a motor rickshaw run into by a truck. He died instantly, so the police said. I am glad he felt no pain.'

'Was his name Glover?'

'Yes, Ras – Erasmus was his first name. So you heard about it? I suppose you would really, as a doctor. The British Embassy have been very helpful, but I just wanted to tell someone I knew, about . . . about something else. I feel guilty.'

'About what?'

'I wasn't sure whether I was going to marry him after all. Someone told me he was two-timing me. I couldn't bear a third marriage that failed – for whatever reason. Third time unlucky wasn't for me. And I wrote and told him I was worried. I wanted to talk to him, face to face, not just writing letters or talking on the phone when often you can barely hear for atmospherics.

'And there was something else about him that worried me. He had suddenly come into money – I don't know how. He'd bought himself a Porsche car. I know he was clever, but he was only a salesman. *And* he was putting a deposit down on a flat in Docklands. A lot of money – on mortgage. A hundred and fifty thousand. And he'd taken to drinking. Like Jack.'

'Perhaps he was working too hard?'

'There was no need to cheat on me. I hadn't cheated on him.'

'Who told you he had?'

'My mother. She didn't like him. Said there was something odd about his eyes. So I told him I was having second thoughts, and next thing, he rang me and said he was on his way here. He had to go to Bangkok and he would stop off in Islamabad to sort things out.'

'Maybe you are better out of that marriage?'

'I suppose I am. But he was very attractive. And I really loved him. I didn't love my first, looking back. But he was the first man I went to bed with, and it seemed wonderful. I was in love with the idea of love.

'Jack Lambourn was a good fellow – when he was sober, but we had nothing in common, really. Nothing. But with Ras, I sort of felt I had found someone with whom I could live, whom I could like. And then he did this to me, and before I could tackle him face to face with what I'd heard, and find out whether it was true or not, he was killed. And I feel I'm in some way responsible.'

She paused, and her shoulders hunched and her whole body sagged as she started to sob. Love let her cry; there was nothing else he could do. What she really needed was a double brandy and he had not even got a single.

'How are you off for money here?' he asked.

'I'm all right,' she said. 'The engineer's generous. He's a nice man, really.'

'I can't help you in any way except as a father confessor, to try and cheer you up and say you have no need to feel guilty about anything,' Love told her. 'Accidents happen. If you'd married him, that might have been an accident that lasted all your life. And his.'

'Yes,' she agreed, 'I suppose so. But there *is* something I wonder if I could ask you to help me with?'

'If I can.'

'It is rather difficult to say this, but I don't know where Ras's body is. He had a suitcase. He said he was bringing me a present. I suppose his case must be somewhere but the police aren't very helpful. Whenever I go to the police station, they say come back, or the officer involved is on leave, off duty, gone away, on a case. You are of good standing, Doctor. Could *you* ask where his belongings are? I'm afraid someone could just go through them, might steal things.'

'Of course,' said Love. 'I'll do that willingly. How can I find you?'

'I don't want you ringing up my employer's house. He doesn't like that.'

'Well, I've got to deliver them somewhere, if I find them.'

'I'll ring you, Doctor. Or I'll come back here. That's the easiest way. It's not like at home out here, you know.'

Love showed her to the door, went back into the room, kicked off his shoes, lay on the bed until it was time to ring

189

for breakfast. He should have felt sorry at Mrs Lambourn's sad story, but something jarred in his mind like grit on an engine bearing.

She had said she had read in a paper that Dr Love was in Peshawar to look at a Cord car. It seemed very reasonable, therefore, that she should come to see him. There was only one flaw in this reasoning. Nothing whatever had been published in any paper about Love's arrival in Pakistan, in Rawalpindi or in Peshawar.

Hossein dumped the leather airline bag on Parkington's bed, looked up at Love and Parkington triumphantly for their words of thanks and praise.

'How did you get it?' Love asked him.

'A matter of contacts,' explained Hossein proudly. 'Who you know Beats what you Know. I know someone in the police. I told him that the Midland Widows Insurance Company, with whom the dead man had a policy on favourable terms, wished to check his belongings, as they had insured them, and they would not like his relations to be short-changed. That could only reflect badly on the police.'

'Admirable,' said Parkington. 'Now let's cut out the crap and open the bag.'

He pulled on a pair of rubber surgical gloves.

'There's no need for that,' said Hossein. 'Everyone has been touching this.'

'I haven't,' said Parkington. 'Not yet.'

The bag was divided into two compartments; he opened both zips. The top section contained an electric razor, underwear, socks stuffed into suede shoes, a guidebook to Pakistan. He turned over the pages. Some towns had been ringed, Rawalpindi, Peshawar, Darra. He put the book on one side, sifted through neatly folded shirts, ties, a blazer with lacquered brass buttons. He opened the other side of the bag: a plastic sponge bag, two suits, a towel, a Canon camera in a case, and three rolls of film still in silver foil wrapping. Parkington put them on one side, zipped up the case.

'Can you get these developed quickly?' he asked Hossein.

'Of course.'

'Then please do that, as Othello said on another occasion, with all convenient speed.'

'Right away. Never Delay a Major Decision.'

At that moment, they heard a gentle tap on the door of the room. The three men exchanged glances. Parkington nodded. Hossein opened the door, went out. Mrs Lambourn was standing in the doorway.

'Oh,' she said, seeing Love, 'I thought this was Mr Parkington's room?'

'It is.'

Love introduced them.

'Why, that is Ras's bag,' she said. 'Did you find my present in it?'

'I don't know what your present was,' said Love. 'You didn't tell me, so you had better look for it yourself.'

He unzipped the bag and she tipped the clothes, the toilet articles, the camera, unceremoniously on the bed. Love watched her face as she did so. She turned the bag upside down, shook it, felt alongside the bottom in case anything should be concealed in it.

'It's not here,' she said.

'What was it?'

'A beauty box of an unusual kind.'

'How unusual?' asked Parkington. 'Dodgy to carry, those things, in the hold of an aircraft. It is unpressurized and scent bottles can leak.'

'It was a metal one – useful out here where luggage can be treated pretty roughly. But, anyhow, it is not here. Has anyone else had a look through the bag?'

'Only the police.'

'I see. Well, if you do see them, could you ask about it? It is quite an ordinary item, sort of grey.'

'You've seen it then?'

'Well, I know the sort of thing it is, and he knows – knew – I like grey. My favourite colour.'

She looked disappointed, saddened.

'I'd better be going, then,' she said. 'I've a taxi waiting outside.'

After she had gone, Parkington went into the bathroom, came back with the tin of aftershave, shook out the last spoonfuls of whisky.

'Here is where we could use someone to follow her,' he said morosely. 'After what you tell me about her seeing a reference to you that never appeared, and this crap about Glover bringing her a present, she seems to be rather more than a children's nurse. On the other hand, we *may* be reading too much into it.'

The telephone rang; Parkington picked up the receiver. Hossein was on the line.

'Those films, sir.' he said. 'There's nothing at all on them. They are all totally blank. They have never been used.'

'Well, well,' said Parkington. 'Thank you for finding that out so quickly.'

He put down the receiver.

'You heard that?'

Love nodded.

'What do you think?'

'I think we've got a lot of loose ends, and not one of them ties up with anything else. By all reasonable accounts, one of those films *should* have been of secret equipment of some kind. But – nothing. The bag's clean. Know what I'm going to do?'

'What?'

'Keep my balls in the air.'

'Speak for yourself,' said Parkington.

'I mean, like the juggler. Concentrate on what we *do* know, little as that is. When you see me again, I'll have a theory.'

'And if you don't?' asked Parkington.

'You won't see me,' said Love.

192

PART EIGHT

Jason Love sat in a carved wooden chair, one of two dozen arranged in rows, as for a lecture, in the lounge of Pink's Hotel, facing a fireplace filled with plastic flowers. He had been sitting like this, concentrating, for nearly two hours.

What secret could make a man kill himself rather than face what he must have believed would be an interrogation in which he might be forced to give it away? Had he been searching for a single jewel of enormous value, hidden somewhere in the Cord? Or if not – then, what? A solution seemed to hover on the perimeter of Love's thoughts, like the birds that fluttered over the hotel's dried-up lawns watching for worms. But the answers to his questions seemed as elusive as those worms.

Suddenly, the explanation seemed so obvious, he felt astonished – almost ashamed – that it had escaped him for so long. He had assumed that the man must have been trying to find something immensely valuable hidden in the Cord. But what if, instead of this, he was attempting to *hide* something of great value? The threat of discovery and the fear of having to admit failure to whoever was employing him had then been so great that he had chosen to die rather than face the consequences of failure. That could mean he had not been able to hide whatever it was he wished to conceal. And since then had anyone else been able to succeed where he had failed?

Love stood up. He must examine the Cord at once with this in mind – not for something that could be removed, but for something that might have been added. He went to the Reception Desk, rang Parkington's room to tell him of his intention. There was no reply. Parkington's key was still on its hook above his pigeon-hole.

'Have you seen him?' Love asked the reception clerk.

'Not now seeing. But half an hour ago I saw him. He said he was going to the insurance office. A cable for him had just arrived from head office in London.'

Love took a sheet of notepaper from a pile on the desk, scribbled a note to Parkington: 'Have gone to re-examine car. Must see you urgently on return.' He sealed the envelope, wrote his signature across the back in case anyone became curious about the contents, and put it in Parkington's pigeon-hole. Then he went out into the bright, cool sunshine. The only taxi in sight was collecting a passenger. He decided to walk out to the road and hail a rickshaw. As he reached the gate, Hossein drove up in his car, stopped.

'Can you give me a lift?' Love asked him.

'Of course. I have just left Mr Parkington in the office. Momentarily, I am free. Where do you wish to go? A long distance?'

'Not really.'

'I am a cautious man, Dr Love. We are short of petrol. It would never do to run out. Forethought is Vital in every successful Enterprise.'

'Not me,' said Love, climbing into the car.

'Tell me, Doctor, are you off duty as well as looking at the old car?'

'A doctor is always on duty,' Love corrected him. 'Why?'

'I have this funny pain, Doctor. In my chest. I wonder if you could advise me about it?'

'Not without a proper examination, and then only with your own doctor's consent. But tell me, you smoke cigarettes?'

'Oh, yes, nearly all the time, many cigarettes.'

'Well, I'd cut that out, for a start. Even so, you look pretty healthy to me. It is probably nothing serious. Indigestion. Nervous tension.'

'You give me good cheer already,' said Hossein. 'In my job I see so many ill people. They wish insurance but they try to conceal from the company that they have weak hearts, gravel, stones. They pass blood, cough up sputum.'

'Sounds a great crowd,' said Love. 'Just like my Monday morning surgery.'

They turned into a Pakistan State Oil petrol station, filled the car's tank. Then Love directed him to the Cord garage. This road, previously almost empty, was now packed with parked cars and trucks half on the pavement, half in the street. At last, they found a space.

'Could you wait a moment?' Love asked Hossein. 'I will be as quick as I can. I just want to check something.'

'No problem,' said Hossein.

He felt in his pocket for a packet of cigarettes, remembered Love's advice, gave a sigh, did not take out the packet.

Love walked along down the uneven pavement to the garage. To his surprise, the sliding door was not locked, only closed. The padlock hung on its hasp, open. Strange. Had Parkington come here to examine the car himself? Could the message the reception clerk had mentioned have contained new information about it – or new instructions?

Love glanced through the small space between the door and the frame, then wrenched it open. The sun shone over his head, lighting up oil stains on the concrete, circular sooty marks on the far wall from the exhaust of innumerable car engines – and an empty garage. The Cord had gone.

Love searched around for any clue as to who could have taken it. He sniffed the air. There was no smell of exhaust, so the engine had not been running. Therefore, the car had not been driven out, but pushed or towed.

He stood for a moment. The Cord was not yet insured, so there would be no reason for anyone to steal it and then make a claim on the Midland Widows. He closed the garage door pensively, walked slowly up the street.

'I'm down here, Doctor,' Hossein called to him. 'I have had to move my car.'

The reason, Love saw, was that a big, high-sided truck with the chariot-like contraption above the driver's cab, was pulling away from the kerb. Love drew level with it. Close up, the faces of birds, apes, lions, eagles, painted in unequivocally bright reds, yellows, greens, seemed as crude as the inscription on the side, 'Don't touch me.'

From the truck's blue sides, long chains, suspended from chromium hooks, rattled as the driver raced the engine. A cloud of black smoke blew out from the exhaust. Love wrinkled his face in distaste. Between the hinge of the tailgate and the high side was a gap of nearly two inches. Through this, he saw the sunshine glitter on the Cord's distinctive silvery paintwork. Ropes held the car securely in the centre of the floor. This would only be done to prevent it slipping or sliding on a long journey, not one of just a few miles. And even as Love stood, staring in astonishment, the truck began to move forward. He ran alongside, beating on the cab door with his fist. The driver looked down at him in surprise.

'*Kya mangta?*' he asked. 'What do you want?'

'That car in the back!' Love shouted. 'Stop! Where are you taking it?'

'New garage,' the driver replied.

'Wait!' yelled Love. '*Wait!*'

The driver shook his head and shrugged, as though he did not understand. The truck accelerated in a cloud of diesel fumes. A tonga overtaking it nearly hit the side. The tonga driver shouted imprecations and punched his fist furiously on his bell to show violent disapproval. '*Pagal wallah!*' he shouted angrily. 'Madman!'

Love ran back to Hossein's car.

'The Cord's inside that truck,' he told him. 'Follow it.'

'I was going to pick up Mr Parkington at the office, Doctor.'

'This is more important. I'll explain to him. Follow it, man, before it's out of sight.'

'As you say, Doctor. I accept your authority. You are, of course, an expert on this vehicle.'

'I have been called other things,' Love admitted as he searched in vain for a seat belt; in Pakistan's driving conditions, it seemed essential wear.

The truck was now two hundred yards ahead of them. Behind it were other trucks of the same size, the same colours, decorated with the same garish designs. Love had not been able to see the truck's number plate, but on the tailgate was a peacock and a man with a sword in his hand, and underneath in white letters, the warning: 'Keep off my tail'. Whether this advice referred to the peacock, the person, or the truck, was not stated.

'It's three trucks ahead,' Love told Hossein. 'Come on, move yourself.'

They passed one truck, then the second, and the third, and then tucked in behind a yellow and black Morris Minor taxi, with the blue truck just in front.

'Where is he going?' asked Hossein.

'That's what we will find out.'

As Love spoke, he realized that Parkington had no idea of his whereabouts. If he assumed from Love's note that he was in the garage, he would soon find that he was not. Love had no means of telling him now; no car telephone, no one who could deliver a message. If he stopped to write another note in Pink's Hotel, he would lose the truck, and in this country, where every large truck seemed virtually identical, he would never find it again. They passed a cinema, where giant advertisements in bright colours for the current film showed men in strange uniforms fighting serpents, wild beasts and adversaries in even stranger clothes. At the bus station, rows of shabby buses waited in line. The sun reflected on bright blue windows, polished metal ornaments.

Flags of Islam drooped from their radio aerials. With a huge broom of twigs, a man swept dust diligently and uselessly from one end of the station to the other. Long-distance, air-conditioned New Khan Road-Runner Coaches. ('The Choice of Noble Personalities') waited on the other side of the road.

They lost the truck at one traffic light and found it at the next, lost it a second time at a crossroads, where a policeman with a whistle in his mouth attempted to direct traffic, waving both arms frantically as drivers pretended not to see him. Then they picked up the truck, stationary on a double track section of the road and Love noted the number, PES – for Peshawar – 870248. Two men pulling a gigantic block of ice on a wooden wheeled trolley had run into a tonga coming the wrong way. A jam half a mile long built up within minutes, most drivers sounding their horns angrily. For the first time since Love's arrival he felt gratitude for the chaotic traffic. Without this, they could have lost the truck.

'Keep as close as you can,' Love told Hossein. 'One car in between, if possible, in case the driver notices us.'

The truck set off. Cars overtook them, fell back. Motor cyclists, some with two pillion passengers, others with three, cut in dangerously on the wrong side. Then they were out on the open road.

'Where does this road lead to?'

'First, Darra. Where they make weapons,' Hossein explained. 'Then, the frontier.'

'How long will that take us?'

'We can't cross the frontier,' said Hossein. 'We may not even get into Darra without a pass. It all depends who's on duty at the last police post. To some I have sold policies, and they are friends. But the others . . .'

He shrugged his shoulders dismissively.

They passed several police posts. Policemen, perhaps clients, wearing neatly pressed dark blue uniforms, light blue shirts, with red scarves at their necks, waved them

198

through. They appeared more concerned with cars and trucks and buses coming the opposite way, and so possibly carrying drugs. By the roadside, a regimental headquarters had its crest picked out proudly in whitewashed stones.

They bumped over a level crossing where a camel waited outside a café hung with green flags; overtook a car overtaking a tonga, which was at the same time attempting to pass two men in track suits jogging up the road side by side. A mosque reared its huge white onion-shaped dome, circled with flags like a necklace, and then fifty yards on, a crowd blocked the road.

They waved frantically at the truck to slow down and stop. Love heard the angry bray of its horns, and the crowd parted reluctantly to let it through at speed. Some men waved fists angrily after it. As Love approached the crowd, he could see a motorcycle on its side in the centre of the road. Near this stood a tonga down on its axle, with a wheel missing. The horse, terrified and whinnying, was being led out of the shafts. Two bodies, one under the motorcycle, lay like piles of crumpled dirty sheets in the road.

'Damn!' said Love. 'We'll have to stop.'

There were good points in being a doctor, but the obverse was that at any emergency or accident, a doctor was always expected to abandon whatever else he might be doing to tend to the ill or the injured. This took priority over all private arrangements it might interrupt or even ruin.

'Pull over,' he told Hossein resignedly.

'We'll lose the truck,' Hossein said anxiously.

'I know, but we can't help it. I have its number now. And there can't be too many trucks with "Keep Off my Tail" on the back.'

'I tell you, it is a very common sign here.'

Hossein pulled into the side of the road, switched off his engine. Love climbed out of the car, walked without enthusiasm towards the crowd. They parted as he approached,

199

looking at him intently. Why should a Western stranger, doubtless a tourist, stop when others of their own kind went past? Two men crouched by the side of the motorcyclist, who lay trapped beneath part of his machine. His face was contorted with pain, his mouth open in the extent of his agony.

'I'm a doctor,' Love explained.

The two men stood up and nodded.

'It was the tonga driver's fault,' said one of them in English.

Love knelt down, felt the motor cyclist's pulse, gently raised his eyelids in turn. He had fallen on his back and the machine had landed on him. He would be lucky to escape with a broken leg and cracked ribs; more likely, he could have broken his back. But the man had no bruising or grazes on his hands or the side of his face, beneath his crash helmet. Nor could Love see any skid lines where his machine had been deflected. His pulse was normal, and his eyes looked out at him warily, not dazed or vaguely. He had had a miraculous escape. Love stood up.

'He's all right,' he said in amazement. 'He is not hurt at all. A very lucky fellow.'

The man who had spoken to him now thrust an unshaven jaw into Love's face.

'Which is something you're not,' he said, grinning. Love smelled sour, nicotine breath, saw yellow teeth, his gloating and shifty eyes.

'What the hell do you mean?' Love asked him. As if in answer, people lifted up the motorcycle. The rider stood up, dusted himself down. The other man, who had been lying in the road near the tonga, also stood up, grinning sheepishly. Suddenly, Love was surrounded. Men stinking of sweat and heavily scented hair oil encircled him, pressing against him so tightly that he could not move his arms. Elbows, fists, suddenly pummelled his kidneys. Someone kicked him behind his right knee joint. He stumbled, and the crowd closed over him. And all the time, cars raced past in each direction, their drivers and passengers ignoring this commotion. Buses and trucks blew their horns imperiously. An accident was no concern of theirs; they had schedules to keep.

'What the hell is going on?' Love shouted angrily. '*Hossein!*'

He felt himself being propelled up the road and away from Hossein's car by the sheer weight of the crowd. He tried to force his way back through the crowd, punching his way now, using fists, knees, elbows, but the men stood so close to him that his feet barely touched the road. He could scarcely breathe. Sweating, excited, contorted faces thrust aggressively into his. He could not see Hossein's car now. He must have sensed trouble and reversed away before he could become embroiled. Love realized he had walked into a trap, and in that split second of realization and bewilderment, he felt an almost unbearable blow on the base of his skull.

He fell silently, weightlessly, through dark and starless skies. The pace of his descent gradually slowed. He tried to move his arms, his hands, his legs, but this was impossible. He sensed a growing turbulence in the air, as though the darkness itself was moving, taking strange shapes like waves on an unknown sea.

He opened his eyes. He could make out a silvery shape ahead, and a blueness beyond. He tasted blood in his mouth. His shirt was torn and stained with blood. Pain in his head pounded like a steamhammer. He blinked half a dozen times to focus his eyes, shook his head to try to clear his mind. The movement was agony to his neck muscles, but gradually the silvery shape resolved itself into a flank of polished painted metal. His eyes were within inches of the left hand front wing of the Cord; the blueness was the sky above and behind it.

Love tried to move, but his hands were tightly bound behind him, and his ankles tied with a leather strap. His body felt as though every joint had been beaten apart and then nailed together. He moved the tips of his fingers behind his back and felt rough, warm planks of wood that rocked and jumped even as he touched them. He breathed deeply, trying to clear his mind, endeavouring to assess where he was, what had happened, what might happen now.

He had the rattle of loose chains in his ears, and the smell of diesel oil in his nose, its heavy, sickening taste in his throat. He was lying on his side, bound hand and foot, in the back of the truck he had been following from Peshawar.

The whole vehicle throbbed with the beat of its ancient engine. Through gaps between the planks in its sides, he saw other traffic: tongas, bullock carts, trucks. Gradually, fragments of the past drifted into his memory. The driver must have seen him, and somehow stage-managed an accident, though how, he had no idea – or why. He must have calculated that, as a doctor, Love would stop to offer help – but who would work this out? Surely not just the driver? More likely there must be someone who was powerful enough to control a crowd of people, find a tonga, and persuade a motorcyclist to lie down in the road – like extras in a scene for a film. In retrospect, the whole idea of such a trap seemed absurd, and yet it had been totally successful.

The sun was warmer now, and Love felt it burn his face, his neck. He rolled over slightly, looked under the car. He could see three pairs of feet thrust into shabby leather chaplis on the floor of the truck. So at least three men were in the back with him. He heard a creak and the metallic twang of the spring that compensated the weight of the Cord's bonnet. Then the bonnet opened like the giant mouth of a metal alligator. Three faces, frowning in concentration, peered into the engine from the other side of the car. One man held a screwdriver and a small metal box from which a thin rubber-sheathed wire protruded. It was about a foot long, stiff, like the antenna of a mechanical spider. What the devil was this – and what was he doing here?

Love's head was clearing now. His eyes were level with the huge chromium hub-cap of the Cord's left-hand front wheel. The sun reflected on it like a great parabolic mirror, dazzling him. He looked past this, above the mudguard, into the engine compartment. On the bulkhead he could see the familiar factory nameplate with the fake chassis and engine numbers. He glanced above this to the small plate with the body number.

He spelt out the numbers stamped on it and then glanced down at the numbers on the other plate. They were all quite different. So what did this new plate relate to? It had seven figures, 3396940. But the other numbers, fake as they might be, only ran to four figures. He knew he had seen an almost similar seven-figure number also with single letters, quite recently, but where and when? The digits churned around in his tired mind like stones in a constantly revolving drum. Could it have been in Islamabad? 'Pindi? Peshawar? He shut his eyes, trying to concentrate, to focus his mind, remembering the juggler's advice.

The truck bumped on. Love heard the impatient warning of its horns as they overtook a bus, and then the men on the other side of the car began chattering among themselves. He heard the sharp scrape of metal on metal, the squeak of a screw turning reluctantly. That box, he thought, looked like something out of an aircraft. An *aircraft*? Now what faint chord of memory did that strike? Then he remembered. Flying to Islamabad from London; reading the airline magazine, and with nothing else to occupy his mind, comparing the latitude and longitude of the Algarve in Portugal with the figures for Pakistan. Those had been 34 degrees, 3 minutes north, and 71 degrees, 30 minutes east at Peshawar. The number on that plate did not refer to the car's body; it was a map reference, perhaps to somewhere in Pakistan, but slightly south and west. That could place it over the frontier – in Afghanistan.

He did not know where exactly, but he could remember numbers easily enough, and he must remember these. He looked more closely at the plate. It seemed too new to have been fitted to the car more than half a century earlier.

Someone had fitted this plate quite recently. He remembered the Cord screwdriver in Ahmed's pocket. Stevie had told him Ahmed had been in the garage – more, in the back of the car, where the tool kit was stored. He could have picked up the screwdriver, and then lacked time to replace it, or did not dare to attempt this in case he was discovered. Now Ahmed's three pencil lines as he lay dying began to have significance. He had been attempting to sketch the Cord's crest.

As the noise of the truck's engine changed, grew deeper, Love repeated the number to himself, eyes closed, until he knew he would not forget it: *three, three, nine; six, nine, four, zero.* He heard a crashing of straight cut gears. The truck jolted, slowed, turned to the left, bumped over an unmade track that set the chains jangling; the wooden floorboards creaked in protest. Then the engine stopped and the sudden silence seemed to have a sound all its own. Love lay, eyes closed. It could be safer to pretend to be unconscious.

Hossein sat uneasily on the edge of the chair in Parkington's room in Pink's Hotel. He had taken the precaution of bringing with him a bottle of vodka which he had obtained through one of his contacts. Stevie stood, back to the open window, watching him with an expressionless face. Parkington poured out three drinks.

'And then what happened?' he asked.

'Well, sir, after they surrounded the doctor, they took him away in the truck.'

'And you followed?'

'Well, very discreetly, sir. For a time.'

'Who owns the truck?'

'Mr Sharif.'

'And what's Mr Sharif's business?'

'His own, sir. With a share in many other people's. He runs drugs, sells arms, buys arms. He is a very powerful man. He knows a lot of things about important people they would not like revealed.'

'He blackmails them?'

'It is not a word I would use, sir.'

'I'm not asking you to use it, I'm using it. Is that so?'

'That is so, sir.'

'So where's Dr Love been taken to?'

'Who can say? Inshallah. It is the will of Allah.'

'Not necessarily,' said Stevie. 'It is the will of Sharif. I'd put money on the fact that Jason is in Sharif's house.'

'But why?' asked Parkington.

'Because he refuses to say the Cord is worth so much.'

'What's Sharif got to do with the Cord?'

'He owns it,' said Stevie simply.

'What the hell? I thought *you* owned it?' said Parkington angrily. 'We've been corresponding with you as the owner.'

'I've never said I was the owner. I just said there was a car to sell.'

'And what's your share of ten million pounds sterling?'

'I've been promised ten per cent. I want to use it to help the refugees.'

'You'll be lucky if you ever get a cent, a penny, an anna,' Parkington told her.

'I'm beginning to think it will be lucky if *anyone* ever gets *any* money for this car.'

'Well, we can't just sit here,' said Parkington irritably.

'What do you think we should do?' asked Stevie.

'I don't know what you're going to do, but Hossein here is going to take me to Sharif's house.'

'No, sir, I'm not going there. That is death to interfere.'

'You mean that?'

'This is a rough country, Mr Parkington. This is not Leadenhall Street and the headquarters of the Midland Widows office, with all the computers chattering. I have seen the place. That is civilization of a kind. This is civilization of an older kind. Here the man with the muscle, the gun, says what goes.'

Parkington sipped his drink, poured himself another.

'You have a very good point,' he said. 'But I look on

myself as the man with both of these necessities. And you still want to be the senior representative of Midland Widows out here?'

'That is my ambition, sir. Before I am thirty-one.'

'And a very good ambition, too. So I'll tell you how we can accelerate your promotion. We wait for a few hours – just in case our reasoning is wrong, and the good doctor is picking wild flowers or something. Then you drive us to the Sharif residence before Love can start pushing up the daisies. Do I make myself clear?'

'Abundantly clear, sir. The Secret of Success is Clear Communication.'

'What I always say,' replied Parkington, and poured out three more vodkas.

Love heard men jump down from the truck, shout to each other; then a rattle as the tailgate chains were undone and the tailgate lowered. Two men dragged Love out of the truck, and held him upright as his feet touched the ground. He opened his eyes carefully. One man took a penknife out of his pocket, slashed the strap around Love's ankles. He flexed his muscles thankfully, breathing deeply.

'Who are you?' he asked weakly. 'What is happening?'

No one replied; he had not really expected they would. Someone dug a fist into his ribs, nodded towards a nondescript house across a wide compound. The concrete was stained by oil from parked trucks, and around it stretched a wire fence on concrete posts. Each concrete post had a large green glass insulator to support the wires; clearly, they carried a very high voltage. Beyond the fence a brown arid wasteland marched to foothills shimmering in the sun. Clouds covered the tops of distant mountains like huge white hats. The air had a sharp metallic tang to it, almost a flavour, quite different from Peshawar. Love guessed he was at a higher altitude and near the Afghan border.

The men prodded him across the courtyard, through a side door of the house, and into a room sparsely furnished with a chair on each side of a simple varnished desk. On the desk stood a telephone and a blotter, and to one side of the room was an old fashioned telex machine, silent now but, from the glowing red warning light, connected up and ready to work.

Another door opened and a middle-aged man entered. He wore light blue cotton trousers, a white shirt, green tinted glasses. His skin was dark, but he was not Pakistani. He could be Maltese or Goanese.

'You are the Dr Love who refuses to believe the car outside is worth what I say it is worth?' he asked sharply.

'And who the devil are you?' replied Love. 'What is the meaning of this assault and kidnap?'

'The answer to the first question is that my name is Sharif and I own the Cord car which has such a fascination for you that you attempted to follow it here.

'Dr Khan, who first got in touch with the insurance company, is a woman of idealistic principles. She hopes to receive some money from the sale to help refugees.

'To answer your next question, you are here for two reasons. One, because, for reasons quite unknown to me, you obstinately refuse to agree that this car is worth ten million pounds.'

'For the best reason of all. It isn't.'

'That is your opinion. No matter. I am sending a telex today in your name to the insurance man, Parkington, copy to Hossein, which you will sign to say you have had other thoughts.'

'And if I do not?'

'Then, Dr Love, it will still be sent – and in your name.

'There is another reason for inviting you,' Sharif went on. 'A more personal one but of equal importance. The other night you went to see this car in Peshawar and while you were there a young man came into the garage. Yes?'

'He had a gun,' Love explained. 'He tried to shoot me.'

'He did not *try*. He could have shot you easily had he so wished. But somehow you disarmed him, and rather than admit defeat, for he was a proud young man, he took his own life.'

'That was his affair,' retorted Love. 'We cannot say when we come into this world, but we have the option of saying when we leave. He took up that option. But what has that got to do with you?'

Sharif came round from behind his desk, crossed the floor. Love could see hatred in his eyes.

'Just this, Doctor,' he said bitterly, his voice clotted with anger. 'That young man was my son.'

Stevie's cordless telephone began to ring as she came into her bedroom. She closed the door, slipped the bolt automatically. She had lived close to violence for too long ever to leave a door open when it could be closed, or unsecured if it could be bolted. She picked up the instrument, listened to the usual whirring and asthmatic whispering and wheezing that seemed endemic with telephones in the East. Then, without pleasure, she recognized the man's voice.

'We have some news for Dr Khan,' he said.

'Speaking,' she replied, wondering what the news could be, anticipating it, almost dreading it.

'I am just now speaking to Dr Khan?'

'I've told you so,' she said sharply.

He began to talk then, in a singsong voice. She said nothing, so eventually he asked: 'Are you still there, Dr Khan?'

'Yes,' she said. 'I'm here.'

'Have you anything to say?'

'Nothing, at the moment. Nothing.'

The line died. Stevie put down the telephone on its charger, stood for a moment looking out of the window. From the turret of the mosque across the road, loudspeakers began to blare a twentieth-century electronic call to prayer. She wondered idly whether this call was taped on a cassette that rewound itself automatically, or would it be on a disc? Not that it mattered: however the message was delivered, it was still the same. The days of the muezzin personally calling the faithful to prayer seemed somehow as distant as the days of the emperors who had marched along the Grand Trunk Road.

She sat down on the bed for a moment, put her face in her hands, not quite sure of her own feelings. She remembered her husband quoting from a seventh-century Muslim caliph: 'Half of knowledge is the question; the other half is the answer.'

Stevie had heard the question now, and she wished she had never heard it, for she alone must find the answer.

At last, she stood up, went into the bathroom, washed her face with cold water, paying particular attention to her eyes. She was due to see Parkington, and she did not want him to know she had been crying.

Love stared Sharif out coldly. The older man lowered his eyes first.

'You have no son,' Love told him. 'You are not the marrying type.'

Sharif punched him in the stomach.

'You bastard!' he cried – and then roared with laughter, but laughter without mirth, a hollow, bitter sound.

'You are quite right, Doctor. I have no sons, but I tend to regard all young men as sons I might have had – and this was a very special young man. He was so proud he could not bear to face failure. Death was for him a matter of resolving his honour. It is written, when honour is lost, it is a relief to die. That was the measure of his dignity.'

Sharif sat down behind his desk.

'Now,' he said, 'this telex. It is immaterial to me whether you sign it or whether you don't. I am sending it in any case, as I say, in your name.'

'What good will that do?' asked Love. 'The insurance people will know I haven't signed it.'

'How can they possibly know that, Doctor? Apply your mind to the problem. Concentrate on it. *You* will not be there to tell them this. *You* will be here – and beyond all ability to communicate with them. *They* will receive a message, signed by you and so unquestionably sent by you.

'The insurance man, Hossein, who was driving the car that followed my truck, will report that you were on the way to my house, and keeping the Cord in sight. They will deduce you are here with me – as, of course, you are.'

'So why kidnap me – just to tell me this?'

'Because, Dr Love, if you were allowed to remain in Peshawar, it would be obvious, even to the indifferent intelligence of the dullest insurance representative, that you had *not* sent the telex. Surely I do not have to explain things to you in such basic terms?

'In any case, you have become a nuisance to me, getting in my way. I cannot tolerate such interference. My driver radioed me from the truck that you were following him so I organized a little play-acting for you. I guessed that you would stop to offer help. And so you did. Folly. In this life, Dr Love, one must only look after one's personal interests. Always. A lesson, I fear, that you have learned too late to be of any advantage to you now.'

'Where is this telex?' Love asked briskly. The homilies could wait, but the longer he could keep this madman talking, the greater were his chances of escape – or so he assured himself. Scheherazade had proved the wisdom of this when she had told the Sultan Schariah her stories for a thousand and one nights. Love's aim was the same as hers: survival, but a discussion over a very much shorter period.

Sharif crossed to the machine, brought back a sheet of paper.

'Let me read it,' said Love. 'And so that I can do so, please release my hands. This is no way to conduct serious negotiations. I am unarmed, as you can see.'

'You are unarmed *now*, Doctor,' Sharif corrected him gently, 'but in the truck my men removed a toy pen pistol from your pocket, so you are clearly not as innocent a physician as you might like to appear.'

Sharif took a sheath knife from his belt, cut the cord around Love's wrists. Love flexed his muscles, feeling circulation return to his fingertips, tingling, like life itself. With its return, his spirits began to rise.

'Do not be so foolish as to attempt any heroics, Doctor,' Sharif warned sharply. 'Look behind you. We are not alone.'

Love turned. The men who had brought him in were now standing, one on each side of the door. They wore soft-soled chaplis; he had not heard them enter. Each had a Kalashnikov slung around his neck, with a bandolier of cartridges over his shoulder. Love's spirits abruptly stopped rising.

Sharif handed the telex message to him. Love read: 'To Parkington, Midland Widows Insurance, Pink's Hotel, Peshawar. Copy to Hossein, Local Office, Sir Syed Road. Urgent and personal from Dr Jason Love. Have further closely examined Cord car over several hours. Car has fascinating and unique historical associations which have never been publicly revealed. These totally reinforce estimated value. Will inform you fully in writing when we meet. Pleased to confirm herewith that ten million pounds sterling under these most unusual circumstances is fair valuation for car's comprehensive insurance. Regards.'

'I am not signing that,' said Love, handing it back.

'As I have already told you, there is no need for you to do so. This message is going, and you are staying.'

'What are these associations?' asked Love mildly. Experience with hysterical patients had taught him the virtue of calmness in dealing with them.

'Let us consider rare cars in the context of their time,' said Sharif expansively. He had this English doctor beaten. Nothing Dr Love could say or do now could change the course of events. At such a moment of triumph, Sharif relished the unusual prospect of a — literally — captive audience.

'In 1935, Hitler was anxious to increase Nazi Germany's influence in the Middle East. Of course, he had his eyes on their oilfields in the event of war. The British were already

211

there, so were the Americans. Hitler therefore determined to stake his country's claim.

'In those days, monarchs were more powerful than any have been since. Hitler decided, as a first move, to ingratiate himself with King Ghazi of Iraq. He presented the king with a magnificent Mercedes 500K sports car. The body was specially built – the only one of its type in the world – by the illustrious Berlin firm of coach-builders, Erdmann and Rossi.

'Like the Cord, Doctor, the headlamps on this car were sunk into the front wings. It had outside exhaust pipes – again as on the Cord – and it was painted a special and unique metallic colour known as silver fish – which is also the colour of the Cord. The Mercedes was presented to the King of Iraq with all the dignity and ceremony that such a superb gift demanded.'

'And did it influence him towards the Nazis?'

'I have no doubt that it influenced the king personally, because everyone is flattered to receive an expensive gift on which so much care has been lavished – especially a rich and powerful man. And certainly Hitler's influence on Iraq was strong. Only a British occupation stopped it falling totally under Nazi domination.

'At the end of the Second World War,' Sharif went on, 'your Prime Minister, Mr Churchill, was also understandably eager to increase Britain's influence in the Middle East because of its oil production. With this in mind, he presented King Ibn Saud with a Rolls-Royce. Mr Churchill had hoped to make him the gift of a new car, as Hitler had done, but production then had not recommenced. However, a Rolls limousine built in 1937 and never sold, never even driven, was discovered in a showroom. The body was quickly removed, and Hooper, the Royal coach-builders, constructed an open tourer specially for the king.

'The rear compartment had an electric fan for the hot climate – there was no air-conditioning in cars then – a solid silver washbasin with silver-backed hairbrushes, crystal goblets and so forth.'

'A magnificent gift,' agreed Love in admiration: anything to keep the conversation going. His troubles could only worsen when Sharif stopped talking.

'Of course, Doctor,' said Sharif. 'As you say, magnificent. But, as so often with the English, insufficient study had been given to every aspect of the matter. The car was naturally right-hand drive – and no one had seen fit to explain that, for reasons of protocol, the King of Saudi Arabia would *never* sit to the left of a driver, but only on the right.

'You will recall that much the same mistake was made in the last century when, in an attempt to improve British relations with China, the British government of the day presented a coach to the Chinese Emperor – never realizing a basic fact, obvious to others, that the Emperor of China would *never* sit beneath an inferior person like a coachman! So as little benefit accrued from that early gift as from the Rolls-Royce a hundred years later. Some people – and you are one, Doctor – never learn.

'Now, the Cord that concerns you so much.'

Sharif paused; his mind was running ahead of his speech.

'Tell me, Doctor,' he asked, 'do you know what happened to the company that made it?'

Love nodded. Every *aficionado* knew how the Auburn-Cord-Duesenberg concern split up in the late 1930s. Errett Lobban Cord, the founder, had received kidnap threats against his children, so he decided to sell out. The Auburn side of the company eventually became American Kitchens; the Duesenberg plant went to a firm building trucks. Cord body dies were sold first to the Hupmobile car corporation in Detroit, who brought out the Skylark, based on them. Then they were resold to the Graham concern, who called their car the Hollywood. Neither was a success. Finally, the dies were sold to a firm in Russia.

Love knew how, at that time, the Soviet Union was eager

to cut costs and development time in building an indigenous motor industry. A Soviet trade delegation in the United States had bought body dies from other companies as well as Cord. A factory in Moscow then produced the ZIS based on General Motors and Packard designs. The initials stood for Zavod Imieni Stalina – Stalin Works.

The ZIS changed its name after Stalin's death to ZIL, the 'L' standing for Likhacheva, the former director of the plant who had pioneered the infant motor industry after the Russian revolution. Both cars were close copies of American designs, and intended for party officials and professional men.

'The Cord dies were delivered to a truck factory outside Leningrad set up to produce cars for Party officials,' Sharif went on. 'In fact, the car never went into production. The factory was destroyed by German bombing during the Second World War, after they had built only one car, and there the venture indeed might have ended, if it had not been for Stalin, who was determined to ingratiate himself with the ruler of Afghanistan.

'Russia, under the Tsars as well as the Communists, has always wanted to control that country. From Afghanistan, their plan has been – and is – to advance through Pakistan to the Indian Ocean, where, of course, they already maintain a very large naval presence. They seek, above all, a warm-water naval base.

'Stalin decided to copy the West and give a special car to the King of Afghanistan as a mark of *his* friendship. He did not choose the Russian ZIS, which was a dull vehicle, and decided to give the king a unique and beautiful car – but one made in Russia. There could never be another, and Stalin hoped that the king would appreciate the individuality of such a present. So on Stalin's personal order – which meant instant death to disobey – this first and last Russian built Cord was painted the same colour as Hitler's gift to the King of Iraq, and delivered to the Royal Palace in Kabul.'

'But it did not help Stalin to get his way?'

'Not to any great extent. In 1973, the king was in Italy for eye treatment, there was a coup and Soviet influence increased. When the Russians invaded the country, the royal garages were ransacked, and this car came into my possession.'

'How, exactly?'

'That, Doctor, is my business. I acquired it, shall we say, for services I had rendered to certain parties.

'I have kept the car here, awaiting the best moment to sell. I saw that interest in old cars is world-wide, and such vehicles fetch increasingly princely sums in the auction rooms of Christie's and Sotheby's and in the United States. Originally I set my sights at a million pounds. But as soon as prices rose, so did my valuation. The price is now ten million.'

'How did Dr Khan become involved?'

'She has lost her husband in Afghanistan. I made it my business to discover what I could about him, because I wished to use her. She is an American citizen and a medical practitioner, and on these two counts a more trustworthy person, surely, to sell a car in the West than someone like me, who has no such distinctions? And, of course, I will give her a contribution towards the refugees she appears so keen to help.'

'How much?'

'That again is my business.'

Love said nothing. He had been playing for time, and it seemed the game was all but over. It was difficult now to follow Sir Thomas Browne's advice: 'Let not Disappointment cause Despondency, nor Difficulty, Despair.'

Sharif's voice cut into these thoughts. 'I do not think you quite understand your position, Doctor,' he said. 'This ten million pounds is only a fraction of a much bigger negotiation which I am conducting and which also involves the Cord. As a goodwill gesture, the car now goes back to Kabul, but for insurance purposes, it will have disappeared.

Now we have talked long enough. I had hoped you would see sense, but you will not – or you cannot.'

He crossed the room, handed to one of the guards the pen pistol Love had taken from Professor Ahmed's jacket.

'This will be the manner of your death,' he told Love. 'There have been many accidents with these lethal toys. They are very dangerous.'

'So I had no hope of survival, even if I had signed the telex?' Love asked him.

'Correct. None. If you had signed and survived, then you could have repudiated your signature. Since you have refused to sign, you still could – if you lived – claim the message is a forgery. To use the quaint English expression, it is like a double-headed penny. You lose either way. And you have lost, Dr Love.'

The two guards manhandled Love out of the room into the courtyard. The truck in which he had travelled was still there; so was the Cord. Within hours, minutes maybe, it would be on its way to the border. But its fate was academic now; his was not. It was imminent.

The guards led him around the side of the house into a small walled yard. A thick brown blanket and two khaki vests hung from a clothes line. A wooden tub of soapy water stood in a corner. Rank weeds sprouted between cracks in the paving stones. A tethered goat warily watched them arrive.

The walls shielded this yard from all other eyes; it was an ideal place to stage a mortal accident. Sharif was clearly no amateur in these matters.

'In the far corner,' the guard ordered. Love walked slowly across the yard, feeling the sun warm on his back, his mind in a turmoil. Never had a day seemed brighter nor life more precious. There *must* be some way of escape. If only he could deflect the attention of one guard, he was certain he could deal with his companion. The prospect of impending death sharpened his awareness like steel on a carving knife. If only . . .

Love's scalp tingled at the realization that only paces away a man whose name he did not even know – would never know – was about to project him instantly into the endless, unmapped mists of eternity on the orders of a megalomaniac. Once again, the words of Sir Thomas Browne seemed apposite: 'Life itself is but the shadow of death, and souls departed but the shadows of the living.' Love had never been one for shadows: hot sunshine was more to his liking; death was altogether too dark, too permanent.

He thought of ducking as soon as he saw the guard about to fire. But that still left the second guard with his machine gun. The first might miss with his pen pistol; his companion would never miss with a gun that could fire five hundred rounds a minute.

'Stand where you are,' the guard ordered him. 'Now turn around.'

Love faced the two Pathans. His only hope now was to drop to his knees just before the man fired, and chance his luck that he could deal with his companion before he could aim his Kalashnikov. This was not a prospect on which he would offer any odds, but then, with his Presbyterian background, Love was not a betting man. If he failed, he would never have the chance to become one.

Slowly, from less than six feet away, the guard raised the pen pistol, holding it like a revolver, with both hands to keep it steady. A blind man could not miss at that distance, thought Love despairingly. He could see the tiny bright point of the bullet beneath the gold nib. Through narrowed eyes he watched the muscles in the man's hands tighten as he compressed the clip – and at once dropped down on all fours.

As though from a vast, almost immeasurable distance of time and space, Love heard a tiny *phffttt* like a bicycle tyre bursting far away.

The guard collapsed, spread-eagled in front of him. The pen pistol rolled out of his opened hand across the paving stones. The goat bleated madly as blood spouted from a wound in the guard's chest. Then Love remembered the plastic plug on the end of the pen: this weapon was lethal to the shooter, not to the person shot at. Could that have been what Ahmed had been desperately trying to tell him before he died? Not that it mattered now. What mattered was that he was back in with a chance.

The other guard stared at his colleague in horrified amazement – and in that second of distraction, Love jumped.

With all his strength, he drove his bunched knuckles up under this man's chin, felt the bone crack. The guard reeled away, lost his balance and fell, screaming in pain, tearing at his splintered jaw. Love seized his Kalashnikov and bandolier of spare ammunition, ripped them up over his head, then brought down the butt in the man's face. The screaming stopped.

Love tore the blanket from the line, wrapped it around his face and shoulders and then, holding the machine gun ready to fire, walked as casually as he could out of the courtyard. His flesh crawled with the expectation of a bullet in the back, but he had to force himself to walk. A running man would immediately arouse suspicion; a walker could pass by and be unremarked on.

Love calculated that no one would have heard the minute explosion of the pistol, or the screams of the second guard, but he could not be certain. He had a chance, he told himself. Not much of one, agreed, but if he lost this he would never have another.

He pushed the safety catch on the Kalashnikov to the firing position, then began to cross the main courtyard where the lorries were parked. As he did so, he saw – too late – the tiny unwinking glass eye of an intruder alert on a pole and cursed his folly in not anticipating such a hazard. He had escaped from one death trap into another.

Alarm bells clanged furiously on a wall above his head. Others began to peal along the perimeter fence; a siren wailed its warning.

Men who had been out of sight working on the trucks

now came running into the centre of the compound, spanners and crowbars in their hands. Love heard Sharif shout orders to them in some unintelligible tongue. Ahead, a man peered out cautiously from behind a bus, a revolver in his hand. Love fired a burst. The man dropped. Love started to run. Others held off for a moment, waiting for orders, for reinforcements, not quite sure what to do, and all uneager to risk a hail of fire from his Kalashnikov that could cut them to pieces.

Love raced towards the gateway – then saw that the gate, in its strong metal frame eighteen feet high, was closed and padlocked. He could not possibly escape that way. He was trapped in an electrified compound – surrounded by armed men.

All they need do was to wait until he tired or used up his ammunition – and then dispatch him or, worse, capture him alive. But, as Sir Thomas Browne had rightly declared on another occasion, 'obstinacy in a bad cause is but constancy in a good.' And to lose heart or determination now would be fatal.

Other guards were coming out of doors he had not previously noticed. He fired over their heads. He did not want to kill hirelings – unless they directly threatened him. His whole training had been to save life, not to take it, and now the life he wanted to save most urgently was his own.

Two men fired down at him from the roof. He fired back, this time aiming at them – and his gun jammed. He wrenched at the activator handle. It had seized solid – possibly a round had entered the breach at an angle. He could free it easily enough, given time, but he had no time.

Without a weapon, he would be shot or overwhelmed within seconds out in the open yard. Love dived back into the house, raced along a corridor. Surely there *must* be another way out somewhere – through a cellar, maybe a back door in the perimeter fence? As he ran, he heard a door slam behind him. He paused, turned. A steel safety door had slid from one wall to the other. He could not go back.

He could only go forward – to what, to whom? He carried the Kalashnikov like a club, approached a corner slowly, carefully now in case of an ambush.

As he turned the corner, a small plump man wearing a crumpled linen suit stepped out of a side door. In his hand he held a .38 Smith & Wesson aimed at Love's groin. Love guessed he was a professional who knew that a revolver bullet rises above its target. An amateur would have aimed at Love's heart or head – and if he fired could probably miss him altogether. No way could this fat man miss.

'Don't move, Dr Love,' he said now. His voice was surprisingly harsh for such a cheerful looking person, which made the incongruity all the more grotesque. 'Stand right where you are, and drop your gun.'

'I can blow you to pieces with it before you make first pressure on your trigger,' Love warned him.

'You can – when it works. But it's jammed. I saw you outside. Do not waste time on impossible threats. Throw your gun on the ground. *Now!*'

Love did so. The man kicked open the door behind him.

'Go in there,' he ordered, and followed Love into the room. He shut the door, locked it, pocketed the key.

'Keep your hands up, and don't try anything at all, or you're dead,' he said bluntly.

'I am unarmed,' Love replied. He felt the man's expert fingers run over his body, then the man moved away.

'Sit down,' he instructed, his voice less tense. Love obeyed. He was in a nightmare world, lost in the heart of an electrified maze, thick with armed guards out to shoot him on sight – and here he was sitting in a locked room while a total stranger held a gun aimed unwaveringly at him.

'Who the hell are you?' Love asked weakly.

'I have many names,' the plump man replied, as though this was a reasonable question and so deserved an equally reasonable answer.

'It depends who I am with, and where I am. But as we are talking here together, and since no one even knows you are with me, I will give you the name I like best. The go-between.'

PART NINE

At the crackle of gunfire, the two Russian scientists looked at each other across the table in the outer room. For years in Afghanistan they had grown accustomed to the sudden spasmodic chatter of machine-guns, the roar of an exploding missile that splintered the peace of moonless nights. But here in Pakistan they had not expected any firing; Pakistan was another country, in a safer, saner world.

Sergei, the smaller of the two men, crossed the room to a window, keeping well back, out of sight to those in the courtyard. He could see men running, guns in their hands. Some seemed to be running aimlessly, first in this direction, then in that, as chickens run when their heads are cut off. The only explanation must be that they were frantically searching for someone. He went to the door, unlocked it, looked out nervously into the corridor.

A guard came towards him.

'Do not be alarmed,' he said. 'There is an Englishman out there who has started to shoot. He will be apprehended.'

'But what is an Englishman doing here?' asked Volkov, the other scientist. 'What sort of Englishman is he?'

'He is a doctor, so I understand. A very dangerous man. Mr Sharif was questioning him, and suddenly he went mad.'

'Mad? You mean violent? Is he armed?'

'Now he is, yes. But he was not in the beginning,' the

guard explained. 'He is trying to run away. Of course, it is impossible to escape from here. There is an electric fence.'

'Maybe. But if he got in, he could get out, couldn't he?'

'That is so – but only through the main gate. And that is locked and guarded. Very soon he will be caught. You have my word. This is a safe place. Please be reassured.'

'But what is an English doctor doing here? We were not told any foreigner was here.'

'It is a private matter with Mr Sharif,' the guard explained nervously. 'You will have to ask him. This is none of my concern. I only wish to calm your fears.'

The implication was that the doctor's presence was none of the Russians' business, either, but both scientists felt alarm run like fire in their blood. However, explanations would have to wait. They had been sent here on a specific assignment of the highest priority and importance. All other matters must remain totally subordinate to this until they had conducted their tests and produced their report.

The scientists went back into their room, locked the door. On the table, spread out on a freshly laundered white sheet, because cleanliness was absolutely essential with equipment of this delicacy and accuracy, lay a small grey metal box. Wires of different colours protruded from it, and a copper rod as long and thin as a knitting needle trembled on a coiled spring. On one side was a square red plastic button, with a metal guard above it so that it could never be pressed by accident.

Sergei cleared his throat to conceal his nervousness.

'Are you satisfied?' he asked. Volkov nodded slowly, almost reluctantly, as though he still had doubts.

'The diagrams we already have match these circuits,' he said slowly. 'Everything seems to be in order, but . . .'

'But *what?*'

'We cannot say definitely that it works, until we see it working,' he said firmly. 'You know that. We must test it.'

'But how can you test it here?'

223

'We can send a sample test transmission. Very short. A second or two. No more.'

'Won't that be dangerous?'

'Not here. Who can pick it up here? We are miles from any Western listening post. You know that as well as I do.'

'What about the satellites? They pick up everything.'

'We know the times when they are due to pass overhead, so we can rule them out.'

He glanced at his watch.

'The next one is not due for nearly three hours,' he said, as though he was talking about a bus, a train. 'So the transmission will be over nearly a hundred and eighty minutes before it could be picked up. Isn't *that* a large enough safety margin for you?'

'If you feel it is an acceptable risk, we will have to take it,' said Sergei without conviction.

'It is more than acceptable, Comrade, it is *essential*. We cannot risk what would happen if we give this equipment clearance without testing it. Assume it does not perform as we are led to believe – and as we would have informed our superiors – think of our position then.'

'I am thinking.'

Sergei's blood slowed at the thought of what would happen if they were found wanting on this most secret mission.

This harmless looking box contained the heart of the West's most advanced electronic guardian. Every radar designed to track a target had the ability to listen only around the moment the echo from the target was expected. This system was known as 'gating'. Once selected, the target would be positioned in the centre of a range gate whose width would allow for every effect of range changes due to the speed of the target. This little box held the key to what the West called 'range gate stealing'. This occurred by retransmitting a duplicate of the true radar echo from the target at exactly the same time but at an increasing strength.

The controller would now introduce a carefully increased

delay before returning the false echo and the tracker would be totally deceived; the shell or missile would be sent off beam.

For some reason, Sergei suddenly thought of the body of the European traveller clad for centuries in its thick coat of ice. He had never known any corpse so cold, not even those that had been frozen deliberately for weeks before they were sent back for military funerals in Moscow. Now the chill of other mens' deaths touched his own heart.

Volkov had already opened a large metal box. From this, he took minute transformers, wires, an assortment of instruments. He worked quickly, methodically, his eyes magnified enormously through the pebble lenses of his glasses. He was probably the best man at this sort of thing in the Soviet Union, and that meant one of the three or four best in the world. In the United States, his qualifications and unique skills and sheer brilliance of intellect would have brought him princely rewards. In Leningrad, where he held a Chair of Electronic Science at the University, they had earned him a two room flat, a Moskvich car and a small dacha, the size of a tiny bungalow, on the Black Sea.

At last, everything was in place. Sergei looked at Volkov, eyebrows raised. Volkov nodded. Sergei switched on the power. Needles trembled on hair springs against black figures on white dials. A bank of computer screens displayed green images, a mass of moving figures, complicated graphs. Orange, blue and green lights pulsed and winked. A subdued sound of humming filled the room, a noise like a distant swarm of bees.

'We're ready,' he said, watching the screens closely. 'Make it as short as possible.'

Volkov did not reply. He was feeding data into a computer – time, date, temperature, altitude, expected wavelength. Then he pushed away the guard over the square red button, pressed down firmly with his thumb. Instantly, the coloured lights flicked off; a larger red light glowed like a single angry warning eye.

From loudspeakers a signal crackled like burning twigs. Volkov pressed the red button again and computer images shrank to tiny green pinpoints and died. The warning lights faded and went out.

'That was brief,' said Sergei with relief.

'One point eight five seconds.'

'You are satisfied, then?'

'I would have liked a longer test, but at least we do know that it works. And when we can decipher what is on the tapes and discs we will know exactly how well.'

He lit a bitter-tasting Pakistani cigarette, looked across the compound. All seemed quiet now. Men were lolling against the trucks, machine guns slung around their shoulders. They did not appear to be looking for anybody now; they could be off-duty – or waiting. But for whom or what? He guessed that the English doctor, whoever he was, had been found and dispatched. He had no quarrel with that. He felt totally unmoved by other people's deaths, their injuries and pain. Only when these things could in any way affect him did he feel disquiet. He was content to stay in the secret engine rooms of war and revolution, always out of the firing line.

And, of course, as both men knew from their own experience, those who knew when to take a cautious approach were much more likely to live longer than those who rushed ahead bravely – and sometimes blindly. Pioneers were often expendable, and as frequently discredited. Wiser ones waited, prudently keeping away from danger or contumely until they thought it safe to accept the glory and claim the rewards.

Lenin had realized this in words Volkov liked to quote: 'One step forward, two steps back . . . It happens in the lives of individuals and in the history of nations.' He was content to follow this philosophy wherever it might lead him.

Love faced the go-between, bewilderment showing in his face.

'What do you mean, a go-between?' he asked, his mouth dry with reaction. He felt almost unbearably weary, mentally and physically.

'I deal between people who need me, and can afford my services, paying in one way or another, not necessarily in money. Governments, politicians, businessmen from many countries, sometimes even yours. They find me obedient to their instructions.'

'So who are you working for now?'

'Primarily, Dr Love, as always, for myself. Survival is man's most important instinct. Certainly it is mine – for without survival what use is success?'

These questions and answers seemed bizarre, lines rewritten from Kafka, without any bearing on Love's own desperate situation. This man might be a lunatic, but he had a gun – and possibly, just possibly, he was not hostile. He had to humour him – as he had tried to humour Sharif.

'You will never get out of here unless someone helps you,' said the go-between simply, as though reading his thoughts. 'There is only one way out, through the main gate which is locked and bolted. The fence is charged with 10,000 volts. Everyone on Mr Sharif's staff is now looking for you, with orders to shoot you on sight as a dangerous intruder. Nor is this description altogether wrong. You have already shot one guard, and another has been found dead. You cannot look for mercy or leniency. And even if you did, you would not find them.

'I am the only person who can – *possibly* – help you to escape and survive. Nothing guaranteed, Doctor, you appreciate. Nothing is ever certain in this life – only that one day we are all required to leave it. And this departure I may be able to postpone for you. On strict conditions.'

'What are they? I am not in a position to drive a bargain.'

The go-between allowed himself a small smile. He put away his revolver in a shoulder holster.

'You see, Doctor,' he said, 'I trust you. To a limited degree, that is, for trust does not come easily to me. I must therefore warn you, I have a remote control button in my jacket pocket. The slightest pressure on it from my arm will bring everyone running – *here*. Now that I hope we understand each other, to business. First, you *are* a doctor of medicine, I assume, and not of music, literature, history or philosophy, or of some other esoteric subject?'

'No, medicine, first and only. Why? Don't tell me you have a health problem?'

'We all have health problems, Doctor. We are dying before we are born. I am not concerned with my personal health, but I have a daughter who is unwell.'

'Look, I can't treat her now,' cried Love desperately.

'I'm not asking you to. She is, in fact, at this moment in a clinic in London. Money is no object for me, but so far as her treatment is concerned, I must know I am not wasting it. I want her to have the best specialists in the world to treat her condition.'

'Which is?'

'I am not proud to have to tell you she is a heroin addict.'

'That is serious,' Love admitted. 'But there are several people I know who report progress with even the most desperate cases. Patients of whom other specialists have despaired.'

'So I believe. And I want to find them. *Now.*'

'Can't her doctors in London help?'

'Probably. But I do not know them. I have not met them or spoken to them as I am speaking to you. Nor are they beholden to me as you are, Doctor. I give them money. I can give you your life – if *you* find the best specialist for her, the best treatment.'

'How can I possibly do that here?'

'I will get you out of here. But first, I must have your word to honour your part of the deal.'

'You have it here and now. If I do escape, we can meet in Peshawar or London, anywhere. Then I can give you introductions. But I cannot promise miracles.'

228

'Only God has that gift,' replied the go-between. 'I was brought up a Catholic.'

For a moment, he recalled his childhood in Central Europe, in a country long since swallowed by neighbours, its name only now appearing on old maps. Once more, he heard the Angelus, saw the candles burning on the altar, smelled the sweet, reassuring scent of incense as the priest intoned the ancient Latin words.

How simple life had appeared then, how full of promise had seemed the future – and how terrible the reality! And how far he had wandered from the true faith. Perhaps his daughter's illness was a judgement on him and his ways? Or was this simply superstition?

'So,' he said, dismissing such uneasy remembrances of lost peace and certainty. 'We are agreed.'

He held out his hand. Love shook it.

'I am putting my faith in you, Doctor,' the go-between added. 'But in case you should think of double-crossing me, remember, I know many people who owe me important favours. In such an ill-advised situation, you would not live to old age. You understand me?'

'Perfectly. But I never go back on my word.'

The go-between opened a wall cupboard, took out a Pathan hat made of brown fustian.

'Put that on and drape the blanket right around your head as well as your shoulders. Cover your face and you will come with me, as my driver, my bodyguard. Do not look up and, above all, do not speak to anybody.

'If anyone addresses you, I will answer. And do not let anyone see your eyes. They are blue. Stay close, and if I give an order, do *exactly* what I say, when I say it. No argument or hanging back. One false move and no one can save you. Remember that.'

'I don't need reminding.'

'Then we will leave.'

Love followed the go-between along the corridor, out into the courtyard. The sun felt warm through the blanket, which smelled slightly of camphor. He kept his head down so that no one could see his face as they walked across the yard, past the trucks, to a black Mercedes. A driver was sheltering from the sun in the shadow of a bus. The go-between spoke rapidly to him. The man nodded, gave a gesture of salute, began to walk to the house. He did not look back.

The go-between motioned to Love to climb in behind the wheel, while he opened a rear door.

'Now, start the engine.'

The air-conditioning system hummed. The car moved forward. A guard opened the gates and saluted smartly as they drove through and out on to the main road.

'You're staying at Pink's,' said the go-between as they approached Peshawar.

'How did you know?'

'It is my livelihood to know such things.'

Love stopped the car outside the hotel.

'Come into my room,' he said. 'I will put a call through to London to someone who may be able to help your daughter.'

'Already?'

The go-between looked surprised and pleased.

'If you pay for the call – already.'

They went into Love's room. Love looked through his address book for the number of the specialist he sought, a contemporary at Oxford and Bart's. He dialled the number and waited impatiently. Sighs and whispers and clicks and electronic bleeps spoke into his ear as circuits opened and closed half-way across the world. Then a bell trilled discreetly. A voice – Roedean and the London College of Secretaries – announced: 'Sir Richard Guthrie's office. Can I help you?'

'I hope so,' said Love. 'Can you hear me?'

'Perfectly. Where are you?'

'In Peshawar, Pakistan. Dr Jason Love. A part-social, part-professional call to my old friend, Sir Richard. Is he available?'

230

'He is with a patient, Doctor. Can we ring you back?'

'That is possible, but I think it unlikely that you will get through. It is only by the grace of God that I have reached you so quickly now. Please apologize to Sir Richard, but explain that if I could have a word with him before we're cut off altogether, I would appreciate it very greatly.'

'Please hold on.'

Minutes passed. More beeps, ticks, whirrs from unknown electronic instruments processing the call. Then he heard Guthrie's voice, in his bluff, breezy doctor-to-doctor way. The tones he reserved for patients were altogether more serious; after all, huge fees were then involved.

'Jason, my old sport! What are you doing in Pakistan? Opening a British takeaway? Tea and chips all round?'

'Just trying to stay out of trouble,' Love replied. 'And not succeeding too well. But that's not why I am calling you. I have with me a gentleman who has just saved my life, so I owe him a favour. He has a daughter, a heroin addict, in a London hospital. He would like an independent opinion on her condition and the best available treatment, either in England or the States, cost to be absolutely immaterial. Can you help him, his daughter, me, and, of course, yourself?'

'I will do my best,' said Sir Richard cautiously. 'Let me have the patient's name and the clinic.'

Love handed the telephone to the go-between.

'Speak to Sir Richard yourself.'

'I am much indebted to you, sir,' said the go-between, suddenly not so confident, just another father wanting advice. 'What Dr Love here has told you is quite right. Money is of absolutely no consequence. I hope you hear me right, sir?'

'Perfectly,' said the specialist quickly. 'Perfectly. Keep talking.'

The go-between gave him the name of the clinic where his daughter was a patient, the name under which she had been admitted, and the names of the specialists treating her. When the conversation was over, he replaced the receiver and for a moment turned away, but not before Love saw that his eyes were unexpectedly moist with tears.

'Doctor,' he said at last, his voice hoarse with emotion, 'when I first saw you in Sharif's house, I *thought* that you looked honest. You have more than repaid your debt to me, but you may still need help out here. Sharif is not a man to antagonize unnecessarily.'

'I had no wish to do so, necessarily or unnecessarily. I came here to value an old car, which Sharif tells me is his property, a fact I did not even know until today.'

'That is a car I would advise you to leave alone, Doctor. In itself, it may only appear to be an engine, a body and four wheels. But it is also a symbol, and more important, it . . .'

The go-between paused for a moment, as though realizing he might give too much away. Then he shrugged his shoulders.

'Let me just say that it means a lot to a number of important people,' he said briefly. 'A great deal. Odd we should meet as we did. I was going to visit you here, but you arrived at Sharif's house, albeit unwillingly, and so saved me the trouble. Such things may be fate, chance – or the work of Providence. Another word for God. There are many things we do not know about such matters.'

The go-between took out a blank card. He wrote down an unusually long telephone number, handed the card to Love.

'Should you be in any trouble, I mean *real* trouble, Doctor, not the troubles we all experience every day but, as you medical people sometimes say, a matter of life and death, telephone that number.'

'If I was in that situation, I might not be able to do so.'

'Then get someone to telephone *before* you approach that situation.'

'Who shall I ask for?'

'I have not given you a name,' said the go-between, 'because, as your poet said, what's in a name? I have as many names as Mr Sharif. So do plenty of people with

232

whom I deal. But give your name and your call will be answered, and if it is within our power, it will be acted upon. And when I come to England, I will call on you. We will find your address in the Medical Register.'

Love noted the lapse into the royal or editorial plural, watched the go-between's Mercedes drive away. Then he went back into the bedroom, poured himself a vodka, drank it.

He had escaped from Sharif, but only temporarily. Sharif had money and power and political muscle; as the go-between had hinted, he was not a man to accept such a setback. It could only be a matter of very little time before Sharif came after him. He believed Love knew too much, and so could be dangerous to him. Whereas, as Love admitted ruefully to himself as he poured another drink, the truth was that he knew too little about Sharif and the Cord; in fact, he knew almost nothing at all.

MacGillivray had intended to leave the office early that evening; it was his wedding anniversary and he had promised his wife a modest celebration. They would go to the theatre, have dinner at his club, and then take a taxi back to their flat off the Brompton Road. Here, as on every previous anniversary evening, they would look through old photograph albums together.

Yellowing sepia pictures showed MacGillivray as a lieutenant, a captain, a major, with his wife, in various outposts of a vanished empire: Rangoon, Lahore, Aden. In their wedding photograph they looked absurdly young and pleased with themselves outside St John's Church in Calcutta. The MacGillivrays posed in tennis clothes in the grounds of the Galle Face Hotel in Ceylon (even that country's name had changed now); with naval friends on the beach near Kota Bharu on the east coast of Malaya, now Malaysia.

Every picture carried poignant memories. Only weeks after the beach photograph was taken during the Second

World War, the Japanese landed in Kota Bharu. Their advance troops set off a trip wire which exploded a defensive mine buried in the sand. The defenders thought that this had been activated by cattle grazing nearby, as had happened on other occasions. Presumption took the place of proof – with calamitous results: the fall of Singapore and the opening of the Empire's arteries, as centuries of white supremacy in the East began to bleed away.

MacGillivray, brandy in hand, always found something soothing and reassuring about these old photos. The faces that stared out of the fading prints seemed somehow more straightforward and, in an odd sense, innocent, than the plump discontented faces he saw every day in the Strand, Whitehall, Piccadilly. People now expected so much more – demanded so much more – not only out of life, but from their marriages, children and possessions, and dissatisfaction, as desire outran performance, showed increasingly in their faces. They talked continually about their rights, but in the last analysis, everyone possessed only one right: the right to die. Did they wish to exercise that right sooner or later?

MacGillivray locked his desk, and was putting the keys into his pocket before switching on the room's electronic surveillance system, when his deputy hurried in to see him. He held a sealed folder.

'So glad to catch you,' he said breathlessly. 'I heard you were leaving early. This has just come in from CIA Liaison.'

'What luck,' MacGillivray said ironically. Why was it that, so often, when he wished to leave the office, not early, as his deputy assumed, but actually on time, instead of hours late, something inevitably arrived to delay him?

'One of their AWAC aircraft has picked up a signal near the Pakistan border with Afghanistan.'

'What sort of signal?'

'An unidentified transmission.'

Why could the man not come to the point quickly? He

loved long convoluted sentences, would always prefer to say, 'It is known by me,' rather than 'I know'.

'Well, although they can pinpoint the area fairly accurately, it is a transmission of a kind they have never encountered before. They have put it through every computer and so on, for comparison and evaluation, but it just doesn't add up.'

'Is it in speech? In clear? Signals?'

'A mass of electronic chatter. A very short burst. Barely two seconds.'

'What has this got to do with us, then? How can we help? If they don't know the answer, how can we?'

'Well, it *is* our area, sir. We have responsibility for it. And we do have someone out there.'

'A part-time man, Parkington,' MacGillivray confirmed. 'And a country doctor who has worked for us once or twice in a roundabout way. He's out there to value an old car, of all things. The Americans probably have a hundred full-time operatives on the ground.'

'I agree our establishment is rather depleted in that area, sir. Actually, I had not realized just how drastically.'

'Well, you do now.'

'Even so, sir, I think you should alert him – them.'

'Why? Is there a report as well?'

'Yes. A brief one. More of conjecture than hard facts. But I think you should read it.'

'Why didn't you tell me this at the beginning?'

'I was coming round to it, sir.'

'Well, let's see the damn thing.'

MacGillivray put on his half glasses, read the single typed sheet.

'I see what you mean,' he said slowly. 'Make a signal to Parkington. Most immediate. How are we contacting him, by the way?'

'In a rather unusual and roundabout way through the insurance company that employs him. The Midland Widows.'

'I know them well. They refused a burst pipe claim I made on my flat last year. I hope they are more accommodating here.'

The deputy forced a dutiful smile.

'You were on your way out, sir,' he said, as though he had forgotten. 'Shall I sign the signal for you?'

'No. Get it coded, and I'll sign it.'

MacGillivray's anniversary was a private matter, but this cable could be of national concern. Once more, duty had overruled and overridden his personal feelings. His contemporaries of long ago would have approved his strict order of priorities. That writer fellow, L. P. Hartley, had been quite right: the past *was* another country, and they did things differently there. And a bloody sight better, too, MacGillivray thought, as he lit a cigar and wondered whether he could reach the theatre before the second act.

An overweight, red-faced man in a crumpled lightweight grey suit jumped out of his Range Rover outside Pink's Hotel, went up to the Reception Desk. His bulk made him seem middle-aged, but he was actually in his thirties. By the time he was forty, if he lived that long, he would be an old man.

'You have a Dr Love staying here?' he asked the clerk, making the question sound like a command.

'I would like to see him.'

The effort of walking had made him perspire; he mopped his forehead with a yellow silk square.

'I will ring his room, sir.'

Jason Love came out to the Reception Desk, introduced himself. The fat man said: 'We can't talk here. All these damned people have ears as long as your arm. What about your room?'

'What have we to talk about?' Love asked him bluntly.

'A young woman.'

'What young woman? Do you want me to treat her or something?'

'No. She came to see you the other night. She was going to marry some poor devil who was killed in his rickshaw. One of these goddamned idiot drivers you get round here, charging about, going against the traffic.'

'Oh, yes. Mrs Lambourn.'

'Right,' said the fat man. 'Well, she's gone.'

'What do you mean, *gone*? Gone out of her mind, out of her home? Please explain yourself. You appear to be under some tension.'

'So would you be. Wife going crazy because she's gone. Kids screaming their heads off. She was a sort of nurse to our two. My lady wife went in to see why she hadn't bathed them tonight – and she wasn't in her room.'

'You're the engineer?' asked Love.

'Yes, yes, I'm the engineer. She told you that, did she?'

'Yes. How did you know I was here?'

'She had written on a bit of paper: Dr Love. Pinks. So I thought I would come round and see you in case you knew where she's off to.'

'I have no idea. But is there anything sinister about her not being in her room? Perhaps she has just gone down to the shops, or something?'

'No way. People out here don't just go down to the shops. They take a car, a taxi, or they send a servant, more like. It is too far to walk, and too hot. Anyhow, it's not done. Her clothes have gone, too. Her suitcases. She's cleared out. Done a bunk, lock, stock and barrel.'

'Cleared out? You're sure? Not left you a message, a note?'

'Nothing,' said the engineer grimly. 'That's why I came round here. I wondered if you knew anything.'

'Absolutely nothing. We had a brief chat and she left. Back to you, I thought.'

'Well, you thought wrong. She's gone, I tell you. What do you think I should do, Doctor? Tell the Embassy? She's taken every single thing she owned. The room is cleaned out.'

237

'Except for one piece of paper with my name and address on it. Sounds odd.'

'Why odd?'

'Doesn't it seem strange to you?'

'Can't say so.'

'Were there any other names on the paper? Any other messages, notes, things she should have bought, telephone calls she's had, or wanted to make?'

'No, nothing.'

Love nodded.

'So in my view she left a note knowing you would come round to see me at once. But why?'

What could Ruth Lambourn gain by that? What could he lose by that?

'If I hear anything,' Love said, 'I'll tell you. Let me have your address.'

The man handed him a card. Love put it in his pocket, wished him good-day, watched him stride importantly across the tarmac, climb into the Range Rover. He wondered where Mrs Lambourn was now. And whether she had left of her own free will – or whether others had insisted she leave, perhaps against her wishes.

He crossed the lawn, knocked on Parkington's door. A key turned in the lock. Parkington let him in, locked the door behind him. Stevie was sitting in an easy chair, a whisky in a toothglass on the table. Love felt a sudden – and, he assured himself – totally irrational twinge of jealousy at seeing her there. She looked pale and unhappy.

'You saved us a journey,' said Parkington. 'We were coming out to rescue you.'

'I rescued myself – with a little bit of help,' said Love. He explained about the go-between, and told them about Mrs Lambourn's disappearance.

'What's Sharif doing?' asked Stevie.

'Nothing, so far as I know,' said Love, 'but I can think of a lot I'd like to happen to him if I had any say in the matter.'

238

'I can give you a say,' said Parkington. 'We're going to see him. All of us.'

'But why?'

'Better to go back to him than wait until he comes to see us. Or you in particular.'

'I'm not so sure,' said Love slowly.

'Nor am I,' said Parkington. 'Not entirely. But we've got to do it. Attack is always the best defence.'

He pushed a piece of paper across the table. Love read: 'FOR PARKINGTON MIDLAND WIDOWS CARE PINKS PESHAWAR STOP EX-HEAD OFFICE LONDON WE SERIOUSLY CONCERNED OVER CONTINUED DOWNTURN BUSINESS OPPORTUNITIES INDO-PAKISTAN AREA STOP SUGGEST YOU IMPLEMENT POSSIBILITIES ALREADY SENT TO YOU REGARDING LIFE COVER IN KARACHI BOMBAY DELHI STOP PLEASE KEEP HEAD OFFICE FULLY INFORMED YOUR MOVEMENTS AND PREMIUM RATES BEING CHARGED STOP'

'Means bugger-all to me,' said Love inelegantly.

'Not too much to me, either,' agreed Parkington, 'until it is decoded. Then it makes a lot more sense.'

'Like what sense?'

'Like this.' He picked up another sheet of paper, read out the pencilled writing. 'An early warning aircraft on a routine flight has picked up an unidentified radar transmission from map reference 34 55N 71 20E. The transmission was compressed, and lasted one point eight five seconds precisely from a hitherto unknown and untraced transmitter. MacGillivray wants me to check it out. Now *Ek dum*, as they say out here. So, obedient as ever to his instructions, that is what I must do. And I need you to help me.'

Parkington unfolded an ordnance map, moved a plastic ruler across its glossy surface.

'This is the map reference, about thirty miles north west of Darra.'

'The transmission seems to be coming from Sharif's house,' said Love.

'Exactly. Now you understand why we've got to see him.'

'He's not going to tell us who's transmitting – or what or why?'

'Depends on how we ask him,' said Parkington.

'And you're coming?' Love asked Stevie.

'I know the area. I also know the language. That could be useful.'

'I can think of almost anything I'd rather do than this,' said Love. 'When you're under sentence of death, as Doctor Johnson says, it concentrates the mind wonderfully. Or as Sir Thomas Browne put it, "The long habit of living indisposeth us for dying." I am not disposed to die just yet. I have no intention of going back. I came out here to examine an old car. I've examined it. I've told you it is not worth what the vendor says it is worth. That is the end of my job. Over and out.'

'Over and in,' retorted Parkington. 'It's not the end. It's barely the beginning. You can't refuse a challenge.'

'Try me.'

'I am. That's my answer. And yours,' said Parkington firmly. 'Come on. We've not got all day or night. If we hang about much longer, Sharif will be here to see us. And that, we all agreed, would be very bad news. Maybe fatal news. Let's be on our way.'

They heard a timid knock at the door. Love opened it. Hossein was standing outside.

'I am very sorry, sir,' he said sheepishly. 'I would not like you to think badly of me, by not staying with you.'

'I never think badly of anyone,' Love told him magnanimously, and not altogether accurately.

'When I saw there was a lot of trouble, I realized I could do more to help if I myself were not also captured.'

'You realized no such bloody thing,' said Parkington shortly, coming up behind him. 'You wanted to save your own skin and whatever other parts of your anatomy you value.'

'Please, Mr Parkington, I am a married man. I have others to consider. I am not like you, sir, a single person. And I wish to rise in the company. Teamwork is the Theme. We are all Links in a Chain. If I can help you in any way, I wish to do so.'

'I can tell you what you can do,' said Parkington. 'We are going back to see Sharif.'

'*We*, sir?'

'You are driving us.'

'I have a very busy schedule here,' said Hossein nervously.

'Listen,' replied Parkington, 'you won't have any schedule at all, unless you drive us. The Midland Widows will make other arrangements. Do I make myself clear?'

'Abundantly, sir.'

'I would like you also to arrange something else for us,' Love told him, feeling rather sorry for the man. 'I want you to hire a truck the same colour as the one we followed. Don't bother about a driver. I'll drive.'

'I can do that, willingly.'

'Good. I saw a café on the road, beyond a level crossing, decorated with lots of green flags. Arrange for us to pick up the truck there late this afternoon.'

'You have a plan of Sharif's place?' Parkington asked Hossein.

'We insure the house, sir. I have a plan of the building, with positions of fire extinguishers, floodlights and burglar alarms.'

Hossein spread out a shiny, folded sheet of paper on the table.

'The fence is electrified, ten thousand volts. Death to touch,' said Parkington, reading notes on the plan.

'We can short that easily enough,' Love pointed out.

'Possibly,' Hossein agreed. 'But that would immediately set off the alarm.'

'How is power taken to the alarm system?'

'By an armoured underground cable in case overhead lines should be damaged. There are also storage batteries to keep lights and alarms in operation for twenty-four hours.'

'So it doesn't really help us to cut the wires?' asked Love.

'Not at all helpful,' said Hossein.

'So how can we silence the alarms? Every weapon has an antidote. As an old character I like quoting put it: "In venomous waters, something may be amiable. Poisons afford antipoisons."'

'Not in this situation,' Hossein assured them.

'Thomas Browne, you should be living at this hour,' said Parkington drily. 'What's the best way in, then?'

'There is only one way – through the front gate. But that, as you saw, Doctor, is eighteen feet high and locked, bolted and guarded.'

They looked at the plan for a moment, then Love spoke.

'Here's what I suggest we do,' he said. 'We have registration plates made up with the number of the truck that carried the Cord. Then we put them on our hired truck, and drive up to the gate. The guard opens it, lets us in – and the rest is up to us.'

'*Will* they let us in?' asked Stevie dubiously.

'Who can say?' replied Love. 'The answer is written on the wind.'

'And the wind cannot read,' added Parkington.

'Agreed. But the guards can. And there is a precedent for this. During the Russian Revolution, the Tsar's loyal troops shot all kinds of people who arrived at the palace wishing to help the Tsar and his family. They showed passes and letters and laissez-faires, you name it, and *still* the guards shot them. The reason was that the Tsar's guards could neither read nor write. They had been told that *anyone* not wearing uniforms like theirs was a traitor and should be shot on sight. I'm gambling that Sharif's guards will have a list of their truck numbers.'

Parkington sat in the front of Hossein's car, Love and Stevie in the rear. Love had bought two sets of Pathan clothes, the kemize or thick shirt, tweed jackets and pantaloons for Parkington and himself, with round pillbox hats made from long woven tubes of khaki cloth that could be pulled down to conceal their faces. Steve wore her husband's clothes of similar style and pattern. None of them spoke until they reached the outskirts of Darra. Then Love tapped Hossein on the shoulder.

'We will need three flak jackets,' he told them. 'Who makes them here?'

'I know just the place, sir. He is a distant relation.'

'Then get close to him.'

They turned off the main road, parked in an alley. Goats rooted in piles of rubbish, and when Hossein switched off the engine, Love could hear an insistent whine of electric drills as armourers fashioned weapons in their open-fronted booths. From the background came a constant rattle and crackle of gunfire as others tested the newly-made guns, firing at targets in the foothills. The air felt thick with the smell of cordite and boiling oil used to blue rifle barrels.

Hossein was away from the car for barely ten minutes and returned carrying three jackets. They put them on under their coats.

'There is not one for me,' Hossein complained.

'You won't need it,' said Love. 'As soon as we collect the truck, you can go back to watch over the interests of the Midland Widows – and your schedule.'

He turned to Stevie, handed her the card with the go-between's telephone number, explained why he had given it to Love.

'You have your mobile phone with you?'

She nodded.

'Then, if things get too bad, give him a bell. Mention my name. He might just be able to do something. Or again he might not. Only time will tell.'

'Old Father Time hasn't been too communicative so far,' retorted Stevie with a wry grin.

'Well, give him this chance,' Love told her.

Five miles further on they stopped outside the café with the green flags. Half a dozen trucks were parked off the road. Their drivers sat on benches at trestle tables drinking mugs of unsweetened green tea. Most had a Kalashnikov slung around one shoulder, with bandoliers of ammunition; others wore revolvers in open webbing holsters on their belts. The sun glittered harshly on the sheets of hammered polished tin that decorated the sides of each truck. Their crude, brightly coloured paintings of peacocks, tigers, lions, serpents, which Love had thought so unusual when he first arrived in Pakistan, he now accepted as part of the scenery. One could get used to anything, he thought, excepting the possibility of violent death. Everyone believed that such an event could never concern them – until it was too late.

They sat down on a bench warmed by the afternoon sun, ordered four mugs of tea. They did not wish to give any impression of urgency; Sharif might have an informer in the café. After tea, Hossein took them to the truck he had hired, and then drove off thankfully back to Peshawar.

Love climbed in behind the wheel of the truck. There was no ignition key, not even a switch, only two bright, bare-ended wires.

These sparked as he tied them together to fire up the engine. The silencer had split; the noise sounded like constant gunfire under their feet. Stevie climbed up next to him, then Parkington, and they set off.

Half a mile up the road, Love pulled in to one side, unscrewed the truck's number plates and replaced them with the ones ordered in Peshawar. Parkington passed over the automatic he had taken from Ahmed's killer. Love slipped it into his jacket pocket. Stevie already had a gun that had belonged to her husband.

'I hope you won't have to use it,' said Love. 'As doctors, we should be saving life, not taking it.'

He raised the truck's bonnet. As he had expected, the engine was thick with oil and dust from the road. They ran the tips of their fingers through this, then rubbed the oily grit on their faces to darken them. If they reached Sharif's house at dusk, they might just pass for Pakistanis.

They climbed back into the cab, drove on slowly. The

steering was heavy and the brake shoes had worn down to the rivets. It would be madness to risk an accident – and not easy to avoid one in the chaotic traffic. Buses and other trucks crammed with people, livestock, and huge amorphous bundles sewn into canvas covers, overtook them with an impatient blare of horns. Others cut in, cut out, stopped abruptly for unknown reasons in the centre of the road. Dusk was falling; soon it would be dark. Shadows began to stretch out towards them from the foothills. In the weak yellow glow of their headlamps, Love swerved to avoid tongas, cyclists, all travelling trustingly, without lights.

To one side of the road, he saw a flickering of oil lamps. A generator lit the sign he had noticed earlier: English Pure Honey. Love pulled off the road, cut his engine.

Parkington looked at him enquiringly.

'An idea,' Love explained. 'This man is selling honey. I'm going to see if he'll sell the bees.'

'Are you mad?' Parkington asked him incredulously.

'Medical statistics prove one in every three people can be. Maybe I'm the one out of us three.'

Love approached the honey vendor, who was stacking the lemonade bottles full of honey into the back of a pick-up; there would be no customers along this road after dark.

'Salaam,' the man said. 'You wish pure honey? From English bees?'

'Aleikum, salaam,' Love replied. 'I don't want to buy the honey, but the bees.'

'They are my livelihood,' the man replied with quiet dignity.

'I will pay you accordingly,' said Love.

The man's face brightened.

'How many hives – and how much?' he asked briskly.

They did a deal for two hives, carried them to the back of the truck, which was littered with chains, coils of rope, pieces of wood to act as wedges for unwieldy loads.

Love tied the two hives tightly together by their legs and then fixed one end of a long rope around the front legs.

'What's the idea?' Parkington asked him.

'I hope we never find out,' Love said grimly, and climbed up behind the wheel.

Minutes ahead, they saw a red light winking on a distant roof, a warning to low flying aircraft.

'We're here,' said Love. 'Fasten your seat belts.'

'We haven't got any,' said Parkington.

'Then go through the motions.'

He turned to Stevie.

'Keep right down out of sight, in case there's a reception committee. No need to tell them you are here – yet.'

He felt unusually protective towards Stevie and wished to minimize any danger to her. She slid sideways and crouched, gun in hand, beneath the dashboard on the floor between them.

Love turned off the road towards the high wire fence. He and Parkington unrolled their hats down to shield their faces – just in time, because as they approached the gate, floodlights on poles, unmarked on Hossein's plan, suddenly dazzled them.

Love lowered his window, keeping his head in shadow. A guard unslung his automatic rifle, checked the truck's number plate against a list of numbers clipped to a board, waved them inside, and bolted the gate behind them.

Their headlamps raked several vehicles parked side by side. Through gaps in the woodwork of one truck, Love glimpsed the Cord's silvery paintwork. He felt relief that it was still there. Now – to get it out.

Love parked next to this truck, pulled apart the ignition wires to stop the engine. The guard had his back to them; he was fixing a padlock and chain to the gate. Love and Parkington jumped down.

As Love passed the tailgate, he released its catches and casually threw the end of the rope from the beehives over the top. Love then swung himself up behind the wheel of the vehicle containing the Cord.

So far so easy – but not far enough.

A guard was lying asleep across the bench seat of the truck. He had a Kalashnikov slung across his body.

When Love jumped into the cab, the guard awoke with a great shout of alarm. As he swung himself upright, Parkington wrenched open the other door of the cab, gripped the sling of the man's weapon, heaved him out. He fell heavily on the concrete – and as he fell, he fired. Bullets sprayed the swinging door, burst the truck's front tyre.

Their only hope now was to manhandle the Cord out before anyone raised a general alarm. But the car was at least five feet off the ground, and already other men, alerted by the sudden burst of fire, were running towards them to see what had happened. And then the whole dark compound erupted into a blaze of brilliant light.

Under these unexpected floodlights, Love saw a ramp up which cars and trucks could be driven for servicing. This took the form of two separate stone slopes, level on top. In the space between them, a mechanic could stand while draining oil from an engine or gearbox. If Love could back the truck right up against the top of this ramp, they could then roll the Cord out and down the slope.

'Grab that rope!' he shouted to Parkington. He fired up the engine and reversed the truck wildly. Parkington, in the front seat, held on to the rope attached to the beehives. As the rope tightened, the tailgate of the truck in which they had arrived swung down with a clatter. The hives jerked backwards at the end of the rope and crashed on the concrete with a great splintering of wood. Tiers split. The wax frames and honeycomb inside fell in an untidy heap – and two great black clouds of swarming, furious bees rose into the air. Guards fled in every direction to avoid them.

Parkington let go of the rope and jumped down as Love backed up against the stone ramps. They ran to the rear of the truck, undid the chains, lowered the tailgate.

Love leaped into the Cord's driving seat, switched on the ignition. The engine fired instantly. He slammed in the electric gear selector, reversed across the level part and down the ramp into the yard. Parkington jumped in beside him. Love swung the steering wheel around – and saw that two armed guards at the gate stood with their machine-guns trained on them. Love guessed that the Cord's gearbox, radiator and eight cylinder engine block would give protection against anything they could fire – so long as they kept their heads down. He let in the clutch fiercely, meaning to charge the gate and trust to the Cord's sheer weight and power to burst it open.

Then Love felt a cold metal circle, the size of a wedding ring, press hard into his right temple.

He turned.

Sharif was holding the muzzle of a .45 Webley against his skull.

'Switch off the engine and get out,' he ordered Love. 'Now. Or I blow your head off.'

Parkington was already being manhandled out of the other side of the car. Someone seized his revolver, and began to wave it excitedly. A guard frisked Love, found the automatic, removed it. More armed guards now surrounded the two men who looked over their shoulders, frantically searching the compound for Stevie. What had happened to her? Was she still in the truck? Or had she also been dragged out, and taken away by this shouting, angry crowd?

A guard looped a rope around Love's neck; another twisted both his arms behind him, tied his wrists tightly with the same rope so that he could not bend forwards without choking. Then, having trussed him in this way, the guards led him and Parkington across the concrete, cold and bleak beneath the lights, bees still swarming overhead, into the house – and the room where he had previously met Sharif.

'We were leaving,' Sharif told him now. 'But since you appear so eager to come back, Dr Love, you will both stay here. For ever.'

'Meaning what exactly?' Love asked him, playing for time. There seemed nothing else to play for now.

'There will be a fire after we leave. It will destroy this house – and you with it.'

'You're mad,' Love told him.

'Not as mad and stupid as you have been,' said a girl, her voice sharp with contempt and hatred. Love turned slowly, painfully towards her, recognizing the voice.

Ruth Lambourn was standing in the doorway. She spat in his face.

'You thought you were smart, Doctor,' she said.

'And you?' he asked her.

Whose side was she on – theirs or Sharif's? For a moment, optimism surged. Could this be a rescue attempt in disguise? The idea was infinitely encouraging – but to judge from her attitude, it seemed too heavily disguised.

'When I worked for your ridiculous housekeeper, Mrs Hunter, at Bishop's Coombe, I hated you.'

'Why?'

'Because you seemed to have everything. Money, profession, status. And you never even noticed me.'

'I noticed you,' said Love. 'So did Mrs Hunter.'

How many times had he listened to Mrs Hunter's criticism of Ruth's slipshod work, her frequent mistakes, the lists of things she broke. And as many times, he had spoken up for the girl, explaining she was young, she would learn. Now – this. But then, whenever you helped a lame dog over a stile, you must expect to be bitten.

'When I saw you in Peshawar and told you about that pathetic creep, Erasmus Glover, you believed everything,' she went on.

'Not quite,' Love corrected her. 'I've known too many patients lie to believe everything anyone tells me. And, incidentally, that creep you speak of was a traitor.'

'To what? To whom? Everyone works for themselves in this world. You thought he was bringing out plans, blueprints, micro-films of secret equipment. He wasn't so stupid. Not like you.'

As she spoke, Love realized too late what he should have

249

discovered long before – if he had followed the juggler's advice more closely.

'Of course, he wasn't bringing plans,' said Love quietly. 'He was bringing out the gear . . .'

'Or rather one essential part he could carry,' interrupted Parkington. 'That was your present – which you couldn't find because Sharif here, who had no doubt ordered Glover's death, took it himself.

'Then, my sweet-tongued lady, he decided to cut you out. And there is sweet-nothing-at-all you can do about it except stick close to him, hoping he pays you something for all your trouble. Because if he doesn't no one else will. Ever.'

'Like Ruth in the Bible,' said Love, 'where he goes, you go. To the end of the line. Which cannot be too far away.'

'Shut up!' shouted Sharif angrily. He hit Love across the face – but not before Love saw the anguish and anger of realization in Ruth Lambourn's eyes.

Sharif hit Love again, bringing the edge of his right hand across Love's throat. Love staggered, gasping for breath, choking as the rope bit sharply into his windpipe. Other men now crowded into the room, hitting and kneeing him. Through a deepening red raw mist of pain, Love could see Parkington go down, and then mercifully, under the hail of blows, the faces of the guards faded, and in their place came darkness and peace of a kind.

Love awoke, moved his body slowly, carefully. No bones seemed broken, but every muscle ached. His face was soft and puffy with bruises. His teeth felt loose in his mouth. An unshaded electric light burned in one corner of the room, and he could see Parkington lying on the floor twenty feet away. He called out to him.

'Are you all right?'

An absurd question, but it provoked an answer.

'Alive,' allowed Parkington.

'What's the time?' asked Love. 'Is it today – or tomorrow?'

'I can't see my watch with my hands tied behind my back. Do me a favour. Look at it for me.'

Love rolled laboriously across the bare dusty boards. Splinters dug into his wrists and face as he manoeuvred himself close to Parkington's wrists and read the time: 3.35. That must be in the morning, because through curtainless windows he could see the night sky pricked with stars. But what morning? How long had they been tied here?

'When do you think this place is due to go up in flames?' he asked Parkington, suddenly remembering Sharif's words.

'When did they leave?'

'No idea. We must have been out cold for ages.'

'Then we shouldn't have too long to wait before things warm up.'

They lay for a moment in silence, each man concerned with his own thoughts. They heard the telex machine in another room begin to clatter, sending or receiving a message. But what use was that knowledge to them?

'I wish I had followed your advice,' said Love when the telex stopped.

'About what?'

'That bootlace you offered me, the one with the trepanning saw inside it. That could have cut through these ropes in seconds. I should have taken it.'

'I did,' replied Parkington smugly. 'Never refuse a good offer, has always been my motto. That lace is in my right shoe.'

'Not for long, it isn't,' Love assured him.

He manoeuvred himself around until his back was pressed against Parkington's feet. Then, with hands still tied behind him, he unpicked the lace from Parkington's shoe. He threaded the loops of the flexible saw inside it over his thumbs, and began to hack, slowly but steadily, at the rope that bound Parkington's wrists.

The tiny teeth gradually bit into the stiff hemp. Every so often, Love had to stop to flex his wrists, but he knew he

251

had almost cut through the rope when Parkington cried: 'Steady on! That's not the rope you're cutting, that's *me*!'

Love pulled away the rope, and then Parkington untied Love's bonds.

They both stood up unsteadily, as circulation gradually and painfully returned.

'Let's go out through the window in case the door is booby-trapped,' said Love.

They climbed out over the sill into the unexpectedly chilly darkness, walked carefully around the side of the house, keeping close to the wall in case they operated an intruder alarm which would switch on the floodlights. The back door had been left unlocked. They went inside.

High up on the wall, Love saw the main fuse boxes and high tension switches for the alarm system, turned them off one by one. Then as they came out into the compound, he saw – too late – the glass eye of an infra-red sensor built into a post.

'*Run!*' he bellowed.

As they raced across the compound, the house erupted behind them in a sheet of flame. Its intense heat, and the explosions as cans of kerosene and petrol took fire, blew breath from their bodies and flung them flat on the concrete.

Pieces of burning debris thrown into the air by the force of the blast began to shower down all around them, like fiery rain. Canvas covers on trucks started to smoulder; flames sprouted from bales of hay stacked in open vehicles. One by one, trucks and buses took fire. They blazed furiously, as fuel tanks burst in the ferocious heat.

The gates were still locked, and it was clearly impossible to scale the wire. The two men were trapped at the heart of a furnace. Against the angry red heat of the fire, the Cord on top of its ramp stood in silhouette, like a prize exhibit at an all-night, open-air motor show. The flames had not yet reached it because the ramp was about thirty feet away from the nearest burning truck.

Whatever secret the car had ever contained must have

gone with Sharif, otherwise he would never have left it behind – but the car itself could still carry them to freedom. Love raced up the ramp, switched on the ignition. The engine fired instantly. He reversed down the ramp, and Parkington climbed in beside him.

'Where to?' he asked, as though they had a choice.

'After Sharif. He's almost certainly taken with him whatever was so valuable.'

'We'll never cross the frontier in this without any papers.'

'Yes, we will. Sharif told me this car was going back to Kabul in any case. The police and customs will be expecting it – with luck. Now – heads down! We're going through the gate!'

Love accelerated, jammed the throttle to the floorboards, and threw himself sideways to avoid being flung through the windscreen, in case the gate held firm.

Two tons of solid metal, propelled by the supercharged power of two hundred horses, hit the metal frame with the punch of a pile-driver. Bolts sheared, chains snapped, the gate swept open – and they were through and on the road.

Behind them, the house and yard had become an incandescent inferno. Sparks and burning strips of wood and cloth rained down on them for half a mile, and then they were clear. Love wiped the sweat of relief from his forehead. Parkington, his face blackened by soot, gave him the thumbs-up. The glow receded behind them.

They passed trucks going in the opposite direction, ablaze with lights, red, green, blue, like travelling Christmas trees. Here and there by the roadside, in mud hut villages, tiny lamps flickered. Then dawn painted the sky pink and amber and then with gold.

Parkington shouted against the growl of the car's two three-inch exhausts.

'What's your plan if we do find Sharif? We've no weapons, remember.'

'Only the ones the good Lord gave us.'

'Not a lot of use in our situation.'

'We may improve our situation,' Love replied confidently. They had come so far, endured so much; they could not give up now. Curiously, the acute danger of their predicament did not depress them. Instead, the calm quiet air of high altitude, the exhilaration of escape, to be driving fast on an arrow-straight road, in a powerful open car, gave both men an agreeable if euphoric illusion of invincibility.

PART TEN

Love kept an eye on the red pointers of the instruments against the green glow of the car's dash lights. Oil pressure steady at 40 pounds to the square inch; water temperature at 170 degrees; dynamo charging well, engine revolutions of 3000 a minute keeping them at 80 miles an hour. The huge car held the road like a vice. This was the kind of motoring for which it had been intended; not to languish in the garage of a king, but to be out on a main road, almost empty of other vehicles, with the sun coming up behind them, and tomorrow about to begin.

They approached the border. A blue single-decker bus with the words 'Frontier Police' painted on the side, wire netting over its windows and plastic riot shields stacked up on a long rack on its roof, waited in the shadow of a single-storey hut. A policeman had lit a fire, and was crouched down, cooking breakfast in a wide flat pan. There was no pole or barrier to block the way across the border, but Love slowed and stopped.

A Pathan, hung with rifles like a walking firearms salesman, came out of the bungalow, crossed to the car, put his face close to Love's.

'Yes?' he enquired in English.

'Going through,' Love told him. 'Mr Sharif.'

He instinctively followed the quaint but widely held belief of the English in distant lands that if they talk slowly enough and in short abrupt phrases, foreigners must instantly understand them.

This man apparently did. He nodded, as though not greatly concerned either way, then spat on the ground and began to pick his teeth with a split match.

'All right?' asked Love as casually as he could. '*Thik hai?*'

'Okay,' he agreed, and waved them through.

'Sharif must be a magic name,' said Parkington, impressed. 'But I could use some of the armoury that fellow is carrying.'

'Let's hope we don't have to.'

The guard watched them out of sight, then went back into the building. He sat down at a table, and from the drawer took out a piece of paper on which a number had been written. He stared at this for some time, as though memorizing it. Then he began to punch out the figures on the telephone.

The Afghan side of the frontier seemed exactly the same as Pakistan: flat and featureless. The same clumps of spiky grass and bushes grew out of a vast expanse of dried-up earth. In the distance, the horizon shimmered like a lake. But then such similarity was to be expected; this frontier had for generations been a false barrier, drawn up by civil servants in India as an administratively convenient border – and therefore one more difficult to cross illegally than a natural boundary, involving steep mountain passes that lent themselves to ambushes.

The sun came up swiftly, and polished the dust on the car's long silver bonnet until it glowed like an immense drawn sword. They saw no other vehicles now, no other people, only a road stretching to foothills, with layers of mountains behind, each range seemingly higher than the one in front, rising like a three-dimensional backcloth, with the hindmost peaks lost in cloud.

Soon, they began to climb, and the engine started to labour as the gradient increased. Love dropped down a gear, and the car found its second wind and swept on effortlessly around hairpin bends, past tiny houses where smoke from cooking fires spiralled up vertically into the windless air.

The hills on either side seemed to move steadily closer to the road as they climbed; an optical illusion, no doubt, but somehow unsettling, menacing. The beat of their exhaust boomed back defiantly from rock walls in gorges and defiles. From time to time, they heard a muffled banging from the rear of the car as of metal beating on metal. Parkington glanced at Love, eyebrows raised questioningly.

'Sounds like a broken shock absorber mounting,' Love reassured him. 'I've had that happen on my own car – and remember, we hit that gate a hell of a blow. Nothing to worry about, though. It's not serious.'

Gradually, Love became uneasily aware of a vast silence that hung like an invisible shroud over the distant mountain peaks. He felt as though the ghosts of others who had earlier attempted this crossing, east to west, west to east, and had failed to make their destination, were somehow with them. He remembered the macabre inscription over the door of a chapel in Evora in Portugal, which had been built from the bones of hundreds who had died in a plague, centuries earlier: 'Our bones await your bones'.

This was ridiculous, he thought. He was tired and therefore becoming morbid, defeatist. He must accentuate the positive – Look on the Bright Side, as Hossein would have said, quoting from his optimistic manual.

Love was pondering how he might express this admirable intention in other more gracious words when he rounded a corner, dropped down into low gear because of a double-S bend warning ahead – and almost ran into the truck parked sideways across the road on the blind side of the curve.

Love braked heavily. The Cord's huge tyres smoked as they laid rubber tracks on the tarmac.

'Bloody ridiculous place to park!' he shouted at Parkington angrily, steering the car to the far side of the road, intending to drive between the truck and the rock wall. Just in time, he realized the space was too narrow – and the choice of parking was only ridiculous from their point of view. As unprepared as a fish swims into a net, he had run into a road block.

As he stopped the car, Mr Sharif stepped from behind the truck, flanked by two men armed with sub machine-guns. One fired a warning burst into the air six inches above the Cord's windscreen. Love switched off the ignition.

As Sharif came forward, his bodyguard fell into step with him.

'Get out of the car,' he ordered.

Love and Parkington climbed out. As one of the bodyguards frisked him, Love heard the cool tinkling sound of running water; they must be near a waterfall. The air felt chill and clear and crisp. Violence should be millions of miles away, not here in this remote and peaceful place.

'So,' said Sharif, 'you seek my company. You both declined my invitation to stay in my house, and yet you follow me here. This time you will follow me much more closely. And so that you do not attempt to escape yet again, we will go on together – to the end of your journey.'

Sharif took a mobile telephone from his pocket, tapped it.

'The guard at the frontier telephoned me,' he explained, smiling. 'That couldn't have happened in the old days, of course. There weren't such things as these then. But there are now. Time is always on the move, Dr Love. And now you two will move on with it – and with me.'

He called an order over his shoulder. Six armed men jumped down from the truck, grinning. One held two long lengths of rusty chain, another a pair of handcuffs. They came over to Love and Parkington, threaded the open end of each handcuff through the last links of each chain. Then they snapped the handcuffs roughly on their wrists, and tied the chains to a towing hook at the rear of the truck. Something made Love glance up over the tailgate. Mrs Lambourn was sitting in the back, watching him.

'Not had your thirty pieces of silver yet?' he asked her.

'Of course not. If you had, you wouldn't be here.'

She spat at him.

'You won't be so cocky for long,' she retorted angrily. 'You are out of your league. No more gentlemen now, Dr Love, only players – professionals. What would your doting patients say if they could see you like this?'

Love told her. She spat at him again, her face dark with hatred.

Sharif climbed up into the cab of the truck; the driver was already behind the wheel. The bodyguard jumped into the rear of the vehicle, which began to move forward, slowly at first, then with a vicious jerk as the driver engaged second gear.

Love and Parkington had hoped that they could manage to keep upright and perhaps run behind the truck – at least until it picked up speed. But the sudden and unexpected jolt threw them off their feet, knocking breath from their bodies. The chains tightened, and the truck began to drag them along stretched full length and twenty feet behind it.

The rough thickness of their tweed coats and the metal plates inside their flak jackets should save them for a time, Love thought. But then – what? Both men knew that the razor-sharp flints and stones embedded in the abrasive dust would rip flesh from their bodies like the claws of wild tigers. This time, no hidden saw could save them. As Sharif said, this looked like the end of their journey – or at least the beginning of the end.

The truck bumped along at about five miles an hour until it drew clear of the gorge. Then the driver accelerated. The vehicle now began to swing wildly from side to side as he crashed into top gear, and surged into the corners. At times, centrifugal force flung Love and Parkington against the rough wall of the hillside, all breath beaten from their bodies by the force of the impact. And then, as the driver took the reverse bend, they were thrown out on the opposite side, hanging right out over the ravine, like weights on the ends of pendulums. As they came back on to the road again, each rough patch punched their chests with hammer blows.

259

Dust stung their eyes, coated their throats, blocked their noses. They coughed and choked in its hot, grating cloud, gasping for air. The constant jolts and jerking of the truck wrenched their arms in their sockets. The handcuffs scored their wrists and already the metal plates in their flak jackets had warmed unpleasantly from friction on the road. Soon they would be hot enough to burn their flesh.

They tried desperately to haul themselves up close to the truck to try and keep as much of their bodies as possible off the road, in the hope they might somehow climb the tailgate, but they lacked the strength to succeed. Sharif guessed their intention, and ordered the driver to accelerate savagely, and then to slow down abruptly. Sharif kept glancing back at them from the side window, shouting abuse. He had won and they had lost, and he exulted in the fact. Ten million pounds sterling for the Cord, abandoned by the roadside, and soon no doubt to be stripped by locals of all removable parts – wheels, tyres, lights, battery – and then heaved over the edge of the track. As much, or maybe more, from Kabul for the item he had taken from Glover's luggage. Perhaps this really should be his final deal, the moment to bow out and retire to his house in Geneva, or the chateau near Lyons, and enjoy the money he had made? He would think about it, no firm decisions yet; the best deal was always the next one.

Stretched like a man on the rack, muscles aching, Love felt totally disorientated. He had nothing left by which to measure time or distance. He only hoped, weakly now, and increasingly against all reason, that somehow the truck would stop; somehow they could be released, that this nightmare must end. But how, where, when?

And then, as Love and Parkington hovered in the vague hinterland that separates exhaustion from blind oblivion, he heard a roaring in the air only feet above him, like a locomotive in the sky. Was it only the blood beating in his ears, the product of a body tortured to the edge of endurance? Or could it be real?

The noise increased until he felt his head would burst. He peered upwards, forcing his aching eyes to focus through the swirling clouds of dust – and then suddenly the roar receded. He and Parkington were sliding forwards over the surface of the road, through the thick, choking dust – but the truck was no longer pulling them. It had stopped abruptly, totally unexpectedly, and to his amazement was ablaze. As in a nightmare, he heard cries and screams of pain and fear. Someone leaped from the cab, ran to the edge of the road and fell, an incandescent human torch.

The sheer inertia of the truck's speed had pulled Love and Parkington along; now they lay, still chained to the blazing shell, perhaps twelve feet behind it. They felt the fierce dry furnace heat of the fire burn the breath in their throats.

They lay, gasping for air, sobbing with exhaustion and reaction, with a dust cloud above the burned-out vehicle enveloping them. The thunder of an unsilenced engine returned, seemingly now only feet above their heads. An overpowering smell of burning wood, blazing oil, and the sickly sweet stench of roasting human flesh made them choke and retch.

Love peered up again weakly through eyes almost blinded by dust. He could just make out the black shape of a helicopter. It hovered over him, rocket pods hanging like giant pepperpots beneath the wings. He could see the twin air intakes, like huge eyes, that gave the machine the aspect of a giant and evil insect, and above them, the third intake for the oil cooler. A four barrel rotary machine-gun pointed down at them from the nose like an accusing steel proboscis. Under the wings, three air-to-surface anti-tank missiles still hung. There should be four, thought Love weakly, but the fourth must have hit the truck.

As he stared, dazed still and almost uncomprehending, a door in the fuselage swung up and open. Two men in flying gear threw out ropes, were lowered on to the road. One carried a powerful pair of chain cutters. He snipped through their handcuffs, while his colleague slipped safety harnesses

261

around Love and Parkington, snapping the buckles shut. A winchman aboard the helicopter wound them up. Others in the crew dragged them in through the doorway.

They lay on the floor in an extremity of weariness while the two crewmen were winched in and the door closed behind them. Love could see signs written above a mass of hydraulic pipes clipped to a metal bulkhead; another notice on a glycol tank. But the writing was in some strange script, totally meaningless to him.

He heard the crew talking to each other. They all wore black flying suits and round helmets of exaggerated size which gave them the appearance of gigantic insects, like a cartoonist's impression of visitors from some planet lost in outer space.

It was impossible to understand what they said, or to see their faces. Love tried to concentrate, forced himself to recognize one outline of a single letter – or maybe it was a group of letters? Then the truth flashed into his mind: the script was Cyrillic. These men were speaking Russian. Now he realized who had rescued them. They were aboard a Russian helicopter. The three circular intakes and the revolving gun in the nose gave him other clues; only one helicopter in the world had this appearance. They were aboard an Mi-24, known by its crews as Gorbach – 'The Hunchback', from its shape, and by the Mujahideen as 'The Devil's Chariot' because of its ferocious destructive power.

He and Parkington had escaped from certain death to equally certain servitude.

A crewman knelt down by their side, gave each of them a metal beaker of fruit juice. They drank eagerly, choking as the sharp liquid passed down their swollen and parched throats.

'Thank you,' said Love weakly. 'Thank you.'

The man stood up, took off his helmet. There seemed something familiar about him, something Love should recognize. Wearily, he dredged back through all the people he had met in Pakistan. And then he remembered.

262

The go-between stood smiling down at him.

'*You?*' asked Love in amazed bewilderment.

'Me,' the go-between agreed, and grinned. He nibbled a finger nail in his pleasure.

'Where are we going?' Love asked him.

'We'll put down just this side of the frontier. My car will take you on to Peshawar. After that, my friend, we will meet in London. I must tell you that your colleague, Sir Richard Guthrie, has already been in touch with me by telephone. I am happy to report that so far as my daughter is concerned, he feels there is real room for optimism.'

'The same goes for us now,' said Love. 'A lot of room. But what are *you* doing here? How did you hear about us?'

'I gave you my number on a visiting card,' the go-between reminded him. 'And you must have given the card to a friend, for I had a telephone call to say that you and your companion here were in grave trouble. One good turn, as you English say. Androcles and the lion, eh?'

'But where did you get a Russian helicopter?'

'Over the last eight years, my friend, the Mujahideen have captured all manner of Russian weapons and equipment – tanks, guns, trucks, aircraft. They owed me a favour – just as I owed one to you. These men with me are all Afghans.'

'But they look like Russians. They even *speak* Russian.'

'They have had years of occupation to learn the language. After this jaunt the helicopter goes back to its hiding place – and the rest of us about our other business.'

'Can we fly over the road? We left the Cord there when Sharif ambushed us. No one would move that, surely?'

But someone had. They flew so low, following the winding road, that the spinning rotor stirred the dust like a whirlwind, flattening bushes, young trees, clumps of grass. But there was no sign of the car which, with its distinctive colour and from that height, would be impossible to conceal.

'We can't stay any longer,' said the go-between nervously. 'It's too dangerous with these Russian markings. We could even be shot down by our own side.'

Love nodded. The Mi-24 gained height and headed towards the frontier.

'Who telephoned you?' asked Love.

'I have no idea. I did not take the message myself, of course. It was relayed to me. But does it matter, my friend, who does a good deed – so long as the deed is done?'

The go-between's car dropped Love and Parkington at Pink's Hotel. Apart from huge bruises on their faces and bodies, their hair scorched and faces blackened by smoke and soot; apart from ripped, tattered clothes and the bared steel plates of flak jackets that gleamed in the mirror of the hotel entrance hall like suits of burnished mail, they told themselves they might never have been away. And for all they had achieved, they both felt they could have been wiser to have stayed in Pink's.

Indeed, for all the interest in their return, they might never have left the hotel. Room keys still hung on the hooks outside their numbered pigeon-holes. There were no messages for them. No one had called or written; no one had telephoned.

With a strong feeling of failure, and an almost unbearable sense of anti-climax, they bathed, changed, took a taxi to Stevie's house. The manservant they had seen on their previous visit greeted them gravely.

'No Dr Khan here,' he explained.

'Both gone? *Both*?' asked Love sharply.

The man inclined his head.

'Dr S. Khan not here. Her husband not here for much longer time.'

'Do you know when she will be back?' Parkington asked him.

'No knowing,' he replied. 'Therefore cannot be telling.'

The logic of this was unarguable, so they drove back to the hotel. Their spirits had now sunk to zero. True, they personally had survived – but at what unknown cost?

Stevie had disappeared. She could well have been shot

before Sharif left the compound – or more likely had been taken prisoner. She could have been in the truck, and died when the go-between's helicopter attacked it. This seemed most likely. Either way, she had vanished – and Love felt that it was surely too much to hope that he would ever see her again.

In retrospect, the journey to Sharif's house had been agreed with a minimum of planning – as had their pursuit in the Cord. Maybe Mrs Lambourn had been right: the days of the gentlemen really were over; the professionals were in control. And, judging from this fiasco, Sharif's criticism of their countrymen not thinking out things thoroughly could hardly have had a better example. They had also lost the Cord Love had come out to value. And with it had gone whatever secret it had once contained.

Back in their hotel, Parkington found his pigeon-hole crammed with cables. Love went with him to his room, and they sat on the bed drinking vodka from toothglasses while he skimmed through the messages.

He was to report immediately in person to Douglas MacGillivray of Beechwood Nominees in London.

The Midland Widows requested his earliest and fullest up-date regarding the proposed insurance for the Cord car. Before effecting cover for £12,000,000 they wished urgently to reconfirm Dr Love's telex evaluation.

So Sharif had sent the telex, and someone at head office had believed it. But why shouldn't they, thought Parkington bitterly; people believed anything except the truth, which for circumscribed minds was often simply unbelievable.

A claim had also been sent by a Mr Albert Sheriff, a British subject, from an address in Switzerland for US $25,000,000, being the loss of a number of Chevrolet trucks, Mercedes buses, plus a house and outbuildings, with all contents destroyed by fire outside Darra, Pakistan. Love remembered the telex chattering as he and Parkington lay bound on the floor of Sharif's house.

Another Midland Widows message referred to a truck

hired in the name of a Dr J. Love from a Peshawar contractor for a trip beyond Darra – and now missing.

'Let's get out of here,' said Love. They had nothing left to stay for now. 'I'll ring British Airways in Rawalpindi.'

The earliest available seats were on the following morning. They booked them, drove down to Bowker's Hotel. While Parkington went in search of Hossein to tell him they were leaving, Love walked along the edge of the Grand Trunk Road, turning over in his mind what had gone wrong – and why.

Near Bowker's Hotel stood a milestone, eighteen feet across, giving distances to towns and cities in the sub-continent: Lahore, 275; Amritsar, 337; Delhi, 785. These had been carved long ago for other travellers to read, and in a world of jet airliners and air-conditioned New Khan coaches, the figures seemed academic.

Birds that had been silent all day in the heat now began to flutter thankfully around the big trees at the roadside. Soon they would settle, and then entire trees would briefly come alive with bird song.

Workers were going home from offices and factories and shops on motorcycles and scooters, in tongas and cars. All the stumps had long since been drawn on the cricket pitch across the road, and polo ponies were being ridden back to the stables after evening exercise. The day thou gavest, Lord, is ending, thought Love, recalling the words of a once familiar hymn.

Of all ways to end his journey, this seemed the most futile. A woman who had moved Love more than he would care to admit had gone out of his life, probably forever. The thought that he felt at least partially responsible for her disappearance depressed him to the point of despair. Other men had died – possibly needlessly. And neither Parkington nor he had discovered what they had both come east to seek.

Jason Love realized that to many he must appear a person to envy. He owned a country house, ran a medical practice where he was respected, could afford to indulge himself with his splendid car and travel the world seeking new additions to his collection of car nameplates and radiator badges. That was on the credit side of his life's balance.

His father had once told him that when a single man put his hat on his head all his troubles were covered, which was quite true, but the weak word was 'single'.

The debit side of events was that he would continue to come home to an empty house, to messages on his answering machine. Girl friends might flutter briefly into his agreeable life like gorgeous moths, but then they fluttered out again, and soon it was as though they had never been there at all. Here, at last, he thought he had found a companion with whom he could conceivably share his life, and now the hope for the future lay in the past, like the travellers for whom distances on the milestone had once meant so much.

Of course, Parkington and he should never have allowed Stevie to accompany them, but she had appeared confident she could look after herself in any emergency – and once things began to go wrong, they were not in any position to help her. He kept assuring himself of this, but deep in his heart he knew he was rationalizing, making excuses. He did not wish to be on his own any longer that evening, and he walked slowly back to Parkington's room through the sudden brief tropical dusk. Parkington was emptying the vodka bottle into a second toothglass when he arrived. He handed it to Love.

'I was thinking about Stevie,' said Love, sipping the drink gratefully. 'What do *you* think has happened to her?'

'In this business,' replied Parkington flatly, 'it's everyone for himself, women and children included. I hope she escaped somehow. That's not a very positive answer, I know – or, on the face of it, a very likely possibility. But have you a better one? It's what is going to happen to *us* that worries me.'

'In what way?'

'Read these.'

He threw a handful of cables on to the table.

'They are going mad in London.'

'They are always mad in London,' said Love dismissively, and threw them back. 'I take the view that every letter, every cable, answers itself in time.'

'Not these,' said Parkington grimly. 'We have to answer these.'

There was a knock at the door. Hossein came in, grave-faced, carrying a sheaf of papers in a folder.

'I am sorry to bring you bad news, sir,' he told Parkington, 'but the office telex has been running almost constantly all through the day.'

'Switch it off,' said Parkington. 'We'll explain everything when we get home.'

'You don't want to see these messages from London? They are very serious. Mr Sharif's whole property, his fleet of trucks and buses, was insured with us.'

'He won't be making a claim. Mr Sharif has gone to see the great insurance assessor in the sky.'

'Please?' asked Hossein, puzzled.

'Never mind,' said Parkington. 'As I told you, we're leaving in the morning. Anything I should see to before I go that's *really* urgent?'

'Well, sir, there was the matter you recently mentioned. My promotion. You were kind enough to say you would put in the good word for me.'

'Gladly.'

Parkington took a piece of headed notepaper from the writing desk, signed his name on the bottom.

'Go back to the office,' he told Hossein, 'and type yourself a letter from me. I've already signed it.'

'What shall I say to myself?'

'Just this. That I found you loyal, enthusiastic, coura-geous, a man whose concern for the company has always overridden all personal considerations. Dedicated. Totally committed to the company's interests. Single-minded. Etcet-era, etcetera.'

'But I am none of these things,' said Hossein modestly.

'I know,' Parkington agreed. 'So do you. But they don't in London – and what are the two of us against so many? Add that I unreservedly recommend you. Not simply for promotion in this area, but to take charge of all Midland Widows business in Pakistan and India, past, present and future. The Man for the Job.'

'*All?*' repeated Hossein in hushed tones. '*All?* You are very generous, sir.'

'It doesn't cost me a thing,' Parkington assured him. 'Everyone is generous with other people's money. I just hope you have better luck with the next trouble-shooter who comes out from England.'

'Will that not be you?' asked Hossein in surprise.

'I think it unlikely,' said Parkington, and drained his glass.

Miss Jenkins came into Colonel MacGillivray's office.

'Two gentlemen to see you,' she said. 'Dr Love and Mr Parkington. Will you be offering them coffee?'

'No,' he said. 'I will not be offering them anything. Show them both in, please.'

As they came into his office, a green light glowed outside the door to show that he was not to be disturbed. The door locked itself electronically. MacGillivray leaned back in his leather chair and regarded his visitors without enthusiasm as they set down their suitcases.

'We only arrived this morning, sir,' Parkington explained. 'Your driver was waiting for us at Heathrow and brought us straight here.'

'I'm glad something went according to plan,' said Mac-Gillivray drily.

He opened a folder on his desk, tapped the sheaf of memos and telexes.

'You will have seen some of these, I expect?'

Parkington nodded.

'If not those, no doubt others very like them.'

'I don't know what the hell went wrong, Parkington, but

269

you will have to give your reasons in writing – all of them, unpleasant reading though they may undoubtedly be.

'Here we have a prominent businessman, one of the richest in the East, who has died a most violent death with several of his staff over the Afghan border. And he holds a British passport, as did a woman with him, a Mrs Ruth Lambourn. His home, his office, his entire fleet of trucks and buses have been destroyed by fire, widely believed by the police to be arson. Just before it started, two Englishmen answering to your descriptions were seen in the compound where the vehicles were kept. There are reports that another Englishman, I trust not one of you, actually shot a worker there – and let loose two hives of bees. I cannot understand that. I might call you many things, Parkington, but an apiarist, no.

'Then there was the suicide of a young Pakistani. The murder of a retired professor, a most distinguished man. Complaints of invasion of Afghanistan sovereignty. More complaints, couched, I may say, in the most vigorous and outraged terms, from Pakistan's ambassador in London. From Moscow, Kabul. What the hell *has* been going on?'

'If we knew,' said Love simply, 'we wouldn't be here. We did our best.'

'Your best? To do what? Ruin us? Sir Robert, the chief of the SIS, has called me half a dozen times this morning already. The Foreign Secretary wants an immediate and detailed report on the whole matter. The Prime Minister is personally concerned. Questions are tabled to be asked in the House about yet another balls-up by the secret service.

'If it hadn't been for the CIA, an organization for which I admit I do not always have the highest regard, we would have been right up that well-known creek in a leaking canoe without a paddle. But you even seem to have trodden heavily on the CIA's toes – for what reasons, I know not.

'I should tell you that the CIA were apparently on the very edge of discovering something which could have changed the whole economic balance for Afghanistan – after

270

the Russians leave. In addition to all your other errors, you two have to blow that as well.'

'What do you mean, sir?' asked Parkington. 'We didn't come across any CIA people.'

'You wouldn't recognize them if you met them in your porridge,' retorted MacGillivray bitterly. 'You would still be looking for men in cloaks, with false beards and dark glasses – which seems to be about the level of your operation.'

He opened another file.

'Here's the gist of the matter. A few weeks ago, in Afghanistan, the Russians discovered the frozen body of a seventeenth-century traveller. I understand he was a British subject, Ralph Ballantyne.

'Seemingly, Ballantyne had been one of a group of merchant adventurers trying to find an overland trade route to the east. Instead, they found their deaths. The Russians have been actively prospecting for minerals in Afghanistan, blowing up snow and ice so they could put the drills in – and they literally blew his frozen body out of its resting place.

'Ballantyne carried on his person a pouch containing notes on something they believed could be of value, but written in some ancient language. They got this former professor – who, as I have said, was later murdered – to translate it. Then he disappeared – with his translation. Someone knew how valuable this message was – and the Mujahideen blew up a mortuary or truck containing Ballantyne's body and the original document as the only way to stop the Russians getting it properly translated in Moscow.'

'What was the message?' asked Love.

'How the hell do I know? But the received wisdom is that it concerned the whereabouts of rhodium deposits. This metal is part of the platinum family, and so far is only mined in Russia, South Africa and, to a small degree, in Canada. Some Afghan rock formations have been thought to contain it, but no one has ever been allowed in there long enough to

271

find out for sure. The Russians used their years of occupation to try, of course, but without success.

'When I tell you that rhodium makes up only four per cent of all known platinum deposits – and platinum currently fetches at least $500 an ounce – you will have an idea of rhodium's phenomenal market value.'

'What's it used for that makes it so expensive?'

'Up until now, largely for electrical contacts and for treating metal. But it is an essential ingredient in the catalytic converters fitted to car engines to reduce poisonous exhaust fumes. Within a few years, all petrol sold in the West will be lead-free, and then the value of rhodium goes up beyond any estimate. That is why the Russians were desperate to find it – at any cost. The Americans nearly found its location. And that is what you appear to have lost – and with it a whole new economic future for Afghanistan.'

He stood up.

'There is one other thing. That woman, Mrs Lambourn, who died with Mr Sharif. Her parents are also raising hell. Going on TV, pestering their MP and so on. Know anything about her?'

'Yes,' said Love.

'Well?' asked MacGillivray impatiently.

'She is not a woman we need mourn for too much. She was not on the side of the angels. She persuaded Glover to bring out to Pakistan not just plans of some secret device but the heart of the apparatus. She didn't realize that Sharif would never let a low grade operator get away with this. Why should he, when he could have him killed and collect the gadget and the money himself?'

'Why indeed?' asked MacGillivray rhetorically. 'What Glover took out was junk, of course.'

'How do you mean, junk?' asked Love.

'Our people knew he was selling secrets, so they provided him with a harmless secret to sell – not telling him, of course. We wanted to see where he would lead us.'

'But wouldn't the buyers test it before they paid?'

272

'Of course. They did in the house of this man Sherriff or Sharif or whatever he's called. Parts of it were genuine, which they hadn't seen before. But they needed to make a very brief trial transmission – and a United States AWAC plane, on the lookout for any strange transmissions, picked this up. We could then pinpoint the source – right in Sharif's backyard.

'The buyers would know they'd been sold a pup when they took it to pieces in Moscow or Leningrad or wherever. They'd then do our work for us over the characters who had sold it to them. Maybe Sharif was lucky to have a quick death. Mrs Lambourn, too. The fact is, they were only in for the money, a quick buck – or a million bucks. What's the difference when you're dead? They weren't pros, you see.'

'Sort of gentlemen rather than players?' asked Love innocently.

'Well, sort of,' MacGillivray admitted.

'So *I* was just there to be used?' Parkington asked him coldly.

'We're all just here on this earth to be used,' retorted MacGillivray. 'And seeing how you acted and reacted, it's lucky we didn't really have to use you!'

'Do you know what happened to Sharif and Mrs Lambourn – how they died?' Love asked.

MacGillivray inclined his head.

'We employed the services of another man of Sharif's type, a freelance, if you like, who works for almost anyone, any country, if the price is right. And here, since the CIA were involved, it was.'

'A sort of go-between?'

'You could call him that, yes. A go-between.'

The telephone rang. MacGillivray picked it up. Miss Jenkins said nervously: 'Sir Robert on the green phone for you.'

'Tell him I am out but will ring him back,' said MacGillivray.

'He said it is very important.'

'When Sir Robert says that, he means it is very important to him,' MacGillivray told her, replaced the receiver.

He stood up.

'You see? It never stops. You can have no idea of the hornet's nest you've stirred up. And what your blundering activities have cost so many people. I will see you out.'

'In case we touch the silver?' Love asked him ironically.

'In case you touch *anything*,' MacGillivray replied. 'I cannot afford anything else to go wrong.'

He led the way down the stairs, opened the front door.

At the kerb, glittering in the eleven o'clock sunshine, stood the Cord car in which Love and Parkington had driven over the Afghan border, and been forced to abandon at the roadside.

Stevie sat at the wheel. She waved a cheerful greeting.

'Can I drive you gentlemen anywhere?' she asked.

'Not me,' said Parkington with feeling. 'I'm beginning to feel I am accident prone. I'm taking the bus. Let a stranger do the driving.'

Love could hardly believe that Stevie was actually sitting in front of him, only feet away. He had imagined her dead, wounded, captured. And here she was in London, looking lovelier than ever. *How?*

MacGillivray was grinning at his amazement.

'What do *you* find so funny?' Love asked him.

'If I didn't laugh, I'd cry. If only you hadn't loused up those rhodium details, I could almost forgive you the rest. This could have the makings of a reasonably happy ending.'

'Now I know why Stevie searched my belongings in my hotel room,' said Love. 'You are in this business? As the colonel would say, a pro?'

She nodded.

'Hurrah for the CIA,' said Parkington sarcastically and set off for the nearest bus stop.

Love walked to the front of the Cord.

'I can make it a more than reasonably happy ending for you,' he told MacGillivray. 'If I have a mind to.'

'How?'

'I know the map references for those rhodium deposits.'

The colonel looked at him in astonishment, his smile fading.

'Is this *your* idea of fun?' he asked coldly.

'Not at all. Nor was my trip to points east. But before I do give it to you, I want you to change your views about Parkington. Your circus or the old firm or whatever you care to call it, really means something to him. It doesn't do much for me.'

'I'll change my views about anyone. Parkington, you, anyone at all, Doctor. I'll say the world is flat, and day is night – if you're not fooling.'

Love opened the bonnet of the car, pointed to the thin strip of metal screwed on the side of the Cord's bulkhead.

'There's your map reference,' he said. 'Metal on metal. About metal. Brought to you at the cost of the life of a brave professor.'

MacGillivray copied down the figures in a notebook, took a penknife from his pocket, unscrewed the metal strip.

'That's travelled far enough,' he said. 'It stays right here with me.'

'As a bargaining point?' Love asked him.

'Something like that. Collateral is probably a better word.'

Love lowered the bonnet.

'I've left my Cord at Heathrow,' he told Stevie.

'I'll drive you there,' she said.

'I hoped you'd say that.'

He climbed into the car beside her, looking back as she accelerated away. MacGillivray was still standing on the pavement looking at the strip of metal. He did not wave goodbye.

Love and Stevie sat in silence, relishing each other's company, until they reached the Piccadilly underpass. There, the deep exhaust beat booming back from the tiled walls brought back to Love memories of his trip through the Afghan gorges.

'How did you get out?' he asked her.

'In this car,' Stevie replied. 'When we drove into Sharif's yard in the truck, I took your advice, remember, and crouched down out of sight, so the guards didn't know I was there.

'When they took you and Richard into the house, I wasn't keen for them to discover me, but couldn't escape because of the electric fence. All those bees buzzing around made the guards run for cover. The compound was deserted for a few minutes. I couldn't find a hiding place, so in desperation, I climbed into the luggage boot of the Cord – where I'd once told my father-in-law to hide. I didn't think anyone would look there – and they didn't. It was very hot and uncomfortable, especially when you drove fast along that winding road. Didn't you hear me banging on the floor?'

Love nodded, remembering the thumping sound he had told Parkington was a loose shock absorber.

'And then?' he asked.

'When you stopped the car, I was about to come out, but I heard Sharif's voice so I stayed where I was. When he drove away, I got out of the boot. I saw that you and Richard had also gone so I got on the phone.'

She tapped the mobile telephone that lay on the seat by her side.

'Who the hell did you ring?'

'The number you gave me.'

'I see.'

Love paused.

'MacGillivray also claims the credit for our rescue.'

'Well, he would, wouldn't he? After all, he's a total professional. I'm not that dedicated. Medicine is equally important to me. This is his living, his life.'

'And his pension depends on his performance. And maybe a K when he retires.'

'Exactly.'

Maybe MacGillivray had activated the go-between, or maybe it had been Stevie – and the go-between wanted to help Love because of his introduction to Sir Richard Guthrie. But did it really matter? As the go-between had asked him: 'Does it matter who does a good deed – so long as the deed is done?'

Love turned towards Stevie, seeing the wind in her hair, her blue-grey eyes fixed on the road. He took a deep breath.

'You're coming back with me to Wiltshire . . . Aren't you?'

Love tried to make the question sound like a statement.

Stevie did not answer. They came up over the Hammersmith flyover, circled the Hogarth roundabout, accelerated out on the M4 motorway. Love looked at her sharply.

'You *are*,' he repeated more confidently.

He could see Stevie's eyes were surprisingly bright. Her lower lip trembled ominously. Still she did not speak.

She turned off the approach road to the airport and stopped the car outside the long-term car park, switched off the engine. Over their heads, aircraft took off, painting streams of vapour on the morning sky.

'No,' she said flatly. 'I can't. We had better say goodbye here.'

'Goodbye?'

She nodded. Love saw her eyes glisten with tears she did not bother to wipe away. He took both her hands in his, looked across at her, trying to will her to change her mind. Her fingers felt very cold, although the day was warm. She kissed him then and he felt the saltiness of her tears on his tongue.

'If I came back with you, it would be even harder to say goodbye,' she said. 'I'm a coward about such things. Here is so impersonal. Hundreds and thousands of journeys starting, ending, people greeting each other, saying goodbye. An airport is the only place in the world to end something you hoped, you wished, you dreamed might have gone on for the rest of your life.'

'What are you saying?'

'Goodbye. That is what I am saying. And, in any case, you don't really know me.'

'I could spend all the years of my life trying to remedy that.'

'It wouldn't work out.'

'It won't unless we give it a try. I have never asked anyone this,' Love continued more hesitantly, 'but there must come a time even to a bachelor like me . . .'

'Don't go on,' she said. 'Please.'

A tear rolled out of her left eye; he brushed it away from her cheek, his touch soft as a feather blown by the wind. She did not move.

'I want you to marry me,' Love told her. 'We could set up a practice together, here in England.'

'My place is not here,' she said. Stevie's voice was very soft, barely above a whisper.

'Your place is with me, and my place is wherever you are. If you want to go back to Pakistan, I'll go willingly. Or to the States. Anywhere. It doesn't matter, so long as we are together. Don't you see that?'

'I see that,' she agreed, not looking at him now, but looking away beyond him at aircraft landing, taking off, circling above them in the sky.

'Will you marry me?' Love asked her.

She took her hands out of his and drew back slightly.

'I cannot.'

'But you are a widow. You *can*. Don't you want to?'

Stevie looked intently at him now, as though storing up the image of his face in her mind.

'You know I do. I care for you more than I have cared for anyone in all the world. More than I thought I could ever conceivably care for another person. I love you.'

'Well, then?'

'I cannot marry you,' she explained. 'I would if I could, as you must know. But I am not a widow. I have heard my husband is alive, and back in Pakistan.'

'But he was killed. You said you had proof.'

'So I thought. He was badly wounded, but he lives. Paralysed and blind. I had a telephone call before I went with you and Richard to Sharif's house.'

'Who rang you?'

'Someone on Sharif's orders. He thought I would be pleased. As I should be.'

'But you never really loved your husband?'

'What is love but a Western word?' she asked bleakly.

'It's more than that,' Love answered her. 'It's being with someone, wanting them, missing them if they are away, feeling your heart beat more strongly at their footstep outside the front door.

'It's the special way they laugh – and cry. Their scent, their taste – everything good and bad about them. A day without them is like a day without the sun. That is more than a Western word, surely?'

'I agree,' she said, 'but I am married. It is my duty to go to my husband. I cannot abandon him in his state. You must see that. Life is like a one-way street. We can stop or we can go on. But we can never, ever go back.

'I cannot go back now, dear Jason, but always remember that I wanted to. And when I am old I will remember what it felt like to be loved by a man to whom I could give myself physically, mentally, every way – to be two halves of a peach, as the Pathans say.'

'Your mind is made up?'

She nodded.

'Events have made it up for me. But remember, you are also loved. And you always will be.'

'I will remember.'

Stevie turned the ignition key; the engine fired. Love climbed out of the car and stood for a moment leaning on the door, feeling the metal warm on his elbows, storing up in his memory a picture of her face, beautiful and tragic, moving out of his life forever.

'Life,' Sir Thomas Browne had written, 'is a pure flame, and we live by an invisible Sun within us.'

279

Love knew now that for him this sun had risen the moment he first met Stevie in his hotel room. She might leave him now, but somehow, some time, somewhere, they would – must – meet again, or else that inner sun would set. He knew that, and as he watched her drive away, he hoped, believed, trusted that she did, too.

Love carried his bag into the car park, found his car, drove to the entrance, handed in his ticket, and sat at the wheel, his thoughts on his practice; his locum would not be expecting him to return so soon.

The attendant in the booth glanced at the ticket, rummaged in a desk.

'Are you Dr Jason Love?' he asked. 'From the West Country?'

'The same.'

'There is an envelope here for you. Sort of official. A despatch rider delivered it a short time ago. Said it must be signed for.'

Love scribbled his signature on the slip of paper the attendant handed to him, opened the envelope. The address in Leadenhall Street meant nothing to him. Then he recognized the ornate logo and embossed letterhead of the Midland Widows Insurance Company.

'The directors wish to inform you that, in view of the fact that the company accepted a premium for the Cord car in Pakistan, and your efforts were instrumental in saving an outrageous and doubtless fraudulent claim, they have decided unanimously to show their appreciation of your actions by presenting the car to you as a gift.

'Documents will be forwarded to you in due course.

'We would add that this gift has been approved by our new General Manager in Pakistan and India, Mr K. H. Hossein, who wishes to be remembered to you most warmly.'

Love smiled ironically. So now he owned a car which had meant so much to three people. To Sharif, who had attempted to use it to make another fortune. To Ahmed,

280

who had risked his life to hide inside it a message of inestimable value to his country. To a traitor who had planned to use the car to transport a secret of another kind across a frontier to an alien power.

Three people, thought Love, with totally different motives, lives – and all now dead. He looked at the Cord's crest on the dashboard: three hearts, three arrows which had all found a target.

There could not be too many people who owned one Cord. Now he owned two – but only temporarily, he told himself. He would auction the second one and send the proceeds to Stevie to help her refugees. That might even persuade her to return to thank him. And if she did come back, would she do so only to go away again?

The car park attendant gave up trying to read the letter over Love's shoulder.

'Good news, sir?' he asked, hopeful of a tip.

'Yes,' answered Love.

'Been away abroad, have you, then?' the man went on.

'Yes, again. In Pakistan.'

'Bet you're glad to be back here in this country, sir. Not a lot ever happens out there, eh?'

Love nodded gravely.

'Not too much,' he agreed, and let in the clutch.